The Earth Commission

For William,
Seek the Truth always!
E Talley Mg—
Sheridan A. Morris

E. TALLEY MORGAN
AND SHERIDAN A. MORRIS

PAGE PUBLISHING, INC.
New York, NY

First originally published by Page Publishing, Inc. 2017

ISBN 978-1-64027-079-4 (Paperback)
ISBN 978-1-64027-080-0 (Digital)

Printed in the United States of America

CHAPTER ONE

A S DARKNESS GAVE way to the streaks of red in the early morning sky, Jake climbed on his chestnut brown horse, Chester, for his morning ride. It was early spring and the calving was well under way. Jake, with his wavy, reddish brown hair, broad shoulders, and lean, muscular build, was the quintessential cowboy. He liked to spend the first hours of sunlight riding around his thousand-acre ranch, checking on his cattle. The beauty and magnificence of nature inspired him, while the peace refreshed his soul. This was his favorite part of being a rancher.

When he arrived at the crystal clear lake on the edge of his ranch, he stopped for Chester to take a drink. He heard a faint cry on the far side of the lake and instantly knew a calf was in distress. As he reached the location of the cry, he saw a newborn calf had wandered into the reeds and was stuck in the mud. The lake water was up to its neck. Jake grabbed his rope and jumped off of his horse. Wading into the lake, he thought how glad he was that his snake-proof boots were also waterproof. He leaned in over the calf, who was very weak, and looped the rope over its head and front legs. With a gentle tug, he tightened the rope around the calf's chest and began slowly backing out of the mud. At first the calf struggled, but within moments, Jake had the calf safely on the bank. The mother cow approached as Jake was gathering up his rope. He put the rope around the mother's neck and wrapped the calf in an old blanket he had in his pack. He hoisted the calf up onto his saddle and climbed on behind it. He was going to take them to Alo's stable. Alo was the chief of the neighboring Mintaka tribe; he also happened to be Jake's father-in-law.

The spring-fed lake was on Jake's land, only fifty feet from the property line of the Mintaka reservation. Soon after Jake purchased his ranch, he went to the Mintaka chief to give the tribe full access to his lake. Even though the lake belonged to him legally, he felt the lake also belonged to the Mintaka because they had used it for generations. Alo was impressed by the generosity of this kind-hearted, young white man, and he wanted to get to know him better. They talked for hours that first day.

Jake's father had accumulated his great wealth in the oil business in Texas, but Jake had no interest in being an oilman. He was acutely aware of the shallow, selfish nature of his father's associates, who didn't care what kind of damage the oil did to the planet or that the oil drilling turned beautiful land into a smelly eyesore. They only cared about one thing and that was making money. Jake loved the beauty of the land and the wide open spaces. He enjoyed watching the animals and caring for them. His father never failed to remind him that it was the oil business that afforded him the right to experience "all the finer things in life." Soon after he graduated from college with his degree in animal sciences, his parents were both killed in an automobile accident. The accident was caused by a drunk driver, who was driving, of all things, an oil tanker truck. Being the sole heir to his parents' estate, it didn't take him long to decide to liquidate everything and buy a ranch. He wanted to raise grass-fed cattle in a natural way.

Meeting Alo had been a very positive turn of events in Jake's life. Alo and his tribe had been raising grass-fed cattle for years, and they were doing it in harmony with nature. This is exactly what Jake wanted to do. They spent a lot of time together, working on both the reservation and on Jake's ranch. While Alo taught Jake the old ways, Jake taught Alo some innovations in genetic selection and breeding that allowed them both greater success and sustainability.

During the twenty-minute horseback ride to Alo's stable, the exhausted calf stopped shivering and fell asleep. Jake, with the cow in tow, arrived to find his nephews playing in Alo's yard.

"Is your Grandfather home?" he called out.

"No, but Grandmother is."

Just as the kids ran off, Kaia, Alo's wife, stepped out of the back door. "Good morning, Jake, what have you got there?"

"Good morning, Kaia, one of your cows calved down by the lake last night. This little fella ended up stuck in the mud. I think I have him warmed up now, but I thought you had better check him out."

Kaia was an herbalist and healer for the tribe. To each patient, she gave love, acceptance, and the best care possible. It was her gentle, nurturing nature that made everyone feel as though she was their grandmother. There were no medical facilities on the reservation other than the small building behind the house where Kaia processed and stored her healing herbs. She went back into the house to grab her medicine bag, then met Jake in the stable. Once inside the stable, Jake took the old blanket off the calf as the mother cow watched nervously.

Kaia looked the calf over carefully and after a few minutes had passed, she stood up and said, "I have some good news and some bad news. The good news is, once that calf gets its belly full of milk, it will be just fine. The bad news is that blanket of yours is a goner."

Jake smiled and said, "It was worth the sacrifice. We should let the mama and her baby stay inside here until it warms up. Where's Alo?"

"He was out last night looking at the stars and saying his prayers. He should be home soon. Would you like to come in and have some coffee with me while we wait for him?"

"I would love a cup of coffee," Jake replied.

Jake had just finished the last drop of his coffee and was about to ask for another cup, when he heard Alo at the back door. "Morning, Jake, what brings you here so early?"

"I found one of your calves stuck in the mud at the lake. The baby and mama are now safe in your stable."

"Thank you, Jake, I'm glad you found them. I would have hated to lose a baby calf to the wolves I heard howling last night."

Changing the subject, Jake said, "It sure was a beautiful night. Did you see those strange lights?"

"Well, as a matter of fact, I did, Jake. It was the Star People." Alo searched Jake's face for his reaction. "They came to talk about something that concerns them. Well, actually, it concerns all of us."

"All of us? What are you talking about, Alo?"

"It's complicated, Jake. I think they can explain it to you much better than I can. Would you be willing to come with me tonight to meet the Star People?" Alo asked.

"People, you mean, people, like, like physical people? I thought when you said Star People you meant some kind of spiritual beings, I thought you were...well...people, really? You've been talking about Star People as long as I've known you, but I thought it was some kind of a spiritual experience. I never imagined you were talking about real physical beings. Are we talking about space aliens?" Jake exclaimed.

Alo noticed the color had drained completely out of Jake's face. "Well, yes, they are not from this planet, and they are definitely physical, but they are not the scary monsters you are imagining."

"Whoa, you're not kidding. Kaia, he's serious. Is he kidding? Sure, that sounds like fun. What should I bring besides an extra pair of pants?" Looking over at Kaia, Jake asked, "Kaia, do you have something to calm my nerves? I'm sure I'll be okay in a minute. I'm just a little...stressed...no more coffee for me..."

"Jake, I know this is a little shocking, but something has changed and they asked me to bring you to them. It is important that they talk to you. Will you come with me?"

Kaia handed Jake a glass. "Here, dear, drink this Peaceful Warrior and take a deep breath. You will be okay in a minute."

Jake drank the Peaceful Warrior and took a deep breath as he tried to regain his composure. After a few minutes, he said, "Thanks, Kaia, I feel much calmer now. What was in that?"

"Just a little lemon balm, St. John's wort, skullcap, and a whole lot of love. I am glad you are feeling better." Putting her hand on his shoulder, she gave him a reassuring squeeze.

Jake looked Alo straight in the eye and said, "My friend, I trust you completely, so, yes, I will go with you. What time should I be here?"

"Eight o'clock tonight. Bring Naomi."

CHAPTER TWO

O N HIS WAY home, Jake's mind was going a mile a minute. Unfortunately, his horse was only going a mile every twenty minutes. This was destined to be a very long three-mile ride home.

Talking to himself, Jake said, "Well, I might as well relax and get my thoughts together. Okay, so let me get this straight. This morning I was minding my own business when I took a leisurely ride to Alo and Kaia's house. After a cup of coffee with the best mother-in-law ever, Alo comes in and mentions he's been hanging out with his friends, the Star People, and they want to meet me. Yup, that about sums it up. So now I'm going home to tell my wife that her Dad's friends want us to come over tonight. Yeah, that's it. Good ole Mom and Dad want us to come over tonight to meet some of their friends from…out of town. That's it."

Jake and Naomi had been married for thirty years, and he realized they had never talked about Star People.

"Why haven't we ever talked about Star People? Why hasn't she told me about them? Oh yeah, maybe it was because I never asked. Does she know they're physical beings?"

He had never thought about this before, but now that he was thinking about it, it seemed obvious.

"Of course. She has to know!"

Growing up, Naomi was very close to both of her parents, and she learned everything that she could from each of them. She learned about the sacred ceremonies and beliefs from Alo. Kaia trained her from the time she was four years old, and now she is a gifted healer in her own right. He couldn't wait to talk to her about Star People.

Finally, he was on the crest of the hill that led to their driveway. As he entered the gate, he could see his favorite little "pig terrier" guard dog, Bailey, sleeping on the front porch. Bailey heard the horse, jumped up, and ran toward them barking just to be sure everyone knew she was on duty. Bailey was part bull dog, part Welsh corgi, and some other things that made her look more like a little pig that anything else. Most people would call her a mutt, but Jake preferred to call her a handmade original.

"Hi, Bailey. Where's Naomi?" Bailey didn't answer; she just ran back to the front porch.

Once he got the saddle off of Chester and rubbed him down, he led him out to the pasture and headed for the house. "Hi, honey, I'm home," he bellowed as he entered the mud room and took off his boots.

"Good morning, Jake. It sure was a beautiful morning. Did you enjoy your ride?" Naomi asked.

Naomi was a striking beauty with long, straight black hair, high cheekbones, and a tall, thin build. She still took his breath away every time he saw her. He wrapped his arms around her and gave her a kiss before answering. "It was a beautiful morning, and I have so much to talk to you about."

"Wash up. We can talk over breakfast." After filling their plates with browned potatoes, scrambled cheesy eggs, and cinnamon raisin toast, they sat down. Naomi said, "I'm all ears, talk to me."

"I stopped by the lake for Chester to get a drink. When I heard a noise on the other side of the lake, I went to investigate and found a calf stuck in the mud. Once I got the calf out of the lake, the mom came over and I saw they were Alo's."

Jake paused to eat some breakfast. "So how are Mom and Dad?" Naomi asked.

Jake continued eating while he pulled his thoughts together.

"Alo was out praying when I got there, so after Kaia and I took care of the cow and calf, we went into the house for a cup of coffee. I finished my coffee and that's when it happened." He paused to eat some more.

"What happened?"

"Alo came home." He paused again, trying to figure out what in the world he was going to say.

"Is Dad okay? Why are you acting so weird? Just tell me what happened."

"Well, Alo said the Star People, who are physical beings, want us to go over there tonight to meet with them. You and me tonight at eight, go to Alo and Kaia's, then we will go out together to meet the Star People. Okay? Sounds good, right?"

Jake held his breath and watched as a smile broke on Naomi's face. When she reached over and put her hand on his hand, he started breathing again. Smiling at him, she said, "I see you just realized that Star People are not mythological or spiritual, and you're a little freaked out. I understand, but I can assure you they are warm and loving beings. You have nothing to be afraid of."

"Really? You've met them before?"

"Yes, I met them when I was a teenager, when Dad took me with him to pray under the stars. Several times we saw their ship fly over and Dad told me about them. One time when we saw the ship, they landed and came over to talk to us. After twenty minutes or so, they said good-bye and left."

Jake interrupted, "Why didn't you tell me this before?"

"The last time I saw them, I was nineteen and I haven't thought about it much since I met you. And, well, just like you struggled to bring up the subject just now, what was I going to say? Besides, I didn't want to be the one to freak you out. Star People have been visiting my people for hundreds of years. There is no fear or ridicule associated with believing in Star People in our culture, but there sure is in yours."

"Yeah, I get it," Jake said, as he finished eating. "Thank you for breakfast. I was starving and it was delicious. How do you always manage to have breakfast ready right when I walk in?"

Naomi smiled, thinking of Bailey barking, and said, "We women have our ways." She kissed him before she continued. "I think now is a good time for me to tell you something else on the subject of Star People. Nathan and all of Alo's children and other grandchildren have met them too."

Naomi paused to give Jake a chance to swallow. "Do you remember how much Nathan used to love going on those camping trips with his Grandfather?"

Jake's state of shock made him a little slow, so he asked, "Are you telling me our son, Nathan, has met Star People?"

"Yes, dear, that's exactly what I'm telling you. They're the ones who inspired him to get his doctorate in Material Science and Engineering."

"I want you to tell me everything you can about the Star People," Jake insisted.

Naomi nodded. "I will. Relax and enjoy your breakfast. We have plenty of time."

After they finished cleaning up, they went out onto the porch. Bailey was lying on her bed next to Jake's favorite chair. He sat down and started scratching Bailey's head. As soon as Naomi sat down across from him, Jake blurted, "Now start from the beginning and tell me everything."

Naomi was struggling to figure out where to start and how she could best alleviate his anxiety. "Okay, so how about you ask me anything you want to know and then we'll see where that leads?"

"Okay, well, what did they look like?"

"The ones I met were human-like, a little less than six feet tall, light-brown skin, light-colored hair with blue or green eyes. They had all the same basic features we have: two eyes, two ears, a nose, a mouth, two arms, two legs, and most importantly ten fingers. I would say they were very fit and healthy. And I guess I could say they looked like a blend of the Earth races."

"What did they wear? A space suit and helmet?"

"No, they didn't wear a space suit. They told me they don't need quite as much oxygen as we do, and they can breathe our air just fine. Everything they wore was very practical, like a one piece jumpsuit."

"What did their spaceship look like?"

"Well, that was very interesting, and one thing that Nathan was particularly interested in when he met them. The spaceship they landed in was circular, about fifty feet in diameter. You might call it a flying saucer, but it was more complicated than that. It had a circular top disk that rotated in a clockwise direction and a circular bottom disk that rotated in a counterclockwise direction. In between these two plates was the passenger compartment. It was about nine feet tall and had a section for the pilots and chairs for the rest of the crew and guests."

"Guests?"

"Yes, they let us get on board and look around while they answered questions about the way things worked."

"Did they take you for a ride?"

"No, they said it was not possible then, but one day it would be. Another interesting thing about the ship was that it was like a chameleon. They could make it change to look like its background. So when it took off, it just blended into the sky and vanished."

"How did they talk to you? Did they speak English?"

"That was the most unusual thing about the Star People I met. It seemed like they were talking to me just like we are talking now, but that really wasn't what was happening. They explained that they are telepathic, which means they're completely aware of a person's energy. They understand your thoughts, intentions, and attitudes, and therefore they understand what you're saying. I'm not sure if their mouths were actually moving and they were speaking words or just putting words into my mind telepathically. During the time they have been studying Earth, they have learned all the Earth languages, so regardless, the communication is completely smooth. It's impossible to lie to them since they are listening to your energy instead of your words."

"If humans were telepathic, they wouldn't be able to lie. Life as we know it would completely change. Wouldn't that be great?"

"Yes, it would." Naomi smiled as she stretched out in her lounge chair searching her teenage memories for other important facts she could share.

Jake reached down and started scratching Bailey's head again. He was reviewing the information he had received and noticed that he was feeling calm and peaceful. There was really nothing for him to be afraid of. The fear he felt was really just a fear of the unknown.

Besides, he would be with Naomi, Alo, and Kaia, and it was not unknown to them. He thought, *what else do I need to know?*

Jake blurted, "Why would they want to meet me?"

"I don't know, but I have been thinking about it. There is no shame or ridicule from the indigenous people associated with interacting with Star People. In the white culture, it is the opposite, relentless ridicule and shame, even to the point that pilots and scientists lose their jobs over admitting it. It is not easy for white people to handle the truth about Star People. You are an unusually open-minded white man who has relationships in both of these worlds. Just as our son, Nathan, is racially a blend of these two worlds, you are a cultural blend of these two worlds. They could want your help with something."

Jake contemplated this for a few minutes. "I guess that could be it. Alo did say it was something that concerns them and all of us. We'll find out tonight. Now that we've talked, I have to admit, I'm looking forward to it."

"Good, I'm glad. You're looking a little tired and it's going to be a long night. Why don't you stretch out and take a nap?"

"That sounds like a good idea. Processing this information takes a lot of energy. I couldn't work on fences right now if I had to." Jake leaned back in his lounge chair, felt the cool spring breeze on his face, and quickly fell into a deep sleep.

Naomi got up and quietly went into the house. Just as the door closed, she heard the phone ring in her medicine kitchen at the back of the house. Naomi answered the phone. "Hello."

"Hi, dear, how is Jake doing?"

"Hi, Mom. He's sleeping peacefully now. He was pretty freaked out at first, but we talked a long time and I filled him in on everything I could think of. Now he's actually looking forward to tonight."

"I am relieved. It was pretty shocking for him, to say the least. Something really big must be happening. We cannot imagine what could cause such an unusual change of protocol."

"I know what you mean."

"Alo and I were hoping you and Jake would come over later this afternoon so we can have dinner together. If you will bring one of your delicious wild berry pies, I will take care of everything else."

"That sounds great. I'll bring the pie and we'll be there around five?"

"Perfect, see you then."

CHAPTER THREE

JAKE AND NAOMI arrived for dinner promptly at five o'clock. As soon as their feet hit the ground, they could smell Kaia's famous slow-cooked roast beef with onions, carrots, and potatoes. After Kaia put the biscuits in the oven, she and Alo came out to greet them.

"Dinner will be ready in ten minutes, come on inside," Kaia said as she leaned in to hug and kiss Naomi.

"Have you had a good day, Jake?" Alo asked.

"Well, it's been a very unique and enlightening day," Jake said, shaking Alo's hand. Alo kissed Naomi on the cheek while Kaia kissed Jake and they went into the house.

"Dinner smells delicious," Jake said.

Kaia smiled and said, "It has been cooking for hours, I hope it's good. I got distracted this afternoon when a neighbor came over in need of some bronchitis medicine for his daughter. I had to mix it for him, so I was afraid I would be late getting the biscuits made. But it seems I got them ready right on time."

"We're glad. We never ate lunch today and we've been smelling that pie all the way over here, so we're really hungry," Naomi chimed in.

Everyone fixed their plates as Kaia took the biscuits out of the oven and put them on the table. They sat down together and held hands. Alo said the prayer. "Great Spirit, we thank you for all our relations, we thank you for your guidance, we thank you for this food, and we ask that you bless it so that it may heal and restore our bodies. Please be with us tonight and bring peace and blessings to our meeting with our relations, the Star People. Thank you, Aho."

Everyone else spoke "Aho" in unison and they began eating.

Except for compliments on the food, they ate in silence. Each of them was deeply engrossed in thoughts about the events soon to follow. Jake was the first to break the silence.

"Earlier today, Naomi told me everything she could think of about the Star People. I feel much better now about tonight's meet and greet. But I was wondering, Alo, is there anything else you can tell me about them? Now that my mind is open and all."

"Yes, I am sure there is, Jake. I have known them all my life, so let me think about it while we finish eating. I will try to boil everything down to the information that I think will help you the most."

"Thanks, Alo. That sounds good to me. Is anyone else ready for berry pie? Let me take your plates," Jake said, as he got up and began clearing the dinner plates from the table.

"Dinner was delicious, Mom. I'm sure you're the best cook this side of the Mississippi," Naomi said with a smile. "I'll serve the pie."

"Thank you, dear. After we finish eating and clean up, let's go sit in the family room and let Alo talk to us about Star People."

After eating their pie and praising Naomi on her baking skills, they all worked together to put the leftover food away and clean up the kitchen.

Once everyone was comfortable in the living room, Alo began, "Great Spirit created all that is, that includes all that is on this planet, as well as all that is in this universe. The universe includes what we can see and much more beyond what we can see. Even today's scientists acknowledge that there are most likely billions of habitable planets in our universe. In their minds, habitable means habitable by beings like us. Who is to say all beings are like us? Or even that all beings require the same conditions as us?" Alo paused to take a drink of water and let everyone consider what he had said. "It follows then that all our relations includes all beings created by our Creator, Great Spirit. The ones we call Star People are our relations, our brothers and our sisters. We are all connected to each other through our Creator and all that has been created.

"Great Spirit is love, the most powerful energy there is. All conscious beings were created in the likeness of Great Spirit as spiritual beings and then endowed with physical bodies in order to have physical experiences. It is not the type of body we have that defines who we are. It is the sum of the everyday choices we make that defines us. Great Spirit gave us free will to choose to be whoever we choose to be in the hopes that we would choose to grow closer and closer to being like the pure love that created us. Our Star People brothers and sisters are really the same as us, just a little different. Not unlike the different races of humans on this planet, we are all the same but with slight differences. We each individually express who we really are through the way we treat each other."

Alo scanned Jake's face for his reaction. He knew that Jake probably thought he was off topic, but you cannot really understand Star People without understanding the context. "Are you with me so far?"

Jake said, "Wow, I mean, yeah, I'm with you. This makes so much sense and yet I've never heard it put this way before. Correct me if I'm wrong, but you're saying Star People are having a different type of physical experience, but the ultimate goal is the same. To make choices, learn lessons, grow through different hardships, all the while striving to be more and more loving no matter what happens."

Alo's face lit up with a huge smile. "Yes, you are correct."

Then he continued. "Star People have been coming to Earth for hundreds of years. They have been working to help humans evolve and develop. For the most part, only the indigenous cultures have remained open to them and their help. They are only permitted to share information and technology in ways that will be for the greater good of all. But unfortunately, the people in power want information and technology so they can make more money. The greed of the people in the position to help the most has stifled advancement for all and led to the oppression of the poor masses."

Alo looked up at the clock and said, "We had better get ready to go. We are going to walk out to the meeting circle that is just outside the back gate on the hill. Soon after dark, the Star People will land in the field just past there. We should get there early, we'll want to see this landing."

They all agreed and soon had their jackets and flashlights in hand. As a group, they headed up the hill to the circle. It was a cool, clear night, and the sky was a beautiful reddish orange as the sun set over the field where the craft was to land. They each chose one of the smooth boulders on the east side of the outer circle to sit on. It was new moon, so as the sun disappeared over the horizon, darkness rapidly settled on them.

Pointing at a light in the sky, Alo said, "There, do you see that light moving toward us? Keep watching it." They watched as the light continued to descend. When the light was just above the tops of the trees, they could make out the shape of a circular craft.

Jake thought he was prepared for this, but as he could see the full shape and size of the craft, his mouth fell open. He was so caught up in the moment that he didn't even realize his mouth was hanging open until the craft was on the ground a hundred feet in front of them and he tried to swallow. "Whoa. That's amazing," he said to himself. When he heard Naomi say, "You're not kidding," he realized that was his out-loud voice. He blinked a few times and told himself to breathe. He could barely believe his eyes. It was just like Naomi described. The top and bottom discs were still spinning slowly as the craft hovered about three feet off the ground. Suddenly a door opened and a stairway was lowered to the ground. Jake gulped. Someone stepped into the doorway, descended the stairs and began walking toward them. Alo got up and began walking, followed by Kaia and Naomi. Jake quickly took hold of Naomi's hand and walked with them.

As they reached the being, Alo stretched out both of his hands and took hold of the forearms of the visitor. They held each other's forearms for a moment and smiled at each other, in what seemed like a warm greeting between old friends. Then Alo turned to Kaia, Naomi, and Jake and said, "I would like to introduce you to my friend, Oscillada. Oscillada, this is my wife, Kaia, our daughter, Naomi, and Naomi's husband, Jake."

Oscillada said, "Thank you for coming to meet with me tonight. I have a lot of important things to share with you. Please follow me, I have a comfortable meeting space on my ship."

Jake found himself nodding because he couldn't really think of anything to say. Nothing he was thinking, like "hell yeah" or "sure" or "you bet," seemed appropriate. There was a formality and a seriousness about Oscillada that commanded a huge amount of respect. He was relieved that no one else was talking either. He just kept holding Naomi's hand as they followed behind Oscillada, Alo, and Kaia.

When they reached the stairway, he reluctantly let go of Naomi's hand to take hold of the railing. What a weird feeling that was. He was expecting it to be cold and hard like metal, but it wasn't; it was solid but soft like leather.

Once they were inside, the door closed behind them. Even though they were inside the craft, he could see through the exterior walls. He could see out in every direction. The doorway was at the back of the craft. Across the room against the front of the craft were the controls and chairs for the pilots. There were five captain's chairs in a circle at the middle of the ship. Oscillada invited them to take a seat.

Jake sat down in the chair next to Naomi and was amazed to find the chair fit him perfectly. He had never in his life sat in a more comfortable chair. He looked over at Naomi, and said, "I can't believe how comfortable this chair is."

She responded, "Me neither."

Before they could say anything else, Oscillada came into the circle. "Before we get started, I would like to introduce you to my crew. My pilot there on the left is Captain Elle. She is supported by her co-pilot, Lieutenant Jay. They will adjust the environment on the ship now to make it more conducive for our meeting."

A wall appeared behind the crew so they were out of sight. The see-through outer walls became opaque.

Oscillada began speaking, "We are from the Federation of Orion, which is a cooperative civilization consisting of the planets in the area of the universe you recognize as the Constellation of Orion and the Pleiades Star Cluster. The Federation of Orion created the Council of Intergalactic Enlightenment, which is charged with advancing the spiritual evolution and enlightenment of the beings of the lesser evolved planets in this quadrant of the universe. The Council of Intergalactic Enlightenment assigned our Ambassador, John, the responsibility of establishing the Earth Commission to accomplish this task in regards to your planet, Earth.

"The Earth Commission put a base of operation into orbit around the planet Neptune in your solar system. Earth's astronomers have named our home base Triton after mistaking it for one of Neptune's moons. Triton's retrograde orbit around Neptune provides our base with perpetual energy to support all our operations.

"Now that I have given you some background, I would like to get into more specifics about why I have asked you to meet with me today. I am the Commissioner of Scientific Advancement for the Earth Commission. The purpose of my commission is to influence the advancement of scientific research to improve the quality of life on Earth. One of the main aspects of our involvement is to promote virtually free and sustainable energy for the entire planet. Another important aspect is to try and modify dangerous energies that harm the environment and humans directly. Due to the constraints of our primary directive, we cannot take control of anything. We can only suggest, demonstrate, or influence indirectly.

"Direct contact is prohibited without permission from the Earth Commission Ambassador. If there is contact without permission there must be extenuating circumstances that warrant this contact. Any contact not previously approved must be reviewed to make certain that little or no harm was done and to determine if further action is warranted.

"If a Commissioner believes that something of paramount importance requires contact or any other breach of protocol, he goes to our Ambassador. If the Ambassador identifies aspects of our request that affect other commissions, or the overall mission, a meeting of the entire Earth Commission is called. As a result of one of these meetings, I have been given the honor of communicating with your family directly due to the seriousness of the current situation on Earth. The main thing we need to accomplish today is to get to know each other and for you to have a basic understanding of how things work and why you have been contacted."

Oscillada paused to ascertain the emotional state of his audience before continuing. "I am certain that you will have questions and will need time to process the information you are about to receive. Please allow me to continue until I have finished and then we will have a discussion." Everyone nodded their agreement.

"During the 1940s, Earth's advanced countries were working with atomic energy to determine how to use it as a weapon. We hoped to advance the understanding of this energy for peaceful purposes. Atomic energy can be used safely if you know how to decontaminate the radioactive materials. We tried to share the process of decontamination with leading scientists and political leaders. We were surprised that they did not want the information because they were concerned it might allow the 'enemy' to reverse the effects of the weapon.

"This type of fear-based reasoning is alien to us. Our science is not used to kill others. Our goal, both as individuals and collectively, is to use science for the greatest good for the most people. This means that we do not invent things based on greed and our decisions are not based on who will make money. We have found time after time that those in power on Earth are not concerned about the planet or the public's good. This lack of stewardship has culminated in the Earth no longer being able to support or nourish all its inhabitants.

"There are some cultures on Earth that honor Great Spirit, God, the Creator and accept their stewardship responsibility as a religious duty. Some individuals in every culture respect Mother Earth no matter what their religious beliefs may be. We can assist only if we are cooperating with those types of people because the purpose of our mission and their desires are in harmony with each other.

"Each of you is that type of person. All of you help others and are good stewards of the Earth. Alo and Kaia, you have always respected the old ways and taught others to care for one another and to be good stewards of the Earth. Jake, you chose to reject a life as an oilman and instead to be a sustainable natural rancher because of your dedication to these principles. Naomi, you chose, as a child, to learn about natural medicines and healing energies, all motivated by a desire to help others. So it came as no surprise to us that Nathan chose to become a scientist because of his desire to help others and decrease the pollution on the planet.

"Nathan is the main reason that I am here in my capacity as Commissioner of Scientific Advancement. We have influenced Nathan's research, and he has had tremendous success. He has invented a process to put controlled flexibility and other qualities into metallic compounds that would revolutionize the transportation industry. Nathan's invention would save thousands of lives from crashes, dramatically decrease the demand for fossil fuels, and reduce waste by slowing the corrosion of metal.

"Last week when he presented his preliminary research to his boss and the head of the engineering department at the university, he was excited and assumed they would come up with other ways of using the new material process to improve lives. Instead they are planning to sell the process to the military and, thereby, shut him and his research down. Nathan does not know this yet, but the demonstration, which is scheduled for Thursday of next week, is for a military contractor. So we don't have much time.

"Jake, Nathan will need to come home before he realizes what they are planning and puts himself in danger. They will be watching him to see if he will cause trouble. Many discoveries that would have helped people and the environment have been destroyed or misused. We have been given permission to, let's say, interfere so that Nathan's discovery will not be lost."

Jake was instantly furious and ready to protect his son. Oscillada reached over and placed his hand on Jake's arm. Jake began to feel peaceful due to the love, concern, and reassurance Oscillada was giving him.

"Okay, what are we going to do?" Jake asked.

Oscillada answered, "First, get him to come home before the end of this week, actually the sooner the better. Once he comes home, you need to tell him what the university officials are planning. We will meet back here on Friday night. Together we will come up with a plan.

"Next time we meet, I will bring with me, my associate, Kevin, who has special talents that can be used to help Nathan. The plan will include 'cousin' Kevin going back to the university with him to visit for a week or so.

"Please let me assure you we are confident in our ability to protect Nathan and his discovery. Are you okay with this?"

Jake took a deep breath and nodded.

CHAPTER FOUR

"**G**OOD. DOES ANYONE have any questions or concerns?" Oscillada asked.

Naomi spoke up, "If Nathan has invented something that's good for the environment and for people, I can't understand why Nathan would be in danger. Who would want to hurt him and why would they want to stop his work?"

Kaia added, "It doesn't make sense. Why wouldn't the university be happy about his discovery and be supporting him?"

Nodding his head, Oscillada responded, "I understand your confusion. Let me sum it up in a word: greed."

The look of bewilderment on their faces did not fade, so he continued. "The oil companies make money by selling oil, period, so they would not want anything to decrease the demand for oil. When the entire planet is dependent on oil and there are few alternatives, they are in a position to make a tremendous amount of money. All aspects of the oil industry are based on one principle, produce, and sell as much oil as possible. The automobile companies are aligned with the same purpose. Retooling their factories or researching ways to improve fuel efficiency costs a lot of money instead of making them money. The automobile producers and dealerships make money by selling cars, so they don't want cars to last longer. The production of new vehicles, while the old ones sit and rust in junk yards, drives the metal industry. The banks make money by providing the car loans, and they get paid off in four to six years. Banks want cars to be sold more often so they can make more loans. As you can see, the reach of these industries combined with their related support industries is pervasive in this society. This collective consciousness of greed has a stranglehold on your entire civilization. It is preventing the evolution of your species and leading to the destruction of your planet. It is this phenomenon that your President Eisenhower was talking about in his farewell speech to the nation when he referred to the 'military industrial complex.'"

Oscillada could see the depth and breadth of what he was saying was starting to sink in for everyone.

"The wealthy industries provide extensive funding for universities in the form of grants, donations, the lease of skyboxes in sports arenas, and in other ways. The mere suggestion of withholding these funds can get a university to change the direction of any research. Industries donate enormous sums to political campaigns and support politicians in their chosen endeavors. This funding coupled with propaganda in the form of advertising affords them control over the environmental discussion and political debates. War causes huge demand for products like oil, metal, and ammunition as well as huge budgets for militaries and immense power for those in control of the money. Global warming caused by pollution is real, and it has the entire planet in very dire straits. Innovations like Nathan's have to be adopted, and the use of fossil fuels has to be curtailed or the entire planet will be destroyed."

Jake was getting very agitated. "He's right, that's exactly the way it works. I grew up in this world, I know how those greedy bastards operate, and the whole thing makes me sick! Something has to be done about this."

Everyone nodded in agreement.

"That is exactly what we are going to do," Oscillada promised.

Naomi spoke up, "Everything you have said explains why very well. In some ways it explains how. But it seems to me that there has to be something much bigger going on here. It seems too well-orchestrated, too well-organized, and too systemic to be based solely on collusion among the greedy."

"Naomi, you are exactly right. There is, in fact, much more going on that you need to know in order for you to fully understand. Before we get into that, I need to confirm that each of you has chosen to work with us in this endeavor." Oscillada looked at Alo. "Alo, do you choose to join us?"

"Yes, of course I do."

Oscillada directed his attention to Kaia. "Kaia, do you have any reservations about joining us?"

"I have no reservations at all. Count me in. I will do whatever I can do."

"Excellent," Oscillada said, as he directed his attention to Naomi. "Naomi, do we have your full support?"

"Absolutely!"

Oscillada smiled. "Good. Jake, are you fully committed to working with us?"

"Yes, sir, I am."

"Jake, in the morning I want you to call Nathan, and tell him to come home right away. Do not divulge anything over the phone or the internet about what is going on. You must convince him to be here before Friday night when we will meet again. It would be best if he could be home by Wednesday so he can rest that night, then Thursday you can tell him in person about everything that we have discussed tonight. Will you do that?"

"Yes, I'm sure I can get him to come home by then. Why can't I tell him anything over the phone or internet?" Jake quizzed.

"That will be abundantly clear later, when Naomi gets her question answered," Oscillada responded. "Now before we continue, does anyone have any other questions or concerns?"

Everyone was shaking their heads no, so he continued. "Selena, the Commissioner of Politics and Religion is more qualified than I am to answer Naomi's question. We will take a little break right now while we arrange for her to join us."

Jake's eyes widened as he looked around the room. Everyone else seemed a little surprised too. He was wondering what was going to happen next. When he heard Oscillada say, "Elle, initiate the docking procedure."

Oscillada turned to the group and explained, "Another craft just like this one is hovering eighty thousand feet above us right now. I think you will enjoy watching this, so Jay is going to turn on the monitor. Go ahead, Jay, activate the view screen."

Suddenly, the wall behind the bridge lit up. It looked like the biggest television screen Jake had ever seen. Somehow they could see what was happening as if they were sitting outside on the boulders. The second craft was descending and it looked like it was going to land right on top of them.

Jake piped up, "I don't mean to alarm anyone, but I think that thing is going to crush us!"

Oscillada smiled. "Trust me, they will not crush us, however, they are going to land on top of this ship."

They felt a subtle bump, followed by a click sound as they watched the craft land. After about a minute, the view screen went blank. A door opened in the ceiling and a set of stairs descended to the floor in front of the view screen. A woman walked down the stairs. She was just under six feet tall with green eyes and light brown hair. She was wearing a green jumpsuit and the material had circles in the pattern. Jake looked back at Oscillada and noticed his uniform had a wave pattern. As soon as she stepped off, the stairs retracted into the ceiling and the door closed. She and Oscillada greeted each other by grasping each other's forearms.

Oscillada turned to the group, "I would like to introduce you to Selena, the Commissioner of Politics and Religion for the Earth Commission. Selena, this is Alo, Kaia, Naomi, and Jake."

"Greetings. I am very pleased to meet you and to have this opportunity to work with you." She smiled at each of them.

Oscillada said, "We need another chair."

As soon as he said that, the chairs they had been sitting in shifted and a sixth chair appeared in the circle. Selena took her seat next to Oscillada and began, "My job with the Earth Commission is to work to bring about higher spiritual understanding among human beings and to encourage people to be loving, caring, and selfless. While these are the guiding principles that unite the members of the Federation, not all the beings that reside in this quadrant of the universe have chosen to join us because they are not motivated by these same principles and desires. Quite the opposite in fact. Located in the constellation bordering Orion, Taurus, is the Hyades system of stars and planets. This is home to a group of beings collectively known as the Vermosans. The Vermosans originated on the planet Vermosa, but over time they have colonized four other planets. Vermosans are a race of egocentric, narcissistic sociopaths who are motived by any of a number of self-interests, including arrogance, greed, lust, jealousy, hatred, resentment, and laziness. Just as we have been involved with influencing the affairs of your world, so have they.

"My commission has worked to encourage political leaders to make choices that are in the best interest of all people. We have worked through religious and spiritual leaders in an attempt to teach people to be selfless rather than selfish. The success of our efforts could be described as marginal at best.

"In February 1954, I met with President Dwight Eisenhower and explained that humans were on a destructive downward spiral. The planet would be destroyed if they did not stop killing each other and stop polluting and ravaging the Earth. The use of nuclear energy as a weapon is inconsistent with spiritual evolution. Instead, I explained that nuclear power could be beneficial as an energy source, but first they would need to learn how to decontaminate the waste products it produced. I promised we would help with that. In addition, I warned him about the Vermosans. President Eisenhower said he would have to get back to me. Unfortunately, he unequivocally declined my offer and refused further contact. Shortly thereafter, we learned he had signed an agreement with the Vermosans and had chosen to accept their offer of assistance with advanced weaponry in exchange for the right to abduct and perform tests on a limited number of human subjects."

All four of them gasped.

Naomi was furious. "You're telling us that the President of the United States of America gave permission for the Vermosans to kidnap American citizens in exchange for advanced technology that would give him more military power!"

Kaia added, "It never felt right to have a war-hardened military general in control of the whole country, but this is so much worse than anything I could have imagined."

"That's infuriating!" Alo exclaimed. "I can't imagine a more horrible decision."

Jake blurted, "You mean to tell me the lying government has been in contact with Star People all these years, yet they ridicule and shame anyone who ever admitted they thought you might exist. That just makes me wonder, what else are they lying about? Shit! Now I wonder what, if anything, is true!"

"Unfortunately, it gets worse, much worse," Selena warned. "I will explain further when Nathan is here with us. In the meantime, please fill Nathan in on everything we have covered so far. I am looking forward to working with you."

With that, Selena turned to Oscillada, who said, "Jake, you know your assignment. I would like to thank all of you for coming. We will meet you here again Friday night."

Everyone got up and said good-bye to each other. The door at the back of the craft opened and the stairs descended to the ground. When they reached the boulder circle, they turned around to watch the ships lift off and disappear into the night sky.

Jake said, "What a night!"

CHAPTER FIVE

NATHAN ARRIVED HOME late Wednesday night. Though he was anxious to find out why his Dad had virtually ordered him to come home, Jake and Naomi assured him it could wait until morning. He needed to get a good night sleep, and Jake promised to wake him up before dawn. As the sun came up over the hill behind the house, Nathan and Jake were on their morning ride.

"Nathan, tell me about your research project. How is it going?"

"Dad, I'll be glad to tell you about it, but what is the emergency? You sounded worried on the phone and my mind keeps coming up with a bunch of scenarios that I don't like! I want you to tell me why I had to come home, then we can talk about my research."

"I'm sorry you're worried, but your research project is the reason I asked you to come home."

Nathan jerked around to look at his Dad so fast he startled his horse. "What? What are you talking about?"

"Nathan, do you remember the Star People from when you were a boy camping with your Grandfather?"

"Oh boy, yes, I remember. Why are you asking about that? I never talked about it because I thought you would think it was made up, like the monster that lived under my bed. Remember how you had to kill it for me every night for weeks when I was four? I guess I never thanked you for that. So thank you."

Jake laughed a little nervously and said, "You're welcome. Nathan, there are some real monsters lurking under your bed now and we have to come up with a way to deal with them."

"Okay, Dad, you really have my attention now. Let's go to the oak grove and sit at the picnic table and talk face to face, eyeball to eyeball. Okay?"

"Good idea." Jake's thoughts were starting to come together and he was anxious to talk with his son. They were both quiet for the ten minutes it took them to reach the grove. They led their horses to the stream that wound through the trees and sat down on opposite sides of the table. Jake was a little emotional as he remembered having picnics here when Nathan was a boy. They would come here to rest the horses and eat lunch while working on fences or moving cattle. They both enjoyed the work and each other's company. Now some greedy bastards were trying to hurt his son, and Jake would do everything in his power to stop that from happening.

"Nathan, I just have to blurt out the whole thing."

"Blurt, Dad, blurt!"

"Okay. I was taking my normal morning ride Monday when I found one of Alo's calves stuck in the mud. I carried the calf and led the cow back to their stable. Kaia took care of them and invited me in for coffee. She told me that Alo would be back soon and that he had been out looking at the stars and saying his prayers. So far sounds normal, right?"

"Yup. What's the punch line?"

"Okay. Alo came home and told me that he had been visited by the Star People and they wanted to meet me and Naomi that night."

"Oh boy."

"You just said that. I say 'Star People' and you say, 'Oh boy.' See why I couldn't tell you over the phone? This is not easy to talk about. Anyway, back to my 'blurtation.' I was riding home trying to get my mind around going to see a UFO and aliens—"

Nathan interrupted, "I understand, Dad. It's mind boggling. I've met them before and it still seems really weird, but what does this have to do with my research?"

"I'm getting to that. Alo explained quite a bit to me that evening before we went to meet them. He said Star People have been coming to Earth for hundreds of years to help humans evolve and develop. For the most part only the indigenous cultures have remained open to them. He explained that greed and the desire for power over others has harmed our planet. Nathan, does the name Oscillada mean anything to you?"

"Ah…yeah…why are you asking me about Oscillada?"

"Aha, so you do know each other!"

"Dad! Please, just keep blurting!"

"Okay. Alo introduced us to his friend, Oscillada, who is the Commissioner of Scientific Advancement for the Earth Commission. His job is to encourage the advancement of scientific research to improve the quality of life on Earth. The Earth Commission was created by the Council of Intergalactic Enlightenment which was established by the Federation of Orion. The Federation is a cooperative civilization of planets in the Constellation of Orion and the Pleiades Star Cluster. Oscillada went into a great deal of detail about how direct contact is prohibited unless there is a major important situation. Since we were all sitting in a UFO having a nice meeting, I figured something big was up."

"Very astute, Dad," Nathan joked. "Then what happened?"

Jake grinned. "Oscillada said you were the reason for the meeting. You've had tremendous success with your research and have invented a process to change the properties of several metals. Your invention would save lives, decrease the demand for fossil fuels, and reduce waste and pollution, basically making life better on Earth.

"What you don't know is, after you presented your preliminary work to your boss and the head of the engineering department, they contacted the military and various corporate donors to ascertain the monetary potential of your invention. There is tremendous interest in your work. Right now the military is trying to appropriate your research. They'd like to confiscate your invention and classify it as top secret, thereby reserving it for military purposes and making it unavailable for the public good. There would be compensation to the university and a payoff for you. Of course any deal would keep you restricted and under their control. You would get—"

Nathan interrupted and yelled, "What? They're doing this behind my back?"

Nathan was furious. He jumped up from the table, grabbed a stick, and threw it hard. "This wasn't for war and killing people! The process would save lives. It would save people money, millions. It would help people. It would reduce pollution. It would significantly reduce global warming, almost immediately. It would revolutionize the automotive industry. Our need for oil and gas would be reduced by more than half."

Suddenly Nathan started to understand. He sat down heavily on the bench, looked at Jake, and asked, "So what are we going to do?"

"That's exactly what I said. We will be doing something, but we need more information and lots of help. Oscillada promised we will get both on Friday night. He's bringing an associate named Kevin who has special talents. I guess he's like a bodyguard or something."

Nathan felt like he wanted to punch something, but hitting a tree would hurt his hand. What bothered him the most was the betrayal he felt. He thought he and his colleagues were all on the same side, with the same basic values, going the same direction. He was wrong. Very wrong!

Jake debated if he should tell Nathan now about Selena and the things she had told them about the Vermosans. He decided now was not the time. Nathan was going to have to process his emotions and get his mind around the truth he had just received. Jake knew he would have questions that only the commissioners could answer. He felt it would be better if he and Naomi together talked to Nathan about the Vermosans.

"Come on, Nathan, let's get home. Your Mom is waiting for us."

It was a beautiful day for a ride. The sky was a wonderful clear blue. Spring flowers were in bloom. The air was fresh and clean. Unfortunately, Jake and Nathan were so involved with their thoughts that they didn't notice the beauty surrounding them. It was good that the horses knew the way home.

Naomi heard Bailey barking enthusiastically, announcing, "They're home." She had been praying for Great Spirit to give Jake the right words and for Nathan to have the strength to handle the truth.

Nathan came in and stopped to look at his mother. She walked to him and gave him a warm embrace. Nathan only said, "What a morning. I think I'm in shock."

She squeezed his hand. "Come on, sit down, eat a sandwich, and have something to drink." Naomi understood her son well and knew that he was struggling with his emotions. She wanted to comfort him, but it wasn't like kissing his booboo to make it feel better like she did years ago. She thought to herself, *He is a man who needs to fight for what is right. He came from a strong line of warriors and he will have the strength to fight for the good.*

After putting up the horses, Jake came in and saw Naomi had lunch ready for them. He hugged her, poured himself a glass of lemonade, and sat down at the table. He looked at Naomi and said, "Honey, I haven't told Nathan about the second phase of our meeting and the things Selena told us."

Nathan gulped and almost choked on his sandwich. "There's more?"

Naomi reached over and patted his hand. "Yes, son, there's more we have to tell you before our meeting tomorrow."

Nathan took a deep breath and said, "I'm ready, let's hear it."

"We have plenty of time. The meeting is not until tomorrow night. Finish your lunch, play with the dogs, relax, and get yourself grounded. We'll talk later this afternoon," Naomi responded.

Nathan let out a breath, one that he didn't know he had been holding. "That's the best idea I've heard in a while. Dad, do you need some help with anything around here?"

Jake answered, "I need to restack the wood pile to make room for the new wood that I'll be splitting soon. A big oak tree was hit by lightning a month ago. I have it cut up and stacked by the splitter. I would appreciate it if you would move all the split, seasoned fire wood into the south section of the wood shed. That will give me plenty of room for the oak when I get it split."

Nathan quickly got up and said, "I'll do it now."

After Nathan left to work in the wood shed, Jake asked Naomi, "Is he okay? How is he doing?"

"Don't worry Jake, he's going to be fine. Now how about you get back to work in your workshop? You need to smell lumber."

Jake laughed and gave Naomi a big hug and kiss and then another kiss. As he looked in her eyes, his love for her felt like it was going to make his heart explode.

She smiled and said, "I love you too. I'm going to ask Mom and Dad to come over this afternoon. We need to be together."

Jake nodded and felt much more peaceful as he headed to his workshop.

Naomi got up to call Kaia. Kaia answered and said, "I've been waiting for your call. How are things going?"

"Very well. Both men are out working with wood. You know how wood helps them to be peaceful and grounded. I'm calling to find out if you and Dad can come over this afternoon. Jake didn't tell Nathan about the things Selena told us. I think it would be easier if we were all together to talk about that. What do you think?"

"Yes, that sounds like a wonderful idea. We will be there soon."

Suddenly the house was quiet. Naomi decided to sit on the front porch swing, shell peas, and relax. Two hours later, the peas were shelled and Bailey jumped off the swing, barking away. Alo and Kaia were pulling into the driveway in their old pickup truck.

Jake heard Bailey announcing visitors and saw Alo's truck, so he headed toward the house. Nathan had just finished his shower and was sitting the living room. Once everyone had a chance to greet each other, Alo said, "I think it would be good if we smudge and say a prayer before we begin talking. These are powerful things that we are discussing."

Everyone stood up as Alo lit the sage pot. Quietly and respectfully, each of them bowed their heads as Alo said a prayer. "Great Spirit, we come together today in a humble way asking for help and direction. We pray that Mother Earth be healed and restored. We pray for all of Earth's people to have good food and clean air and water. We pray for harmony and peace on Earth. Please help us with this struggle." Everyone said, "Aho!"

Alo smudged each person in turn as they released any negative thoughts, feelings, or energy and opened up to Spirit's guidance.

Naomi started, "I couldn't really understand how greedy people would have the power to stop your discoveries from being used for the good of all. Oscillada told us his associate, Selena, the Commissioner of Politics and Religion for the Earth Commission, would be in the best position to explain it to us. No one by that name was there, so I figured the meeting was over."

Jake jumped in, "Yeah, then the craziest thing happened. This other flying saucer landed on top of the flying saucer we were in, a door opened in the ceiling and in came this woman, Selena."

"You would have loved that part, Nathan," Alo chimed in.

"I'm pretty sure Nathan would have loved the whole evening, Alo. Well, except for the part about what we were being told. Never mind," Kaia said, while shaking her head.

Naomi piped up, "Selena explained that her job with the Earth Commission was to encourage people to be loving, caring, and self-less, and that this was the guiding principle that united the members of the Federation. She told us there were other aliens called Vermosans, who were a race of egocentric, narcissistic sociopaths who are exclusively motived by their own self-interests."

"Evil aliens," added Alo, "from the star system called Hyades of all things. She said these Vermin—"

"Vermosans, Dad!" Naomi corrected.

"That was it. Vermosans were influencing humans."

Jake spoke up, "Selena explained that in 1954, she met with President Eisenhower and offered to provide the technology for using nuclear energy for power and the technology for decontaminating the nuclear waste products in exchange for the elimination of nuclear weapons."

"Eisenhower said no! Can you believe that?" Kaia exclaimed.

"What? He said no? That's crazy. Why would he do that?" Nathan asked.

"Even though Selena had warned Eisenhower about the Vermosans, Eisenhower made a deal with the Vermosans instead of the Federation," Alo explained.

Jake went on, "The Vermosans offered technology for advanced weapons in exchange for the right to abduct and perform tests on a limited number of humans. Eisenhower thought that was a deal he could not refuse. Can you believe that crap?"

"Oh no, that's horrible!" Nathan was completely blown away. Now he knew why his Dad didn't want to tell him this when they were alone. Now all five of them, thinking about everything they had been told, were shaking their heads.

Jake continued, "Finally, she told us the story gets worse, much worse, and she would tell us the rest Friday night. Talk about a cliffhanger!"

"This is awfully difficult to swallow. Maybe we should be relieved that she didn't tell us any more yet," Kaia suggested.

Nathan sighed, "I'll say. I'm glad I have until tomorrow night to think about all I've heard today. I'm sure I have a lot of questions, but I can't think of them right now."

"I agree with Nathan, I think that's enough for now. Dinner will be ready soon. Won't you stay and eat with us?" Naomi asked.

"That sounds lovely, dear. Is there anything I can help you with?" Kaia offered as she followed Naomi to the kitchen.

The men went to the porch to relax. Tomorrow night would be here soon enough.

CHAPTER SIX

NATHAN WOKE UP just before sunrise. He was in his sleeping bag in a hammock hanging twenty feet from the ground and three feet above his nineteen-year-old hand-built wood platform. It had served him well when he was a kid. Years past, in his imagination, the platform had been a raft going down the river, a jungle treehouse, a pirate ship, a flying saucer, anything he could dream up. Now it was a place for him to be peaceful and alone with his thoughts.

Last night while under the stars, he was thinking about his life, past, present, and future. He wondered about the influences on his life and how he had ended up where he was now. This caused Nathan to remember and think about little things that had happened. Things he hadn't really thought about before, especially as a grown man. He realized his Grandfather was deeply connected to the Star People, and he had been conditioned to believe Star People visitations were normal.

When he awoke from his restless sleep, he realized he had made some decisions. He was determined that his invention would be used to benefit Mother Earth and for the good of all people. He understood how close he was to becoming one of the many scientists who had their work taken from them to be misused or destroyed by corporate greed or military coercion or both. It was easy to say and believe, "only idiots or lunatics think it is a conspiracy," until you find yourself in the middle of one. He concluded he was joining the Star People and to hell with the consequences.

Nathan climbed out of his sleeping bag and hung it over the hammock to air out. He was hungry and wanted some coffee. When he walked into the house he heard his Mom and Dad talking softly. He quickly stuck his head in the kitchen doorway and yelled, "Good morning!"

Jake jumped and Naomi laughed. Jake said, "I thought you were upstairs sleeping."

"No, Nathan was camping out under the stars last night," Naomi said, as she finished buttering the toast.

"Did you have any visitors?" Jake asked.

Pouring a cup of coffee, Nathan said, "Just an owl sharing my tree for a while."

Naomi passed out plates of eggs, bacon, hash browns, and toast. Nobody spoke while they were eating except for Jake asking for more coffee and Nathan asking for the elderberry jelly. While they were taking their plates to the sink, Naomi suggested, "Jake, why don't you and Nathan take a ride and check on the cattle? I think it will be good for both of you."

"That's a great idea honey. What do you say, Nathan?"

"Sounds good, let's do it."

As Jake and Nathan got up to leave, Naomi reminded them, "Take your time and enjoy yourselves. We don't have to leave tonight until around seven."

Once she finished cleaning up the kitchen, Naomi went to her medicine room in the back of the house for some much needed private time. After lighting the sage in the pot next to her medicine bag, she picked up her flute and let the music say what was in her heart. She was surprised by how long she played and by how much emotion she was releasing in the music. She was also surprised when tears started sliding down her cheek. Naomi was never a crier and wasn't completely sure why she was crying now. She put her flute down and sat silently looking out the window.

Naomi thought about how brave her people were and how often they had to fight. They always fought with honor and courage. Although her husband had white skin, she knew he would fight with the same honor and courage. This was not a battle between men on horses, or in tanks, each fighting for their nation or a noble cause. This was a battle with a powerful, yet unknown, enemy for reasons only partially understood. This was a war of lies, deception, and trickery motivated by the worst form of greed. Nobody in her family had any understanding of how they were supposed to "win" against such evil. Now she understood why the tears came. She was afraid for her family, but she had faith and courage that Great Spirit would provide what they needed to defeat this evil. Naomi started to relax because she knew that they would win, no matter how difficult the battle. Thinking about her husband and son enjoying their morning ride, she felt love and peace envelop her.

Jake's horse, Chester, loved to race against any horse he saw ahead of him. A horse could be a mile away and Chester would take off. Nathan's horse wasn't competitive like Chester, but Sadie did love to run. When Sadie started running ahead in her jubilant "ain't it great to be alive" manner, Chester took off and the race was on. Jake and Nathan didn't hold back. They raced until they reached the gate, then looked at each other and grinned. Jake said, "That's better."

Jake wanted to check with his ranch hands who were helping watch over the herd during calving season. Jake often hired Matt and Luke, Nathan's cousins, when he needed extra help. Matt and Luke were young, strong, and experienced cowboys. They did not have much of a formal education, but they were hardworking, totally honest, and experts with cattle.

As Jake approached, Matt stood up and said, "Hello, Uncle. Hey, Nathan, it's been too long."

Matt and Luke were like brothers to Nathan. They fished, hunted, explored, and grew up together. Alo taught the boys Mintaka ways beginning when they were very young. Nathan went off to a private school when he was twelve. Although it was hard for him to be away from his family and in a different culture, when he came home and his cousins pounded on him in greeting, he was instantly happy and felt a deep sense of belonging.

Nathan swung off his horse and gave his cousin a hearty punch on the shoulder. "Hey, cuz, it's good to see you. Where's Luke?" Nathan asked.

"Luke's taking a newborn calf to Kaia. She's the weaker of twins and the other calf is hogging all the milk. Kaia has a cow with plenty of milk at the stable and she's going to try to fatten the calf up. Once the calf is stronger, we'll bring it back to the herd. That's the plan anyway," Matt explained.

"That's a good plan. Have you run into any other problems?" Jake asked.

"Does having an eight-hundred-pound grizzly bear passing through count as a problem?" Matt enjoyed watching Jake's mouth fly open.

"What? We haven't had any bears here for years!" Jake exclaimed.

"You can thank the conservationists that the bears are returning," Matt said.

Jake hated the thought of losing cows and calves to bears, but he also admired and respected bears. "What did you do, Matt?"

"Well, Uncle, we did what any self-respecting Native American cowboy would do. We whooped and hollered and waved our hats, from a respectful distance of course, as we stayed between him and the herd. The bear probably thought we were crazy because he high-tailed it to the next county," Matt grinned.

"Good job!" Jake exclaimed. "If you see any more bears, please let me know. I know a man who specializes in training dogs to bark and chase off bears. If I have to, I'll hire him to come over and chase them off."

Nathan spoke up, "Hey, Matt, I'm planning on being home for a few days. Do you think we could do a little fishing?"

"Absolutely! Give us a call when you want to go."

"Okay, will do." Nathan smiled at Matt, and turning to his Dad said, "Do you want to ride over to Alo's now?"

"Yes. I have a few things I would like to run by him."

Jake and Nathan said good-bye to Matt and headed to Alo's. As they rode along, Nathan started thinking about his invention, the Star People, his cousins, his colleagues, the upcoming meeting tonight, and he suddenly felt overwhelmed. "Dad, are you believing all this?"

Jake shook his head and said, "Sort of, not really. Well, maybe." He thought for a minute and said, "Nathan, I know this is all true. I know we are not imagining it. I know Star People are real. I know you have invented something that is amazing and evil people want to take control of it. I know that we're being given a chance to change the course of human history. But when I actually say it, internally I'm thinking, I must be dreaming, this can't possibly be happening."

Nathan laughed and felt relieved to know he was not the only one with these conflicting feelings. Alo sensed that Nathan and Jake were on their way to see him, so he was leaning against the fence gate to his yard waiting for them. He opened the gate to let them ride in and then shut it behind them. Jake and Nathan barely had time to jump off before Chester and Sadie started toward the watering trough and hay bale.

Alo said, "Come on in and have some coffee with me. Kaia is at the neighbors. Their daughter has bronchitis and Kaia went to check on her. She took enough teas and medicine with her to cure the whole family if necessary. Let's sit here on the porch. I'll get the coffee."

"Please sit down, Grandfather. I'll get the coffee," Nathan offered.

"Thank you, Nathan." Alo looked at Jake, saw that he was a little tense, and thought, *Now is the perfect time to share the dream.*

Nathan handed them their mugs and sat down. Alo said, "Great Spirit blessed me with a dream last night that I need to share with you."

Jake and Nathan gave Alo their undivided attention. His visions and dreams were more valuable than gold. They were gifts from Great Spirit that guided and kept them from harm. Alo stood up, lit the smudge pot, and lifted his face to the sky. "Great Spirit, we thank you for the visions and dreams that help us to know the right path to follow. We thank you for protection and guidance. Aho." Jake and Nathan stood while Alo smudged them and the porch.

After they sat down Alo began. "My dream started with a dove flying over a mountain carrying a hawk feather in his mouth. The hawk feather was difficult for the dove to carry. The strong winds made it impossible for the little bird to get across the mountain. The wind was too strong and forced the dove to the ground. The dove was too tired to fly. Nightfall was approaching, soon the dove would be a target for hungry predators like the owl and the snake. The dove looked toward the east and saw a white buffalo walking toward him. The buffalo said to the dove, 'Jump up on my back and rest. I will carry you and your feather. You and your feather weigh nothing to me. The owl and the snake cannot hurt me and they cannot hurt you if you will trust me to carry you.' The buffalo carried the dove safely across the mountain. When they reached the other side, the dove was rested and able to carry the hawk feather and continue his journey."

Jake liked to have things spelled out, and he wanted to make sure that he got the whole point of the story, so he asked, "Alo, could you possibly explain the dream to me? I think I understand most of it, but I would appreciate you telling me."

Alo thought of the jokes about how white men can be deaf, but he would never put Jake in that category. He knew that Jake's love for his son and his sincere desire to understand was what made him ask. "Yes, Jake, I will. This is a serious time and we all need to have understanding.

"Great Spirit is telling us that Nathan is a man of peace and he has a great truth that he is carrying. It is a heavy truth and impossible for him to carry alone. The obstacles that he faces are more than he can handle. Nathan is trying to climb over the mountain of greed and corruption while carrying his invention to help others. Powerful forces are trying to keep him from succeeding. The White Buffalo is a sacred symbol of life and abundance and that all things are connected. We are connected to each other and the Star People. The buffalo protects and nurtures us. Nathan will be carried and supported through his enemies by the Star People and he will not be harmed if he trusts them."

Nathan felt more humble than he thought possible. He looked at Alo and Jake and said, "I am not afraid. I am determined to finish this journey."

The three men stood up in total solidarity and strength. Jake said, "Nathan, let's head home so that we can get ready to come back for the meeting."

Nathan turned toward Alo, "What is the proper attire for the party tonight?"

Alo joked, "You could wrap yourself up in aluminum foil." They all laughed.

Chester and Sadie were quite content and ready to go. Alo closed the gate behind them as they left on the trail for home.

Naomi was waiting for Jake and Nathan. She could tell as soon as she saw them that they were in a good place. They were both smiling and rubbing Bailey. Bailey was doing her famous belly roll trick. She rolls over and you rub her tummy. It is her only trick, but she has perfected it. Every family member has been well trained by Bailey to participate in her trick.

Jake came in, wrapped his arms around Naomi, and gave her a big hug and kiss. "Honey, Alo had a dream last night and everything is going to be fine. Maybe a little weird, but fine."

When Naomi looked at Nathan she saw an inner strength and peace that she had never seen in him before. She thought to herself, *This is my kid!*

Nathan smiled and said, "Dad, could you fill Mom in while I take care of the horses?"

"Sure. We'll be taking the truck this evening so go ahead and put them in for the night. Thanks, Nathan."

"Talk to me. I want to hear all about it." Naomi insisted.

"Sure, honey, sit with me."

As they sat down in their easy chairs in the living room Jake knew he had to be concise and clear while quickly telling the whole story. He started with the important part. Jake explained Alo was at the gate waiting for them and he had a dream to share. Jake told Naomi the dream, word for word, knowing she wouldn't need Alo's interpretation. When he finished, Naomi was in tears. That wasn't anything Jake was expecting. He had seen tears on her face only once before and that was when Nathan was placed in her arms at birth. Jake was at a loss for words.

Naomi said, "I'm fine. I had a moment this morning of feeling scared and overwhelmed. I became emotional thinking about the danger Nathan could be in, but I released it to Spirit and have faith that everything will be all right. I felt God's assurance and became peaceful. But for Spirit to give Alo this dream as a confirmation is a huge gift that fills my heart with joy. Thank you, Jake."

"What are you thanking me for?" Jake asked.

"You are always loving and supporting me and I know that you would do anything for our family. You are a good man, Jake Stevenson."

Jake was again at a loss for words, so he followed his heart and went over to Naomi and hugged her against his chest. They hugged each other without saying anything. Nathan came in, saw them, stopped, and hugged them both.

Naomi said, "Go ahead and take your showers. Dinner will be ready soon."

"Good idea," Nathan said as he headed up the stairs.

Naomi called out to him, "Nathan, your aluminum foil suit is hanging on the back of the bathroom door."

Jake looked at Naomi and said, "How did you know about that?"

"Dad sent me a smoke signal, no wait, it was a phone call. He called when you were on your way home to say everything was fine and he told me Nathan asked about proper attire. He made me laugh."

While Jake and Nathan were getting ready, Naomi was heating the chili and baking the cornbread for supper. In thirty minutes, they were at the table. Nathan had put on his newest jeans, a long sleeved green plaid shirt, and his good boots. Naomi told him that he looked "out of this world." Unfortunately he had a mouth full of water at the time. After they finished their second bowl of chili, the guys cleaned up the kitchen while Naomi got ready. It was almost time for them to leave. Everybody was a little anxious but in good spirits.

CHAPTER SEVEN

I T WAS CLOSE to eight o'clock when they pulled into Alo and Kaia's driveway. Jake, Naomi, and Nathan were feeling excited and a little nervous. Alo and Kaia walked out to greet them.

Alo said, "The Star People will be here any minute. Let's go straight to the circle to wait for them."

They eagerly made their way to the sacred circle. Within minutes of their arrival, they spotted a light overhead coming toward them. They watched in awe as the craft landed. The door opened and Oscillada and Selena emerged.

Oscillada called out, "Hi, Nathan. How is my favorite student?"

Nathan walked toward him. "I'm very glad to see you again. I'm especially happy to have the opportunity to thank you in person for all the guidance you've given me."

"Thank you for listening. Nathan, I would like to introduce you to my friend and colleague, Selena. Selena, this is Nathan Stevenson."

Selena took hold of Nathan's forearms in the customary way. "Hi, Nathan, it is a pleasure to meet you."

"Come in and make yourselves comfortable," Oscillada said as he led them up the stairs.

As soon as everyone was on board, the stairs retracted and the door closed. Jake looked around the room and saw that this ship was much larger than the last one. The bridge with all the controls was above them on a mezzanine level. The view screen was in front of them, but the rest of the ship was not wide open like on the other ship. Oscillada could see they were looking around and very curious, so he spoke up. "This ship which is over one hundred feet in diameter has sleeping quarters for all our guests and crew in addition to other amenities. It is much more well-appointed for longer excursions. Since we are going to be working together, we are set up to be here for an extended period."

After everyone took their seats, Selena began, "When we last met, I told you about the Vermosans and Eisenhower's agreement with them. I would like to pick up where I left off. Nathan, I am sure Jake and the others have filled you in on everything I told them Monday night. Do you have any questions?"

Nathan recapped, "Let me make sure I've got this straight. The Vermosans are a race of egocentric, evil aliens who are here to exploit Earth and its people. They have aligned themselves with the arrogant, greedy people of Earth who share their values or lack thereof. They manipulate everyone and everything to satisfy their own selfish desires without any consideration of the consequences to the planet or its people. Is that right?"

Selena nodded, "Yes, that is the gist of it, but as I was saying, it does get worse. President Eisenhower thought he was being clever when he made his agreement with the Vermosans. He imposed some restrictions on the number of humans that could be abducted, and he established a group within the Central Intelligence Agency called Majestic Twelve to provide oversight of the Vermosans. The Vermosans were supposed to notify Majestic Twelve about each human abduction and insure that the humans did not remember anything. Vermosans are pathological liars, so they did not even pretend to adhere to their agreement. They did not report their activities as required. They refused to limit the number of people abducted and made no effort to insure their victims would have no lasting damage. The Vermosans are the source of the horror stories about people being subjected to frightening tests or being abducted and never returned. They are also the ones responsible for the cattle mutilations you may have heard about."

Nathan was outraged and said, "You're right, this is much worse."

Selena continued, "Unfortunately, I am just getting started. President Eisenhower wanted to protect himself from any political fallout associated with people realizing that the government had a relationship with aliens. In his effort to create plausible deniability for his administration, Eisenhower made Majestic Twelve a completely autonomous division of the CIA. It was Majestic Twelve who began the propaganda campaign denying the existence of aliens and ridiculing anyone who even suggested they might exist. Making Majestic Twelve completely autonomous was a grave miscalculation on his part. After it was too late, he realized Majestic Twelve was no longer under his control. The Vermosans continued to divulge technological secrets to Majestic Twelve, and Majestic Twelve allowed the Vermosans to do whatever they wanted to do.

"In his farewell speech to the nation, President Eisenhower was referring to the threat posed by Majestic Twelve and the Vermosans when he said, 'We must guard against the acquisition of unwarranted influence by the military-industrial complex. The potential for the disastrous rise of misplaced power exists and will persist.'"

Selena heard a soft gasp coming from the audience. She continued slowly, saying, "President Eisenhower fully explained the situation to incoming President John F. Kennedy. President Kennedy was determined to regain control over Majestic Twelve, and he made several strategic moves hoping to accomplish just that. This made Mr. Kennedy very unpopular with Majestic Twelve and the CIA. President Kennedy's efforts to establish his authority over the rogue arm of the CIA, known as Majestic Twelve, ended very badly for him, as you know."

Selena paused as she read the shock on the faces of their five guests. Alo, Kaia, and Naomi each had tears in their eyes. Jake and Nathan were both shaking their heads. None of them could speak for a few moments.

Finally, Jake spoke up, "Are you telling us that Majestic Twelve was behind the assassination of President John F. Kennedy?"

"Yes, that is exactly what I am telling you. I know all this is hard to hear, but it is necessary in order for you to have a full understanding of the dangerous situation we find ourselves in. Are you ready for me to continue?"

After a few moments of being in shock, everyone nodded their heads.

"To go this far, to assassinate a President of the United States, in the pursuit of self-interest is the embodiment of pure evil. Once a human has reached this level of evil, there is no turning back. When a human being chooses to perpetrate this degree of selfishness against another being energetically that person becomes a Vermosan. There is nothing that this anonymous group will not do in order to protect the status quo in this world where they maintain supreme power."

"Holy cow! Are these the guys who are planning to seize my research?" Nathan asked.

"Yes, and make no mistake, these are very dangerous people, and to make matters worse, the alien Vermosans are helping them."

Oscillada spoke up, "I would like to jump in here and tell you a little more about Vermosans."

Everyone shifted their attention to Oscillada, very anxious to hear what he was going to say.

"First, as I am sure you can imagine, not all the beings in the universe are like humans. For example, on planets that are smaller than Earth, where the gravitational pull is less, the average being can be over ten feet tall. On the largest planets, the average height can be as little as two and half feet. Suffice it to say, the differences are extensive. Vermosans are very different indeed. They are physically hideous, ten feet tall, with claws, red eyes, and scaly skin like reptiles. They don't breathe oxygen, they aren't affected by radiation, and they don't drink water. There is no amount of damage that can be done to the Earth that will render it unsuitable for Vermosans."

Nathan asked, "Why haven't they just exterminated us?"

"Great Spirit, God, the Creator won't allow it. The Creator has endowed each of us with free will. Each of us has been given the opportunity to choose how to live our lives and choose who we are going to be. This free will is a gift of the Creator. Therefore, it is sacred and is not to be interfered with. The Vermosans can only lead, trick, coerce, and encourage humans to choose to destroy themselves."

"That explains a lot," Kaia said.

"Exactly," Oscillada and Selena agreed in unison.

"Let me clarify a little more," Oscillada continued. "The Vermosans are the worst of the worst. They are the darkest, vilest creatures in all the cosmos. If they have their way, one of two things will happen. Either humans will become extinct or humans will become their slaves. What the Vermosans are trying to do to Earth, they have already done to four other planets. On three of these planets, the native species has become extinct. On one, the native species became a slave race, totally under the control of the Vermosans. This slave race is sometimes referred to as the Greys. They have been reported by some human abductees and captured by the United States military when one of their ships crashed in the New Mexico desert while they were trying to escape from the Vermosans."

Oscillada took a moment to check on everyone before continuing, "Now I have some good news. I won't be surprised if you have questions about what I am about to say. If you do, feel free to ask. On our side, we have one very unique order of beings known as Midwayers. They are so named because they are, well, in effect half spiritual and half physical."

Everyone was intrigued and listening very intently.

"A Midwayer in its natural state is a ball of energy, which looks like a ball of light. In this state, they can travel at the speed of thought."

"The speed of thought? What is that?" Nathan interrupted.

"The speed of thought is instantaneous, but I realize as a scientist, you would like a more precise answer so let me put it this way. The speed of thought equals the square of eight times the sum of the speed of light plus the speed of sound."

"Okay, well, I would say that is instantaneous. Please continue," Nathan said, wide-eyed and smiling.

"A Midwayer is also a shapeshifter. They can materialize, so to speak, to look like anything or anyone they choose."

"How does that work?" Nathan inquired.

"They utilize more than one technique to accomplish this. In essence, basic shapeshifting involves studying and creating a mental image of something, then using the mind to conjure up this mental image and project it onto their physical form. This can be used easily and quickly to enable them to look like a boulder, a tree, a person, or composite of people they have seen before or just about anything. As you can probably imagine, this could be very useful."

Selena interjected, "Most of the stories of 'divine intervention' attributed to angels were actually Midwayers deploying this technique."

"That is amazing!" Nathan exclaimed. "Please tell us more."

Oscillada continued, "They employ this basic technique mostly for short term, shall we say, assignments. It can be difficult to maintain the projection of this mental image for an extended period of time. It can be done, but it takes a lot of focus and energy. In order to maintain physical form for an extended period, they use a more advanced technique. This advanced technique could be referred to as the doppelganger phenomenon."

"What?" Jake and Nathan gasped simultaneously.

Oscillada chuckled to himself. "This advanced technique requires the use of a DNA sample from a volunteer. Once the Midwayer mixes this DNA with his own and the physical transition process is complete, the Midwayer can materialize at any time as the exact replica of the volunteer, i.e. his doppelganger."

"Whoa, this is really the stuff of science fiction," Nathan said.

"Yes it is, Nathan, except for one thing. It is real, and it is going to give us one incredible secret weapon. Think about it, a doppelganger, who knows what you know and has a vast array of skills far in an advance of yours, including the ability to walk through walls."

"That sounds amazing, I guess the possibilities would be endless," Nathan responded. He was thinking that he might need to sleep in the hammock tonight.

Oscillada went on, "In our previous meeting, I promised to bring my associate, Kevin, to help us. Well, I am not usually at a loss for words, but I realize, this may be a little difficult for you and I am struggling to figure out how to say this."

"In our family, we have a tradition, if you are worried about how to say something, just blurt it out," Nathan suggested.

"Okay, then here goes. Kevin is a Midwayer," Oscillada blurted.

Oscillada felt much better, but he noticed the rest of them looked a little pale. "We can do this however you would like. You can meet Kevin, who is a physical doppelganger of a friend. Or you can meet him in his natural state and witness his conversion to Kevin. My original plan was to introduce you to him in his natural state, and then have him change to Kevin, but now I am concerned that may be too shocking."

Alo jumped in, "May I suggest that you tell us more about Kevin, the doppelganger? Then explain what we will be witnessing. I think everyone would like to meet him in his natural state and witness the transition."

Nathan spoke up, "I agree, I think it would be best for us to ease into this. We don't want to limit Kevin by being unable to deal with the reality of who he is."

Everyone seemed to be in agreement, except maybe Jake who looked like he was choking a little. Naomi reached over and took Jake's hand. He looked at her and began to calm down and breathe again, then he said, "Keep talking, no sudden surprises, and I will be okay in a minute."

Oscillada explained, "In his natural state as a ball of energy, his name is 7-8-9 the eighth. Since this is very difficult for us to relate to, he prefers to be known as Kevin, which is his go-to physical form. Kevin is the doppelganger of a good friend of ours, a man who lives in Ireland and is a high school biology teacher. He has worked with us on numerous occasions and has graciously consented for 7-8-9 the eighth to use the physical form known as Kevin any time he chooses. Kevin has some physical resemblance to Jake, so it will be easy to pass him off as Nathan's second cousin on Jake's side of the family."

Selena, monitoring everyone's reaction, was pleased to see they were starting to relax. She added, "Kevin would be very effective even if you only ever knew him as Kevin. However, if he is free to come and go, as necessary, in his natural state, the possibilities are endless, and everyone will be safer. That is why we want you to be comfortable with the reality of who he is."

Oscillada, seeing that everyone was now prepared to meet Kevin, said, "When you are ready, I will turn on the view screen, and you will be able to watch 7-8-9 the eighth approach from high above the ship. Then he will come through the view screen and stop right in front of it. Next, in the blink of an eye, Kevin will be standing right here. Is everyone ready for this?"

Jake squeezed Naomi's hand and everyone nodded.

"Jay, activate the view screen and signal Kevin he is cleared for entry," Oscillada said, as he turned to face the view screen.

The screen came on and they could see the night sky. In the sky, they could see a light coming toward them. Suddenly it was about six inches in diameter floating right in front of the view screen. Just as they were able to comprehend what they were looking at, it was gone, and a six foot tall, slender man with brown hair and green eyes was standing in its place. "Greetings, my friends. I am Kevin, and it is my pleasure to meet you."

CHAPTER EIGHT

AKE TOOK A deep breath and thought, *That wasn't bad at all.* Oscillada and Selena greeted Kevin in turn, and they joined the circle.

Kevin spoke first, "Jake, you have to admit, I do look a little like your mother's brother, Jack."

Jake nodded in agreement and said to everyone, "It's true."

Kevin continued, "I have been working with Oscillada and others on a plan. We thought this would be a good time to fill you in on some of the details. Nathan, the two of us will be working closely together, so it is important that you feel as comfortable being with me as you do with your other cousins. I was hoping to spend a few days staying with you, so we can get to know each other. Does that sound good?"

Nathan nodded and said, "Sure that sounds fine, maybe you would like to go fishing with me and my cousins, Matt and Luke."

"That is a great idea. From this moment forward, I am your second cousin on your Dad's side of the family, and we need to be completely sure that no one will think anything different. If you are afraid that people will realize I am an alien, you will draw unwanted attention toward us, do you understand?"

"Yes, that makes sense," Nathan responded.

"Jake, Naomi, Alo, and Kaia, the same goes for all of you. I want you to think of me as family and treat me the same as you would treat any other visiting family member. This is the most important aspect of our cover story. Please rest assured, I have lived and worked on Earth among humans for many years, and I am skilled at blending in. I will save the weird alien stuff for behind closed doors or under the cover of darkness, and no one will be the wiser."

Everyone laughed and Kevin was happy to see they were relaxing. "Once we are in agreement about the course of action we will take, Nathan and I will be deploying the plan on the ground. Oscillada and Selena will be monitoring our activities, as well as the activities of our enemies, from this ship in a cloaked position in space. If they need to alert us of any danger or new developments, they will contact me. In addition, I do not have a need for sleep, so I will travel undetected to the ship each night to review the status of our mission with them. Does anyone have any questions at this point?"

Kaia spoke up, "Those Vermosans sound pretty awful. Won't we need more help?"

Selena answered, "Do not be concerned. Let me assure you, we have a lot of help. Under the command of John, the Earth Commission Ambassador to the Council of Intergalactic Enlightenment, there is an entire contingent of beings known as the Watchers who specialize in monitoring the activities of the Vermosans on Earth and the humans they are influencing. Nothing gets past them. Oscillada and I will be here, coordinating with the Watchers and others to make sure Nathan and Kevin stay safe."

Oscillada added, "We know what Majestic Twelve and the Vermosans are up to regarding Nathan's invention. They do not know we know. It is important that it stays that way. That is why there must be no telephone or internet communication about any of this."

Naomi asked, "How will Jake and I know what's happening with Nathan? I'm afraid I will be worrying myself sick."

Kaia added, "Me too."

Selena responded, "Do not worry. We can easily keep Alo posted on the events that are transpiring. At certain times during the mission, if you would like to be on the ship with us, you can watch what is happening on the view screen. We can pick you up here, before significant events. We will coordinate this with Alo, if you are willing."

Naomi and Kaia appeared relieved. Kevin asked, "Does anyone have any more questions before we get into more details?"

Kevin surveyed the room and saw there were no questions. "Nathan, I know this is going to be challenging for you, but I want you to know I will be with you every step of the way. We would not be asking you to do this if we did not already know that you have the courage and the faith to help us pull it off. Please do not be concerned. Over the next several days we will have time to discuss every aspect of the plan in complete detail. We will not proceed until you are ready."

"Okay, that's a relief," Nathan said, taking a deep breath.

"What I would like to accomplish tonight is to give you an overview of the plan and make sure you are willing to proceed with us. One option you have is to reject our assistance, return to your university, and hope that things don't turn out as we have warned."

"No way, that's a no go. What's my next choice?" Nathan asked.

Kevin replied, "This is how I see it. When you are ready, we will return to your university. You will show me around and introduce me as your cousin, Kevin, who is visiting from Ireland. We'll go to a basketball game, hang out, and pretend nothing is up, while you secretly collect your research data, records, and everything you need to be able to continue your work at another location."

"But the university owns the rights to my work and I can't take it," Nathan interrupted.

"I understand, but wait, there is more," Kevin said with a grin. "Once you have everything you need to continue your work elsewhere, you will leave and I will stay at the university as you. By the time I am through with it, the university won't want to have anything to do with your research. I will make subtle changes to the data, the equations, and the results of your work so your invention looks like a failure. It will look like it would work, but it doesn't. They will not be able to do anything with it and Majestic Twelve will lose all interest in it."

"Go elsewhere? Where will I go? I won't be able to get a job anywhere. I will be a laughing stock," Nathan complained.

"You will not be a laughing stock, I will be. I understand that would be hard to take as a human being, but for me it will be fun because I will know we pulled a fast one on them. You'll go to work for our company and by the time we roll out your invention, it will be too late for Majestic Twelve to get hold of it," Kevin explained.

It was all dawning on Nathan now. "So the only thing that is really going to be hurt here is my reputation and my ego, right?"

"Yes, that's right. The deception will be that you are a failure, but in reality you will not be a failure at all. The question is are you willing to sacrifice your ego and reputation for the greater good?" Kevin asked.

Nathan looked at Jake, Naomi, Kaia, and Alo and felt their love and support. "I say let's do this. It's worth it."

"Excellent!" Kevin exclaimed. "Now there's just one more thing we need to attend to. How do you feel about having a doppelganger?"

"Well, to tell you the truth, in one way I feel weird about it. But in another way I feel like it will be cool. Besides, I don't want to stay at the university and be humiliated. So what do I have to do?" Nathan responded.

"Did you ever have a blood brother growing up?" Kevin asked.

"Oh yeah, Matt, Luke, and I have been blood brothers since I was about seven."

"Good, after we have spent some quality time together and developed a friendship, we will have Alo lead us in a sacred ceremony to combine our blood, blend our energies, and our intentions. This will enable me to appear as your exact double, even down to the fingerprints. If you are willing, at that point I will be able to download your memories, so to speak," Kevin explained.

"Download my memories? Last I checked I don't have any USB ports, how are you going to do that?" Nathan questioned.

"You've seen *Star Trek*, right? Do you remember the Vulcan mind meld?" Seeing Nathan nodding his head yes, Kevin said, "It's a lot like that."

"All my memories?" Nathan asked nervously.

Kevin clarified, "Don't worry, all your intimate, deeply private memories are stored in a certain part of your brain, and I will not be tapping into any of those. Just the facts, man, like who a person is to you, your prior conversations with them, where you park your car, what shirt you usually wear with what pants, practical things like that. The information I will need in order to make sure I don't give anyone a hint that I am not you. Please understand, I have the utmost respect for your privacy. This is a very rare and sacred relationship. I will be honored if you will trust me that much. Should you decide you are not willing to share your memories, that is fine, I should be able to improvise after I have spent more time with you."

"Oh, that sounds okay then," Nathan said, feeling a little more confident.

"Once I am your doppelganger, in order to avoid a lot of confusion, you can call me Nate. How does that sound to everyone?" Kevin asked.

"Clever," "That sounds good," and "I like it" were the responses.

Kevin continued. "Unless anyone has any more questions, I think we are ready to proceed."

Seeing everyone was satisfied with the plan, Oscillada spoke up, "Since there are no more questions, I think we can adjourn this meeting. If you need to see us, let Kevin know because he can contact us at any time. We will be cloaked in nearby orbit and we can meet you back here easily. We appreciate your willingness to work with us and we look forward to seeing you again."

Everyone stood up and said their good-byes. Kevin, Nathan, Jake, Naomi, Alo, and Kaia descended the stairs of the ship into the darkness of the starlit night.

CHAPTER NINE

ALO SPOKE FIRST. "Maybe we should go to the house, have some coffee, and talk about this."

Kaia said, "How about some herbal tea instead? I made up a special blend of tea today for people who have just been on a spaceship." Everybody laughed and agreed herbal tea would be better. There was total silence as they walked into the house.

After they sat down, Jake said, "Nathan, would you please share your thoughts with us? You are primary in all of this and it is your life that is being changed so dramatically."

Nathan said, "I don't even know how to describe my thoughts or feelings. My thoughts are not in order or logical. My feelings are so many and mixed that I feel numb."

Jake was sharing the couch with Nathan. He reached over and put his hand on Nathan's shoulder. He said, "Blurt, Nathan, just blurt."

Nathan took a deep breath and began. "Knowing that my invention really works and is important for improving lives makes me happy. Finding out that the government is in cahoots with evil aliens to the detriment of the planet and human beings makes me furious. Realizing that I have to hide, disappear, and leave my family in order to develop my new process because people I trusted sold me out is causing me to have a strong desire to apply war paint. Now let's just add flying saucers, hidden space stations, Vermosans, doppelgangers, Federation of Orion, and the Council of Intergalactic Enlightenment to that. It's a lot to take in."

Alo spoke up, "Nathan, our people have known about Star People for hundreds of years. We trade information and have built a trusting relationship. Some of our ceremonies celebrate that relationship and acknowledge that Star People helped seed Mother Earth. Our friends, like Kevin, are fighting a great war to save Mother Earth and its inhabitants from the ravages of greed, arrogance, and ignorance. In the past, our relationship consisted mostly of us receiving warnings and advice. Direct assistance was rare and from a distance. Now there is imminent danger. We are being asked to participate as warriors. Applying war paint is now necessary. Mother Earth has provided everything that humans need to have a good life. Great Spirit gives us guidance and the strength to do the right thing. All that is required from humans is to listen humbly, have faith and courage, and be thankful. I think I want to add have some common sense."

Nathan looked at his Grandfather and said, "It's a good day to die."

Kevin jerked around and exclaimed, "We aren't expecting them to kill you! We are working to prevent anything like that from happening!"

Alo smiled at Kevin and said, "You haven't personally worked with Native Americans, much have you? Nathan is not saying that he is expecting to physically die today. He is saying that he is ready. His heart, soul, and mind are peaceful, and he is not afraid of any consequences, including his death. Kevin, do you understand that our people were almost destroyed by the same evil? The white men used lies, trickery, and payoffs to corrupt our leaders and weakened our will with alcohol. They killed us by massacring our woman and children. They killed us by slaughtering the buffalo with their long rifles and leaving them to rot. We didn't understand that kind of ignorance and lack of honor. We now have understanding. We are being given the chance to be allies with another race to save the planet from having the same fate. We pray for Mother Earth to be restored, so that she can provide good food and clean water for all people. We want all people to live in peace and harmony with respect for each other. So I agree, it's a good day to die."

"Oh, I get it. It is a good day to die," Kevin agreed.

It was getting late, the UFO herbal tea was gone, and Naomi got up to get the cups saying, "It's late, and I, for one, am very tired."

Jake, Nathan, and Kevin got up, shook hands with Alo, and thanked him for the lessons. Naomi kissed Kaia on the cheek and whispered something in her ear. Kaia nodded and squeezed Naomi's hand.

When they got to the truck Jake jokingly asked, "Kevin, do you want to drive?"

"Sure," Kevin said, holding out his hand for the keys.

Nathan said, "But you don't have a driver's license."

"Want to make a bet?" Kevin pulled a worn wallet out of his back pocket to show them his completely authentic driver's license.

Nathan said, "You're full of surprises."

Kevin laughed, "Just getting started, cuz, just getting started." Kevin proved to be an excellent driver.

Once they got back to the house, everyone said good night and Naomi showed Kevin to the guest room. "Is there anything you need?" Naomi asked.

"No, ma'am, I have everything I need. Good night." With that Naomi closed the door to the guest room and headed to her room for some much needed sleep.

Nathan was already in his hammock. As he listened to the familiar sounds of the night, the owls, coyotes, and crickets, he drifted off into a deep sleep.

Nathan stirred as the morning sun warmed his face. The smell of breakfast cooking was in the air, and he opened his eyes. On the way to the house, he made a quick phone call to Matt. Jake and Naomi were sitting at the kitchen table when Nathan walked in. "Good morning," he said, as he poured himself a cup of coffee. "Has anyone seen Kevin this morning?"

As if on cue, Kevin walked into the kitchen from the hallway. "Good morning all. Are we going fishing?" Kevin asked, smiling.

"Yes, we are. I just got off the phone with my cousin, Matt. He and Luke will meet us in one hour. Does that sound good?"

"Sounds great."

Jake spoke up, "Kevin, have you ever been fishing before?"

"Not like this. About four hundred years ago, I went salmon trap fishing with an Eskimo in what is now Alaska," Kevin grinned.

"Sorry I asked," Jake said, shaking his head. "I guess you don't have a preference about bait casting or fly fishing then."

"No, but I would like to try everything."

Jake nodded, and said, "Not a problem. We have everything a fisherman needs in the back room of the barn. I even have a worm compost bed in an old watering trough behind the barn, if you want to use a bait hook and bobber."

"No, thanks on the worm bait. Reminds me of the folks back on...oh, never mind."

Jake looked at Kevin with a totally shocked expression on his face.

Kevin laughed and said, "I'm kidding about reminding me of the folks, but I do have an empathetic streak that precludes me from putting a hook through a worm."

Everyone was smiling as Nathan and Kevin left to gather their equipment.

Naomi brought out a lunch basket and a gallon jug of water and said, "No reason to be hungry out there." She had packed peanut butter and elderberry jelly sandwiches, apples, and oatmeal cookies. "Kevin, I don't know what your dietary requirements are, but if you let me know, I will try and fix something for you."

"Thank you, ma'am, but I don't really have any. I just have to get used to eating again. I don't eat much because my digestive system uses everything I ingest. I had better stop now. Probably TMI, sorry."

Nathan and Kevin climbed into the old jeep and took off for the lake. It took them fifteen minutes to get to the dock. Matt and Luke were putting the six-horse-power Evinrude motor on the twenty-four-foot bass boat. Nathan waved and hollered out to them as soon as the jeep stopped. They grabbed their gear and headed to the dock. Matt and Luke walked toward them.

Nathan said, "Kevin, these are my cousins. Matt is the tall one and Luke is the short one. Guys, this is, Kevin, my second cousin, on my Dad's side. He's from Ireland and I just met him last night. He has never been fishing. Can you believe what he's been missing?"

Matt and Luke shook hands with Kevin. Luke asked, "Are we cousins by marriage or something?"

Nathan said, "I don't think so, but if we say we are all cousins that is a true statement."

Matt in his usual hearty way pounded Kevin on the back and said, "Glad to meet you, cousin. Let's go fishing."

Once the boat was anchored at their favorite fishing spot, Nathan helped Kevin get his fishing rod set up. Demonstrating how to cast, he told Kevin where he was likely to find a good bass. Following Nathan's instructions exactly, Kevin allowed the artificial night crawler to sink close to the bottom, then he started to slowly bring it in, giving the tip of the rod a little twitch every couple of feet. When the lure was less than four feet from the boat, a five-pound bass leaped out of the water with the night crawler in its mouth.

Nathan yelled, "Keep your tip up, reel it in steady! Luke, get the net!"

Luke tossed Nathan the net. Nathan was able to get the net under the bass and bring it into the boat. The cousins were high-fiving Kevin and saying, "Not bad, catching your first bass on your first cast! Good job, cuz!"

Two minutes later, Matt caught a four-pound bass. Ten minutes later, Luke caught another four-pounder. Nathan was having a great time, but he desperately wanted to catch a fish. He decided to put a live night crawler on a hook, have the bobber about five feet up, and aim for a deep hole on the other side of a tree stump. He was confident that there would be a fish there, but he had to avoid getting caught up in the branches surrounding the hole. It wasn't an easy cast, but he was successful. After a couple of minutes, his rod was almost jerked out of his hand. The fish didn't jump out of the water, but it pulled hard. Nathan concentrated on giving the line some tension without letting it break. After several minutes, Nathan thought it might be a catfish, a large catfish. It was very heavy, too heavy, for his fifteen-pound line to pull it into the boat.

When Nathan finally saw the top of the catfish's head and the tip of its tail, he yelled with excitement. Matt grabbed the net to help him get the fish into the boat. The blue catfish was almost three feet long and weighed forty-five pounds. It was the biggest fish any of them had ever caught in the lake. Now that they had a boat load of fish and everybody had caught something, they decided to head back to the dock.

When they got to the dock, they remembered that they had food and decided to eat. Kevin said he was too excited to eat, but he would have an apple. It was decided that Luke and Matt could have the bass and that Nathan would take the catfish to Alo. Alo made the best smoked fish and he always shared it. Matt and Luke said they would enjoy grilled fish for supper, but right now, they had to get back to work.

Matt asked, "When can we do this again?"

Nathan said, "Sorry, guys, I've been called back to the university. I was hoping to stay longer, but unfortunately, I have to leave in a day or two. I will let you know next time I'm home again. Today was a lot of fun."

Luke shook Kevin's hand and said, "I'm glad to know we have another cousin. You're welcome to go fishing with us anytime."

"I hope we will see you again soon," Matt said to Kevin after he finished helping Nathan load the cooler with the forty-five pound catfish into the back of the jeep.

Kevin and Nathan waved good-bye as they headed to Alo's to deliver the catfish.

"That was a lot of fun. Who knew I would be such a natural?" Kevin said with a grin as he thought about reeling in that fish. "So, Nathan, are you ready to have a doppelganger?"

Nathan thought for a minute and nodded. "I have to admit, at first I thought I should be able to handle everything myself. Now, however, I see the wisdom of having a doppelganger. Smart people stay behind trees. The ones in the open get shot. I like the idea of pulling a fast one on the bad guys."

Kevin laughed. "Nathan, there is nothing about any of this that is easy. We can't guarantee a happy ending. But the bad guys will not get the benefit of your research and you will be able to continue your work in a safe environment. Also, we can, and will, protect your family from hostiles."

Nathan said, "Let's do it."

When they arrived at Alo's, he was waiting on the front porch. Nathan pulled the cooler out of the jeep and said, "We have a huge catfish in here for you to smoke." Kevin took the other side of the cooler and they carried it to the porch.

Alo opened the lid and smiled. "That is the biggest catfish I have ever seen come out of the lake. It will be fine here in the cooler for a while. Come on, we have something else we need to do." Kevin and Nathan looked at each other, then followed him into Kaia's healing room in the building behind the house.

Alo lit the sage pot. Using his eagle feather fan he smudged each of them and the room. He held their right hands and said a prayer, "Great Spirit, as Nathan and Kevin join their blood and their intentions, we ask that you bless them with your guidance, give them strength and courage. Aho." Then Alo used his sacred bone and flint knife to lance the index finger on each of their right hands and put their blood together. Alo put the mingled blood on his fingertips and applied it to the center of their foreheads. "You are now brothers of the heart and soul."

Nathan felt a little strange. He felt energized and alive. It reminded him of the invigorating energy he felt in the air after a thunderstorm. He was shocked when he saw that Kevin's blood was purple. He had forgotten that Kevin was really an alien. Nathan felt lightheaded and was aware that Alo was helping him get onto the bed. Kevin took the chair next to the bed, and held Nathan's hand, saying, "You'll be fine in a little while. Just relax."

Alo knew that Nathan was fine, but he also knew that he was witnessing something much more than a blood brother ceremony. He needed some private time to meditate on these things. He decided he would have a sweat lodge and then go on a prayer walk in the mountains as soon as he could. Alo saw that Kevin was in a deep meditative state and Nathan was asleep, so he quietly left the room.

After an hour Nathan woke up and saw himself sitting on the chair next to his bed. "Oh boy!" Nathan exclaimed. He sat up on the edge of the bed and looked closely at Nate very closely. "Oh my gosh! You even have the old faded scar above your left eyebrow where I took a header on my bike. This is unbelievable. Are you now allergic to wasp stings? How does this work?"

"Okay. Okay. Let me explain. First, anything that is in your DNA is available to me. Anything that is in your DNA that I don't want or would be harmful to me is not transferred. I want everything that allows me to be you. If you have a visible scar, I only have to take a 'picture' of it with my eyes and mind and it becomes part of my permanent projection of Nathan. Since a scar is not in your DNA, it has to be projected like a picture for me to have it. As for wasp sting allergies, I have it because it is well known out there that Nathan is allergic to wasp stings. You are careful to avoid wasp nests, so I will be too. Get it?"

"Yes. Let's have some fun in the morning. You go to breakfast dressed in my clothes, then I'll walk in the kitchen after you have finished eating. Let's see if Mom and Dad can tell us apart. You can eat, Nate, right? Because I, Nathan, spend a lot of time eating."

"Yes, I can eat, but not as much because my body uses every-thing, no waste."

"No shit!"

"Exactly." Both of them laughed, almost hysterically.

"This having an identical twin does have some fun aspects to it." Nathan grinned. "I can't wait till breakfast for the ultimate test."

Nate helped Nathan get up and walk around. "I'm good now, thanks. Let's go thank Alo and head back home."

Alo was putting small, wet apple wood sticks in the bottom of his smoker. The catfish totally filled the racks. Nathan said, "It already smells good enough to eat."

"It will be ready later. The more it smokes, the better the flavor. I will have plenty to share tomorrow."

Nathan said, "Grandfather, thank you for everything."

"It is my pleasure, I am witnessing sacred and wonderful things," Alo replied.

"When Grandmother comes home, please tell her that we're sorry we missed her. I'm sure she is busy helping someone. We'll see you tomorrow night for the Warrior Ceremony," Nathan said, as he and Nate climbed into the jeep and waved good-bye.

Nathan smiled at Alo, then looked over at Nate, but it was Kevin sitting next to him instead of Nate.

"We can't have people seeing double, I will save the Nate look for tomorrow and the test of the parents." Kevin grinned, as they drove away.

CHAPTER TEN

I T WAS A cool, crisp Sunday morning. Naomi was in her kitchen feeling peaceful and content making apple pies, while Jake was happily working in his workshop on shelving for her medicine kitchen. She had always stored her medicine as single extracts, but lately, she had received so many requests for the same formulas for colds, the flu, allergies, and backaches that she decided to mix these formulas and store them compounded. When Jake offered to build floor to ceiling shelving for her, she decided to mix and store all of her thirty plus formulas. She didn't need her medicine for poisonous snake bites very often, but when it was needed, it was going to be beneficial to have it right there on the shelf.

Yesterday, a neighbor had given her a bushel of fresh apples in exchange for her Flu Fighter. As she finished cleaning up the kitchen, the oven timer was going off signaling the pies were ready.

Naomi went to the workshop to see Jake. "Hi, honey, I just finished making two apple pies. I thought I would take one over to Mom and Dad. The other one is cooling on the kitchen counter for you."

Jake stopped what he was doing, walked over, and gave Naomi a warm hug and kiss. "Thank you, honey, I can smell them all the way out here. I guarantee there won't be a whole pie on the counter when you get back." Jake grinned. "Have a good time with Kaia. I love you."

Brushing the sawdust off his shirt, Naomi replied, "I love you too. I'll be back soon."

She returned to the kitchen, put the other pie into her pie basket, and walked out to the truck. Climbing in she decided to open all the windows so she could enjoy the cool morning air on the drive to her Mom's. As she pulled into their driveway, she saw Kaia was outside.

"Good morning, Naomi, what a pleasant surprise. What brings you here this morning?" Kaia asked.

"I just finished making apple pies so I brought one for you and Dad. And I was hoping you had time to visit."

"Oh, yes, I have time to visit, and that is just what I need right now," Kaia said, as they walked into the kitchen. "Would you like a cup of herbal tea?"

"Yes, that sounds wonderful, and from what I'm seeing in your energy, I'm thinking chamomile would be best," Naomi suggested, after noticing her mother was uncharacteristically irritated. "What happened?"

As Kaia served the chamomile tea she said, "Do you remember the man I told you about, the one that came to get Bronchitis Eliminitis for his daughter?"

"Yes, I remember. What's the problem?"

Kaia was very frustrated. She exclaimed, "He is the problem and the reason the little girl is not getting better! The first time he asked for the medicine, he came here to get it. I could tell he was angry about something. When he called the second time, I took the medicine to their house. I picked up on the anger and resentment he had toward his wife. I could tell the little girl was completely aware of it as well. It is making her sick. I explained to them that their fighting was extremely upsetting to their daughter and this emotional distress was causing her bronchitis. The wife knew it was true and was very grateful that I had said it. He refused to hear what I said and stormed out of the room. After he was gone, his wife explained he had been going to the bar every day after work and coming home drunk. When she tried to get him to stop, he blamed her for 'driving him to drink.' She was at her wits end because she couldn't get him to stop drinking and coming home belligerent."

"Don't tell me, let me guess, the little girl has pneumonia now."

"Not yet, but when the mother called me this morning, I went over and found out her bronchitis was much worse. I had to give her an antibiotic to prevent it from becoming pneumonia. I left her with a quart of Grey Beard decoction and told her I would check on her again this afternoon. The husband, who was still passed out on the sofa, came home drunk last night at midnight. I understand he did not yell at his wife when he came home, but his contempt for her was still palpable."

Naomi exclaimed, "What is wrong with people? When will they learn? It's the energy that matters! Acting nice is not the same as being nice!"

Kaia agreed, "People just don't get it. Negative energy causes disease. Holding onto anger and resentment makes one sick. Projecting negative energy toward others makes them sick."

"Exactly!" Naomi added, "Now to make matters worse, the Vermosans are doing all that they can to encourage negative energy, hatred, anger, greed, jealousy, arrogance, lust, and laziness, and human beings willingly walk right into their traps. People would rather take a pill and believe it will cure them, than do their emotional work or stop any of their unhealthy habits. I don't think I will ever understand it."

"I know what you mean. If people would only treat each other with dignity and respect, then they would feel safer to look honestly at what is really bothering them and get it fixed. Like you say, do their emotional work, instead of making matters worse by seeking revenge or masking the problem with drugs and alcohol. You know, Naomi, I have never said this to anyone before, but I think this emotional negative energy that humans are generating is harming Mother Earth."

"Whoa."

"Think about it," Kaia continued, "All living systems emit electromagnetic energy. Mother Earth has a positive magnetic south pole and a negative magnetic north pole. Humans have positive and negative energy, and we are aware of it when we do healing body work. Then doesn't it make sense that if negative energy throws humans out of balance and makes us sick, wouldn't negative energy also throw Mother Earth out of balance and make her sick?"

"Good point. I bet you're right. I've read that the magnetic poles of the Earth were moving at six miles per year during the early twentieth century, but by 1970 they started moving faster. Now they are shifting twenty-five miles per year."

"That is exactly what I am talking about. If Mother Earth gets more and more out of balance as negative energies outweigh positive energies, won't that ultimately lead to the magnetic poles of the Earth flipping over? What would that mean for life as we know it?" Kaia asked.

"I don't know, but it can't be good. Probably some cataclysmic event that would result in extinction of all humans, and the planet would be left to the Vermosans. I bet that's the reason the Star People have permission to intervene more directly to help us," Naomi realized.

"This is a really big deal. I have always found it disturbing and incomprehensible that people cause so much suffering for themselves and each other. Now that we know about the Vermosans, things make a lot more sense, but they aren't any less disturbing," Kaia said.

"Well, this isn't making us feel any better. We probably ought to put some Peaceful Warrior in our next cup of tea."

"You're right. We can't fix this. All we can do is have faith that Great Spirit will fix it in time. Meanwhile, we must keep spreading our positive, loving energy every chance we get. I know what I am going to do. This afternoon when I go back over there, to check on that little girl, I'm going to take half of this pie you brought me and give it to them. A little loving kindness goes a long way. Thanks, honey," Kaia said, feeling better.

"Great idea. Mom, I love you. Do you want to hear a funny story?" Naomi asked.

"Please."

"This morning Jake and I were making breakfast, when Nathan came in to join us. Just as we had finished eating, Nathan came in from sleeping in his hammock, saying, 'What? You ate without me?' Jake and I were dumbstruck. We looked at the Nathan that we had just had breakfast with and then we looked at the Nathan that had just come in the back door and honestly, Mom, we could not tell the difference," Naomi said.

Kaia laughed. "That is hilarious. Alo told me they had the blood brother ceremony yesterday, but he didn't give me any details."

"It was uncanny. I was sure it was Nathan eating breakfast with us because I understood Nate doesn't have to eat. The two of them had a lot of fun messing with us before they revealed that we had eaten breakfast with Nate. I know that was true because Nathan was hungry and I had to cook more bacon and eggs for him." Naomi laughed.

"I am glad the two of them are getting along so well. It seems to me the more they like each other and the more natural they are together, the safer it is for both of them," Kaia said.

"I agree. They had a blast yesterday fishing with Matt and Luke. Today they are talking, getting to know each other better, and working on the specifics of the plan. It seems everything is coming together nicely. There is some bad news though."

"Really, what's that?"

"Nathan's boss called last night to tell him he has to show his research to a company on Wednesday morning," Naomi shared.

"Oh no, that speeds up the time line."

"I know, but ready or not, they leave tomorrow morning to go back to the university. Kevin is very calm about it. He says it's probably better because they won't have any time to make mistakes. He has a good sense of humor like that, but I'm really nervous about it," Naomi admitted.

"Do you know any more of the plan?" Kaia asked.

"All I know is this. Kevin and Nathan will leave tomorrow morning and by early Wednesday morning Nathan will be back at home and Nate will be handling his meeting. I don't think I really want to know the rest."

"I'm with you on that."

"Well, I need to be getting back home. I've enjoyed talking with you," Naomi said, as she stood up and hugged her Mom good-bye.

"I'm really glad you came over. Now I want to get over there and check on that little girl. Thank you so much for the pie. I'll see you later," Kaia said, walking Naomi to the door.

CHAPTER ELEVEN

A s NAOMI PULLED up to the house, she saw Nathan and Nate sitting on the front porch. "Hi, guys, anyone ready for lunch?"

"Thanks, Mom, but I went ahead and ate lunch, so I could eat a piece of that pie."

"The pie looked and smelled so good, I couldn't resist. It was delicious," Nate added, rubbing his belly.

"Mom, can we use your medicine room this afternoon? We have a lot to do to get ready for Wednesday morning."

"I noticed you have some powerful quartz, amethyst, labradorite, and Apache tears that would be very helpful," Nate added.

"Of course, the room is all yours, make yourselves at home. My crystals are at your service."

"Thanks, Mom," Nathan said, as he kissed Naomi on the cheek.

"Thank you, ma'am. We'll see you later this afternoon," Nate said, as he and Nathan turned to go to the medicine room.

Nathan and Nate sat down in the two swivel recliners facing each other. Nate began, "How do you feel about seeing yourself in the mirror every time you turn around?"

"I'm getting used to it. I feel like I've known you my whole life. This morning, I really felt like we were brothers playing a trick on our parents. I feel secure, supported, and more than that, I feel totally understood in a way I've never experienced. It's nice."

"Good. I want you to know, I feel the same way. Like I told you on the ship, being a doppelganger is a very sacred relationship because I get the opportunity to feel all the same emotions that you feel. It's a blessing for me to have a twin brother and feel that love and support. I would like to thank you again for allowing it. Not just for what we are going to accomplish together, but also for the personal experience that I will cherish," Nate explained.

"I appreciate all you are doing and I trust you. So...well," Nathan cleared his throat, "I'm willing to do that mind meld, download thing you told me about."

"Good, that's excellent. Frankly, I'm relieved," Nate admitted. "Let me explain the process to you."

"Do it. Talk to me. I'm all ears."

"Once I download your memories, they will be attached to the physical form of Nate. Therefore, I will have access to this information only when I am in this physical form as Nate and for seventy-two hours afterward. I want to assure you, I have the utmost respect for your privacy, and I honor you for your courage to allow this. In the future, I will only use the doppelganger, Nate, when I need a tall, dark, and handsome, green-eyed Mintaka scientist to accomplish an important physical assignment given to me by the Council of Intergalactic Enlightenment."

Realizing he didn't need to worry, Nathan chuckled and felt his shoulders relax. Nate took a large quartz crystal obelisk off the shelf and placed it on the table between them.

"We will reach across the table and hold each other's forearms. Then we will lean in over the crystal. You may feel a little dizzy as the energies swirl around your head but just hold as steady as you can, it will not take long. Are you ready?"

"Yes, I am ready," Nathan answered.

Holding Nate's forearms, Nathan leaned his head forward and closed his eyes. Soon he felt as though his head was being gently pushed to the left, then back and to the right in a counterclockwise motion. After a few minutes, Nate released Nathan's arms and said, "Okay, Nathan, you can sit back and open your eyes. Are you feeling okay?"

"Yes, I felt a little dizzy, but now I feel relaxed and peaceful."

"Excellent. Download complete and successful," Nate said, as he took Naomi's two Apache tears off the shelf and handed them to Nathan. "Here, hold these. They'll help you get grounded again. Now it's going to be much easier for us to lock down our plan."

"What do you mean?" Nathan asked.

"Now that I have your memories, I know what you know. For example, if you say something about the flash drive in the safe, I can see the safe in my head and I know the combination just like you do. Now we can discuss the plan as if you are talking to yourself and well...you kind of are."

"That's going to be much easier. I was worried that I might forget to tell you something important, but that's impossible, right?"

"Right. Now we can skip right to the plan."

They talked for hours and worked out every detail. Both felt very confident and comfortable with their plan. All that was left to do was draft Jake and Alo for a little assistance and have the War Ceremony to get Great Spirit's blessing.

Standing up they gave each other a brotherly hug and handshake. After putting Naomi's crystals back where they found them, they went to find Jake.

In the workshop, they found Jake grinning from ear to ear and covered with sawdust from head to toe. "Hi, Dad, those shelves look great!" Nathan exclaimed.

"Thanks. I've just finished sanding them. Tomorrow, I plan to put on a mahogany stain. Your Mom says she wants them to be bulletproof, so I am going to use a marine grade polyurethane after that."

"Nice, she's going to be so happy. I hope I can be here to help you install them. Dad, Nate and I have just finished developing our plan, and we're going to need some help from you and Grandfather."

"No problem, you can fill us both in when we go over there tonight for the ceremony," Jake suggested. "I'll be finished in here in just a minute, then I'll get cleaned up for dinner."

Nathan and Nate pitched in, putting Jake's tools away while Jake vacuumed up the sawdust. They got everything cleaned up and walked into the house together. Jake went to take a quick shower while Nathan and Nate relaxed on the front porch until dinner was ready.

"I think it would be best that I go ahead and switch back to Kevin now." Nathan nodded in agreement as they heard Naomi call them for dinner.

After dinner, the four of them went to Kaia and Alo's house. Once everyone had gathered in the living room Nathan spoke up, "As you know, Kevin and I will be leaving in the morning. I will show my cousin, Kevin, around campus, including my office and my lab, where I will gather up my research while Kevin acts as my lookout. Dad, we want you and Grandfather to pick me up in front of my apartment building at three o'clock Wednesday morning. I need to get out of there and stay hidden as long as Nate is on the job. As you drive up, I will walk out of the building and get into the truck. I'll be wearing my gray hoodie and should be able to slip out unnoticed."

Jake asked, "Why in the middle of the night and why so sneaky?"

Kevin explained, "The Vermosans are monitoring Nathan's activities and we don't want anyone to see him leave, since I will still be there pretending to be him. If anyone notices, it might alert them. That could be very dangerous for all of us."

"How would the Vermosans know?" Naomi asked.

"Vermosans are very aware of emotional energies. This is how they know what to tempt different people with. For example, if a man sees a beautiful woman walk by and thinks, 'She sure is pretty,' the Vermosans don't pay any attention to it. But if he thinks, 'I have to get her in bed' and he puts his energy in that direction, they know he is influenced by lust. They will use his lust to guide him down the wrong path."

"I see, they use people's negative energy against them. Like some people are influenced by greed, some by lust, some by arrogance, some by laziness, and others by hatred. All they have to do is tune into the person's negative energy and they know how best to manipulate him?" Naomi surmised.

"That is exactly how it works," Kevin said. "By remaining peaceful and calm during our mission, we fly below their radar."

"I'm glad Alo is riding with me; he's always calm and peaceful," Jake added, looking over at Alo, who was smiling in his customary calm, wise man way.

Nathan continued, "After you pick me up, we will drive back here and be home before the sun is up. I will stay hidden, off the internet, etc. until Nate finishes making me the laughing stock of the science department and moves me home."

Jake nodded. "That sounds like a good plan. I think it'll work."

Alo stood up and said, "I think we are ready. It's time for our War Ceremony."

Unwrapping the buffalo hide that covered his sacred bundle, Alo took out the three thousand year old buffalo skull, and placed it on the stone slab in front of the fireplace. To the right of the buffalo skull, he placed the sacred pipe and to the left, he placed the sacred bone and flint knife.

Kaia placed the candles around the room, yellow in the east, red in the south, black in the west, white in the north. On the hearth in front of the buffalo skull, she placed the green candle for Mother Earth and the blue candle for Father Sky.

Jake moved the cedar and pine, buffalo-skin drum to the center of the room. He placed six drumsticks on top of it in a crossed pattern. Together they placed six chairs around the drum.

Once the ceremonial space was set up, they gathered on the porch. Alo lit the sage in the smudge pot and smudged everyone. He lifted the smoking pot above his head and started singing as he entered the house. He led everyone in a clockwise direction and entered the circle of chairs from the east. After they completed the circle, everyone stood in front of a chair. Alo put the smudge pot down in front of the buffalo skull and said, "Kevin, please light the yellow candle in the east and pass the lighter to the south."

Kevin lit the yellow candle as instructed and passed the lighter to the south. Nathan lit the red candle and passed the lighter to the west. After lighting the black candle, Naomi passed the lighter to the north. Jake lit the white candle and passed the lighter to Kaia, who lit the green candle for Mother Earth. Kaia handed the lighter to Alo, who lit the blue candle for Father Sky.

Everyone sat down and took a drumstick. Drumming in unison, they began singing, "Great Spirit, make me like a strong bear. This I pray, make me strong..." Nathan started the next song. "Fly like an eagle, flying so high, circling the universe on wings of pure light..." When that song was over, Naomi started singing, "We are alive as the Earth is alive, we have the power to create our freedom, if we have courage we shall be healers…"

After that song ended, Alo put down his drumstick and picked up the Talking Stick, which was decorated with feathers, beads, and rabbit fur. It had an animal totem carved in stone on each end; one was a white owl and the other was a black hawk. Alo began, "While it would be traditional for us to have a War Ceremony if we were preparing for a physical battle, this is not a physical battle. The battle we prepare for tonight is a spiritual battle; therefore, we must call upon a different kind of strength. We cannot use weapons or our physical prowess. We have to rely on our courage, our love for each other, and our faith in Great Spirit. We are here tonight to strengthen this loving, positive energy. Aho."

Alo passed the Talking Stick to Naomi. Naomi began, "I've been blessed with a large, loving family. I've always felt secure, loved, and never alone. When I go to homes where there is dis-ease or someone is hurt, I sense that most people feel alone and isolated. Many times I see that drugs and alcohol are being used in an attempt to deaden the pain of loneliness. There is so much negative energy, and it is making people miserable. It can be a struggle for me to resist the sadness. Knowing that we are fighting this negative energy together fills me with hope. Aho." Naomi passed the Talking Stick to Kaia.

Kaia held the Talking Stick in her hand for a moment. "I am fed up with the negative energy that I am witnessing. Mother Earth is out of balance. Everywhere I look there are lies and dis-ease. The influences of advertising and commercialism are making people unable to think critically for themselves. The values that were once commonplace, such as honesty, hard work, and helping one another have been forgotten and are ignored. It saddens me that the good in the world is being diminished. I am honored that Great Spirit has brought us together to fight for the good. Aho." Kaia handed the Talking Stick to Nathan.

Nathan began, "Having an alien doppelganger, blood brother is an amazing, life changing experience. Nothing in my life will ever be the same again. If I didn't have this brother on my side during this, it would be impossible. With his help, we're going to kick ass. Aho."

When Kevin received the Talking Stick, he looked down and hesitated for a moment because he didn't know how to say what was in his heart. Then he decided to blurt, "I love all of you. I am really old and I have met thousands and thousands of beings. Some human, some not so much. You have accepted me as one of your family, part of your tribe, and I feel your love. What we are endeavoring to do together is a really big deal. If we are successful, we will change the course of human history for the better. Aho."

Kevin handed the Talking Stick to Jake. "I am grateful for my family. Kevin, you may be older than I am, but I accept you as my son. I know in my heart that Great Spirit has brought us together to fight evil and to win. Aho."

Alo accepted the Talking Stick from Jake and said, "Thank you, Great Spirit. Aho."

They stood in a circle holding hands while Naomi and Kaia sang. "Walk in beauty, it's all around you, walk in beauty, let love surround you, walk in beauty with love for all…"

In reverse order, they each blew out the candle that they had lit. When the last candle was out, they said in unison, "Aho."

Jake put away the drum and the drumsticks were placed back in their antler holder as Kaia and Naomi went to the kitchen to get Alo's famous smoked catfish dip, crackers, and other refreshments.

CHAPTER TWELVE

ONDAY MORNING, NATHAN was up with the first crow of the roosters. After he finished his morning prayers, he smelled coffee brewing. He found Naomi in the kitchen cooking breakfast. "Good morning, Mom, I didn't expect to see you up so early."

"I knew you would be anxious to get going this morning. Sitting around waiting for something to happen is not a Stevenson trait," Naomi said, as she gave him a hug and a kiss on the cheek.

"You're not kidding, I don't think I slept at all last night. I reviewed the plan in my head over and over. It seems like a solid plan. Even after reviewing it hundreds of times, I couldn't really find anything wrong with it."

"That's because there is nothing wrong with it," Kevin said, as he suddenly appeared as if out of nowhere. "I just checked with the Watchers. They are reporting that the Vermosans are not aware of any of our activities. Our high-flying friends are in position and everything is good to go."

"The truck is packed and I'll be ready to go as soon as I eat breakfast."

Jake came in the back door just as Naomi had breakfast ready. "Good morning. Breakfast sure smells good and I'm hungry."

Deeply engrossed in their own thoughts, they ate in silence. Kevin projected all the peaceful energy he could muster to comfort them. Once they finished eating, Nathan stood up and said, "Let's do this."

Naomi got up and hugged him good-bye. She hoped he wouldn't notice the emotions that were welling up inside of her.

Jake walked Nathan and Kevin to the truck and gave each of them a man hug and handshake and said, "I'll see you Wednesday morning at three o'clock sharp."

"See you then," Nathan said, as he closed his door and started the truck.

The three hour drive to the university was uneventful. Nathan and Kevin discussed the changes Kevin could make to Nathan's research, without it being obvious that it had been intentionally messed up. By the time they arrived at Nathan's apartment, they were feeling confident and focused.

As Nathan was unlocking his apartment door, his next door neighbor walked out. "Hi, Tom, I want to introduce you to my cousin, Kevin. He's visiting me for a couple of days."

Kevin and Tom shook hands. Tom said, "I would love to stay and talk, but I'm running late. Are you guys going to the game tonight?"

Kevin said, "You bet. We wouldn't miss it."

"It'll be a great game. Nice meeting you, Kevin. Later, Nathan," Tom said, rushing down the hall.

Kevin and Nathan went into the apartment and immediately got to work. Nathan gathered his important research papers and put them in his briefcase. Once he had everything he needed from his apartment, they drove around campus to give Kevin a chance to get his bearings. Actually seeing everything made Nathan's memories much more solid for him. As they parked the truck, Kevin asked, "Are you ready for this?"

"Yes, let's do it," Nathan said, as he closed the truck door and they headed for the science building.

Just as they reached the front door, Nathan's boss, Richard Peck, a short, portly man with horn-rimmed glasses and a thin moustache, walked out. "Hello, Nathan. Are you going to be ready for the meeting Wednesday morning?"

"Yes, sir, I am. Dr. Peck, I would like to introduce you to my cousin, Kevin. He's visiting from Ireland, and I'm showing him around campus."

"Nice to meet you, Dr. Peck. Are you going to the game tonight?" Kevin asked, shaking his hand.

"No, I am not into sports. Nathan has a lot to do to get ready for an important meeting Wednesday, so don't keep him out late." Peck scowled, as he turned and walked toward his car.

Nathan and Kevin continued to Nathan's office. As soon as the door closed behind them, Nathan unlocked his fireproof safe and put his three terabyte portable hard drive and all his important documents into his leather laptop messenger bag. While Kevin was listening for anyone approaching, Nathan looked through everything in his office. Kevin sat down in the chair across from his desk and said, "Someone is coming."

Nathan closed his messenger bag and placed it next to his credenza. He quickly sat down at his desk and began nonchalantly checking his email. There was a knock at the door. "Come in," Nathan called out.

Dr. Peck stuck his head in the door. "Sorry to bother you, Nathan, but I just wanted to make sure you are going to be ready by ten o'clock Wednesday morning. This company is really interested in your research, and the university stands to get a significant endowment from them."

"Don't worry, Dr. Peck, I'm working on the finishing touches right now, and I will be getting my demonstration set up tomorrow. I will be prepared."

"Okay then, I'll let you get back to it," Dr. Peck said, as he closed the office door.

After a few seconds, Kevin gave Nathan the all clear signal and Nathan resumed his work.

"Okay, I have everything I need. You can go ahead and do your thing to the data and notes now. After this, we won't need to come back here," Nathan told Kevin.

Sitting at the computer, Kevin's fingers moved like lightning across the keyboard. As he watched the computer screen, Nathan was amazed by the changes being made. It was just as Kevin had promised; it looked similar to his work, but he knew it wouldn't work. Six months earlier, this same error in logic had led Nathan to a dead end. At that time, he was ready to abandon the project. Fortunately he had an epiphany in a dream that had showed him how to fix his error. This was perfect. No one could figure out the process from this data. Kevin finished up, and Nathan looked around his office one last time. He locked the door and they went to the truck.

"Whew, one down, one to go. Let's drop this stuff off at my apartment and get ready to go to the basketball game," Nathan suggested.

"Sounds good. We shouldn't have any problems tomorrow, so let's have some fun tonight."

The basketball game was packed. It was the final game of the regular season and the Bobcats were undefeated. It was a nail-biter of a game that went into double overtime. At the final buzzer, the Bobcats won with a three point shot from the top of the key.

"What a great game, that was fun!" Kevin exclaimed.

"It was awesome. There is only one way to top off an excellent basketball game."

"How's that?" Kevin asked.

"A pizza and a bottle of Guinness."

Kevin looked a little concerned, "Um, well a crowded game is one thing, but—"

Nathan interrupted, "Don't panic. We can pick up a pizza on the way home and I have Guinness in the fridge."

"Oh, great plan." Kevin said, relieved.

CHAPTER THIRTEEN

NAOMI WAS PUTTING away the last of the dinner dishes when she heard the phone ringing in her medicine kitchen. As she picked up the phone, she saw on the caller ID that it was Kaia. "Hi, Mom, what's up?" she asked.

"I need you to bring me some Snake Medicine, a neighbor just got bit by a rattlesnake that was hiding in his barn, and I don't have all the ingredients to make it," Kaia explained.

"Jake and I will be there in just a few minutes."

Rushing into the living room to get Jake, she said, "Jake, something is up. We have to go meet our friends on the spaceship, right now."

"How did you get all that information from Kaia? You were on the phone less than fifteen seconds," Jake asked, as he pulled on his boots.

"She asked me to bring Snake Medicine, and no self-respecting herbalist runs out of the ingredients for Snake Medicine," Naomi explained, as they got in the truck.

Backing out of the driveway, Jake asked, "Who got bit by a snake?"

"No one. That was a code Mom and I worked out. We figured if the Vermosans were listening in on our conversations, they wouldn't think anything of it," Naomi said with a smile. "Don't worry, I brought the Snake Medicine for the sake of authenticity."

"Very clever," Jake admitted. As soon as he parked the truck, he and Naomi rushed to the house.

Alo met them at the front door. "Something has changed and we need to go to the circle and meet the ship right away."

Kaia gave Naomi a wink as the four of them rushed to the landing site out back. The sun had set, and as they approached the circle, they could see the ship already sitting there. The door opened and Oscillada came down the stairs to greet them. "Good evening, everyone. We are glad you could make it on such short notice. Please come in."

Once they were inside, the door closed behind them. After they greeted Oscillada and Selena, Oscillada said, "Everyone, I would like to introduce you to some of our friends." Putting his hand on the shoulder of a distinguished-looking elderly woman with shoulder-length white hair, he said, "This is Anna, the Commissioner of Plants, Medicine and Health for the Earth Commission." The short green tunic that Anna was wearing over flowing long pants was the same color green that the other commissioners wore but hers had a triangle pattern in the fabric.

After everyone greeted Anna, Oscillada continued. "And this is Eli, a loyal member of the Elite Corps of Watchers assigned to the service of John, the Ambassador of the Earth Commission."

Jake's heart was racing as he was introduced to Eli. He was desperately trying to process what he was seeing. Standing in front of him was a seven foot tall alien with short white fur and pointed ears on top of his head.

Jake thought, *Okay, this is a real alien, right when I least expect it. This guy looks like a cat. Well, except that he stands like a man, a really big, strong man. Okay then. Okey dokey. I am breathing. Naomi is here, I am fine. Everything is fine.*

Oscillada said, "Everyone, please take a seat. Before we get started, I want to assure you Nathan is fine, he and Kevin are actually having a lot of fun. Something has come to our attention that presents us with a huge opportunity. Eli will explain this to you in a minute, but first Anna has something to say."

"As Oscillada has told you, I am the Commissioner of Plants, Medicine and Health for the Earth Commission. In addition to inspiring people like Kaia and Naomi to make and use herbal medicine, my job is to keep track of what is being produced and sold as food on this planet. In addition, we try to keep dangerous, toxic products from making it into the food supply. I would like to digress here for one moment and give you my sincerest apology for my colossal failure to stop the very toxic chemical, aspartame, from being sold as a sweetener."

Anna shook her head and took a deep breath before explaining. "Majestic Twelve had an operative in a position to falsify the lab results that were presented to the Food and Drug Administration. At the same time, they had another operative at the FDA who accepted the obviously falsified results. The collusion of these two disguised Vermosans made it impossible for us to stop it. Despite the very informative documentary we helped produce and all the warnings we have managed to get out, humans still consume tons of this horrible chemical daily. This single failure vastly accelerated the destruction of human health."

Naomi interjected, "Every time I see a diet drink in someone's hand, I tell them aspartame is poison, but every time without fail, the person I am talking to refuses to give up their diet drinks and finishes drinking it right in front of me. It makes me sick."

"I understand. This time we are in a position to prevent the next massive poisoning of the population and that is what brings us here tonight." Anna turned to Eli and said, "Eli, please go ahead and fill everyone in."

Eli began. "We have been monitoring the dealings of Nathan's boss, the insatiably greedy Dr. Richard Peck. After he arranged the unscrupulous sale of Nathan's invention, he gained the attention of the Vermosans. Through their associates at American Foods, they have contacted him and offered him a lucrative contract that will pay the university a million dollars and, unknown to the university, Dr. Peck another million dollars. In exchange for the two million dollars, Dr. Peck will head the, so-called independent laboratory at the university that will determine that their product is safe for human consumption. American Foods is the world's largest producer of food seeds as well as pesticides. Long story short, they have determined a way to put the pesticides into the seeds directly."

"Of course, it is not at all safe for humans, and it will lead to the systematic elimination of honey bees and other crucial pollinators,"

Anna added. "Without honey bees the majority of fruits, vegetables, and flowers would cease to exist. It would be devastating to the world food supply and the supply of herbs for medicine."

Everyone was shaking their heads in disbelief.

Eli continued. "Their thinking is that a farmer will pay more for seeds that protect the crop from destructive pests. They aren't allowed to sell these pesticides in the United States any longer, so they want to do something with their inventory. They have millions of dollars invested in this pesticide inventory, and if they put it in the seeds, they can double what they currently charge for seeds. A win-win situation for their bottom line. A lose-lose situation for the rest of the planet."

"How in the world could anyone be so damn foolish!" Kaia exclaimed. "Did somebody put a can of stupid in the water at their office or what?"

"They are intoxicated with greed and selfishness, and you are right, this makes them very foolish," Anna agreed. "This leads us to our huge opportunity."

Oscillada added, "In order to take advantage of this opportunity, we are recommending a change in the plan that Nathan and Kevin are currently deploying. The updated plan will require Nate to stay on at the university as Dr. Peck's assistant for this new project for an extended period."

"Where will Nathan be?" Naomi asked.

"I am just getting to that," Oscillada explained. "Jake and Alo will pick up Nathan as planned. When you get back here with him, I recommend that all five of you join us here on the ship. You should arrive just in time for us to take off before the sun comes up."

"We are going for a ride in this spaceship?" Jake asked apprehensively.

"Yes. We will take Nathan to his new job at FERN, the Future Engineering Research Network, which is located in North Florida. Our contact at FERN is expecting us, and she has Nathan's lab and living quarters ready for him. Nathan will be able to resume his work immediately. With the help of the dedicated scientists at FERN, we expect to have a full-size operational version of his machine up and running by the end of the year. Once they have accomplished this step, they will be prepared to build and install machines of this type as needed in all different types of industries. It will be everything Nathan ever dreamt of and more."

Selena interrupted. "Well, to be fair, Oscillada, it won't be exactly how he dreamt it would be. I doubt he ever planned to change his name, but since he will still be working at the university as Nathan Stevenson, he will need a false identity to work at FERN. How does David Bridges sound?"

Selena braced herself for the backlash she expected from the family.

"What! Change his name? I bet you will tell us he can't come home anymore either. This is not a good plan," Jake erupted.

"I understand how you feel, Jake, but there has to be more to the plan. In a perfect world, none of this would be necessary, but that is just it, this is not a perfect world. So let's hear them out," Alo insisted.

Selena continued. "You are exactly right, Alo. Remember, we have special tools and resources that we are able to employ. FERN has a secret landing facility for our crafts and we can easily take you to visit Nathan at any time. Also, when Nathan wants to come home for a vacation, we just have to coordinate his vacation with Nate's vacation from the university. Nate drives home, Nathan flies home via spaceship 7-8-9 the eighth goes wherever he wants to go and Nathan is home."

"Remember, Nathan's demonstration is going to fail on Wednesday. Nathan Stevenson goes on to do other work at the university. Meanwhile, a totally different scientist, David Bridges, actually succeeds with the invention. It can't be traced to Nathan, the university can't sue for control of the process, and the Vermosans cannot stop it from doing all the good that it will do for the planet," Oscillada clarified.

"That is brilliant," Naomi admitted.

"Okay, I like the plan better now, but how will Nate be able to stop Dr. Peck and the Vermosans from poisoning the food supply?" Jake asked.

Anna spoke up. "In order for you to understand that, I need to explain some more things to you about the nature of Earth and the universe. I have been given permission from the Council of Intergalactic Enlightenment to divulge this information to you as long as everyone is in agreement to proceed with the updated plan. Is everyone willing to continue?"

Anna looked at each of them in turn and received the necessary confirmation that they were willing to continue.

"Excellent." After gathering her thoughts, Anna explained, "Earth was created by Great Spirit, God, the Creator, as a life-experiment planet. For this reason, there is a greater diversity of life on this planet than is normal in the universe. It is this great diversity in people, plants, and animals that makes this one of the most beautiful and unique planets of all. Life on this planet was created to evolve. In common parlance of today, it could be stated that the will of Great Spirit, God, the Creator is for all life on this planet to evolve physically, evolve emotionally, and evolve spiritually. The behavior of your immune system is a perfect example of this evolution demonstrated in the physical realm. Doing your emotional work, as you would say, Naomi, is necessary to become a mature, stable adult. Learning to maintain a forgiving, loving, honest, and sharing nature is to evolve spiritually.

"Every cell on Earth is loaded with potential. Take an oak tree for example. The wood has the potential to be food for insects, to be used to make fire, or to be lumber, which can be used to build things. The way for the highest potential of the oak wood to be unlocked is for someone to choose to co-create something with Great Spirit using the wood. If Jake turns the tree into lumber and makes a desk out of it, he is co-creating this desk with Great Spirit. The oak tree always had the potential to be a desk, even before humans knew what a desk was. During the evolutionary process of finding out the best potential that is in the wood, humans fashioned it into clubs to use as weapons. This was not the best use and it is not used much this way anymore."

Oscillada spoke up. "Anna, if I may?"

Anna nodded her head. "Of course."

"The Vermosans and the people at American Foods have the pesticides, they have the seeds, and they know a way to put them together that will kill the pests. Their greed makes them unconcerned about the damage they will cause, and we cannot stop them. However, Nate can co-create with Great Spirit a process that will kill the bad pests without killing everything else. This is a technology that is very advanced for this planet, but it is already in the potential of the seeds. There is not enough time for humans to discover this potential on their own, so Great Spirit will divinely inspire Nate with the way to do this in order to save the planet," Oscillada explained.

"Won't that make American Foods rich?" Jake asked.

"Yes, but they were going to get rich anyway. So what is the best choice, let them get rich and poison the planet or let them get rich and not poison the planet?" Anna asked.

"Well, not poison the planet of course, but doesn't that make them more powerful?" Jake wondered.

"Not really. They will have a technique that is beneficial for the planet. Even though their motivation is greed, Great Spirit will turn this negative energy into a positive outcome for Mother Earth. This redirection of the negative energy is desperately needed at this time," Anna clarified.

"I am really going to be contemplating this. I think I understand all that you have said, but I believe it is a lot more profound than I realize right now," Jake said. "Anyway, I'm all in."

Anna smiled and said, "Excellent. Before we meet back here Wednesday morning, please make arrangements to be away from home for a few days and bring whatever you need to make yourselves comfortable. After we have concluded our business at FERN, we have permission to take the four of you on a little adventure if you are up for it. Right now, we would like to show you around the ship and the accommodations that we have for you."

CHAPTER FOURTEEN

TUESDAY MORNING, AFTER waking up to the smell of coffee and breakfast, Nathan stumbled into the kitchen.

Kevin was buttering the toast and said, "Good morning."

"You made scrambled eggs, toast, and coffee for me?"

Smiling, Kevin handed him a large mug. "Here, drink some coffee. You need to wake up quickly, my friend."

"Thanks. What's up, cuz?" Nathan asked.

"There has been a change of plans that gives us a tremendous opportunity to accomplish even more."

"Okay, you have my undivided attention."

"Last night, I met with three of the commissioners."

"You what? Are you saying that you were on a spaceship while I was sleeping?"

"Yes, Nathan. Remember, I don't need sleep, I can move as a ball of light, I am telepathic, and I have purple blood."

"Okay, Kevin, I'm really awake now. I've gotten so used to thinking of you as my cousin, it's easy to forget the other complicated stuff."

"It's good that you are comfortable enough to forget. However, it is because I'm not human and can do the complicated stuff that you are safe and we'll beat the bastards."

Kevin sat down and explained, "Short version. After my failure tomorrow at the demonstration, Peck will be furious. Then he will believe that he owns me. Last night, I was told that American Foods has contracted with Peck to provide the 'independent research' that proves their seeds mixed with their pesticides are safe. He will decide to give me a choice between being publicly humiliated, denounced, and thrown off campus, or being his 'flunky' for the fake research project."

Nathan jumped up so fast the table jumped along with him. "That bastard! I would never do that! I'd live in a cave and eat grass-hoppers before I would lie and fake research for money!"

"Exactly, that's why it's me and not you," Kevin reminded him.

Nathan sat back down, looked at Kevin, and said, "What?"

Kevin smiled and clarified, "It's as if I will be undercover like on a TV cop show. While I am working with them, Great Spirit will inspire me to create a way to make the pesticide treated seeds kill only the targeted pests and not harm anything else. We get to inter-vene in this diabolical Vermosan plan in order to give people a little more time and an opportunity to prevent greed from destroying the planet. Isn't that great?"

"Yeah that sounds great, but what will I be doing?"

"You will be continuing your work at FERN, the Future Engineering Research Network, which is run by a friend of mine. Don't worry about anything, your Dad and Grandfather will be able to give you more details tomorrow. Right now, we need to focus on the task at hand."

Nathan was thoughtful for a few moments. "Kevin, I don't know if it is okay for me to feel the way I'm feeling right now."

"I know you are feeling sad, disappointed, and hurt, and I understand completely."

Nathan nodded and said, "I liked it better when I just felt mad and ready to kick ass, a much more manly reaction. This feeling hurt crap sucks."

"So what are you going to do about it, Nathan?" Kevin asked.

"Hell, I'm going to kick ass, that's what I'm going to do!"

"Exactly. Let's head back to the lab. We have work to do," Kevin advised.

When they arrived at the lab, Nathan slid his ID card through the lab's lock and punched in his code. They went to Nathan's pro-totype machine and turned on the control module. The prototype looked like a big microwave oven with a computer keyboard con-nected to the front panel box.

Kevin said, "Let's add a subroutine to the program that will disable the actual process. When aluminum is put into the machine and the magnetize program is selected, it will just make a buzzing noise. When it is obvious it doesn't work, I will say I need to make an adjustment and check the power supply module. By that time, Peck will be going nuts. I'll adjust something, all right. I will change it so that on the third try, the machine blows up. Sparks will fly, there will be nifty crackling sounds, an explosion, and a fire will burn up the machine. I'll grab the fire extinguisher, and with great enthusiasm, I'll spray the entire lab."

Nathan couldn't help but laugh.

Suddenly Kevin said, "Nathan, Peck is coming. I'm disappearing." In a flash Kevin was gone.

Nathan grabbed a towel, started wiping down the prototype machine and straightening up around the table. Peck barged in and said, "I hoped I would find you here getting ready."

"Yes, sir," Nathan said.

"Good. We've given you lots of support for your research, now it's your turn to do something for us, and yourself too, of course. I expect you to be available in the faculty lounge at nine o'clock tomorrow morning for coffee and introductions. The university President and Provost will be there meeting our guests, and we are counting on you to make us proud of what we have accomplished."

"Yes, sir, I'll be there."

"And Nathan, please wear formal business attire, not your usual cowboy regalia. If you don't have any, go buy some. And get a haircut. You can't go around looking like a wild Indian." With that, Peck walked out and slammed the door.

Nathan was furious. Immediately after the door slammed shut, he pounded his fist on the table. When he saw Kevin reappear, he said, "Did you hear that? Where were you?"

"Yes, I heard it. I was on top of a light bulb on a ceiling light. I couldn't think of a better place for a ball of light to hide, could you?"

The sudden realization of the extent of Kevin's abilities stunned Nathan, and his anger started to subside. "Can you believe the arrogance of that guy? It's like he expects me to look like an IBM executive from the eighties."

"Nathan, I want you to look at things from a different perspective."

"I don't think I want to hear this."

"Yes, I think you do. Remember the smart warrior fights from behind the tree. The one out in the open gets shot."

"Okay, you're right. Besides, in a few hours it will be you, not me. Please give me a different perspective."

Kevin began. "Peck was deliberately baiting you to find out how much you want success. Are you willing to dress differently and get rid of the long hair that is a part of your culture? Are you willing to take a subservient position to him? Can he have you under his control because of your arrogance, pride, greed, and feelings of being less than? In other words, are you moldable? He wants to use you for the seed project even now. He wants to use you, period."

"Okay, I get that," said Nathan.

"Good. Let's go get a navy blue suit with a power tie to appease Dr. Peck," Kevin suggested. "By the way, you don't have to cut your hair. Peck will never see you again, but Nate will have short hair from now on."

"You won't be nearly as handsome. I hope you can still pull it off, doppelganger."

"Don't worry about me, I've got this. That Peck has no idea who he is dealing with!"

They both started laughing hysterically.

With tears of laughter leaking out of his eyes, Nathan looked around the lab one last time and said, "I have everything I need. Let's get out of here."

That evening after shopping, Nathan and Kevin were in the apartment preparing for Nathan's departure. Nathan left most of his clothes, boots, and personal items for Kevin. While Nathan was packing, Nate came in wearing his new navy blue business suit with a white shirt and a red-and-blue striped tie. Nathan did a double take. "How do you like the way you look?" Nate asked.

"Very handsome, but I am glad that's your hair and not mine. I couldn't stand having my hair that short," Nathan answered. "Now get out of that suit, it's making me itchy just looking at it."

Nate laughed and went to change. In a few minutes, Kevin reappeared. "Well, Nathan, how do you feel about all this?"

"It's a little surreal. Packing to move across the country while leaving enough for you to be me is a challenge. I have a suitcase of clothes, a duffel bag, my briefcase, and my messenger bag. How many bags are you allowed on a spaceship?" Nathan asked.

"No limit, at least for you. Nathan, I have a present for you. I think you deserve a going-away gift, and I know the university is not going to give you one. Commissioner Oscillada gave me permission to give this to you."

Kevin handed Nathan a small box.

Nathan took the box and lifted the blue velvet lid. There was a card that read Victory Army Alpine Automatic Watch. It was a beautiful watch and looked like it had at least six different functions, probably more. "Thanks, Kevin, this is a beautiful watch."

"Ah, my bro, this is not just a watch. See the button on the bottom left? Turn it and you'll see a single digit. We have preprogrammed five numbers. If you turn it to one and push it, your father's phone will ring. Two is for your mother. Three is for Alo. Four is for Kaia. Five is for me. There are four more numbers that we will program later."

"Cool! This is like a Dick Tracy watch."

"Well, there are a few differences. This communication device does not use any of the satellites, towers, or phone lines on this planet. It is totally untraceable, and the conversation will be completely scrambled. Anyone trying to listen in will hear only static. Your biological signature allows access and it will only work for you. If it is stolen, it will stop working immediately. You cannot harm this watch, period. Also, if you need help, put your thumb on the watch face and hold it there for three seconds. It's like dialing 911. Some friends of mine will come to help you wherever you are," Kevin explained.

"I hope I won't need that function. How do I set the time?"

"You don't. The time adjusts automatically based on your location," Kevin answered.

"How do I set the alarm?"

"Beats me. Read the instruction manual that's in the bottom of the box." Both of them laughed.

"Thanks, Kevin, knowing that I can talk to you or my family anytime without worrying about the Vermosans listening in means a lot to me. I'm almost finished packing. I think I'll take a nap until Dad gets here."

"That's a good idea. I'll wake you up before three o'clock to give you a chance to get ready. When we see the headlights, we'll grab your stuff and head for the truck. Oh, and, Nathan, don't worry about where you are going. I have been there and I promise you it's a fantastic place. I have no doubt you'll love it!"

CHAPTER FIFTEEN

AT PRECISELY THREE o'clock Wednesday morning, Jake and Alo pulled up in front of Nathan's apartment building. Nathan and Kevin came outside in identical gray hoodies. Nathan climbed into the back seat of Jake's burgundy Chevrolet Silverado crew cab with his briefcase and messenger bag and slid over to the far side. Kevin put Nathan's suitcase and duffle bag in the back seat next to him.

"Take care, my friends. I look forward to seeing you again soon," Kevin said, closing the door.

As the truck pulled away, Kevin turned to go back into the apartment. By the time he turned to face the building, he had changed himself back into Nate, and he peacefully walked inside.

"Whew, that was smooth. Hi, Dad. Hi, Grandfather. How are you guys?" Nathan asked.

"We are relieved to have you back with us," Alo answered.

"It's been an exciting week," Jake added.

"I'll say. I'm glad to be out of there. Did you know that jerk, Dr. Peck, told me to cut my hair before the meeting? Not only that, we had to buy a business suit for Nate to wear. I hate to admit it, but he didn't look half bad with short hair and a suit. But it sure is not me. Did I mention, I'm glad I'm out of there?"

Before Jake or Alo could respond, Nathan went on, "I can't wait to show you this really cool Dick Tracy watch Kevin gave me."

"Dick Tracy watch?" Jake asked.

"Well, it's not really a Dick Tracy watch. It is a really cool watch that has alien technology. I have your phone numbers programmed in it, and with the push of a button I can call you, but our conversation will be scrambled and no one can monitor what we are saying. Plus, if I get in trouble, it has this kind of panic button feature that if I use it, some of Kevin's friends will come and save my ass," Nathan explained, as he leaned back and put his hands into his hoodie pockets. "What's this?"

"What is what?" Jake asked.

"I just reached down in my hoodie pocket and found another one of these cool watches. Kevin put a note on it that says, 'This watch is programmed for your Dad. One is for Nathan and two is for Kevin.' How cool is that? You can reach me or Kevin any time with a touch of a button. That Kevin is the best brother ever." Nathan was ecstatic. "Now I won't ever have to feel alone."

"These Star People are really good friends to have, wouldn't you agree, Jake?" Alo asked.

"You aren't kidding. I have learned so much, and I...well, I'm actually having fun," Jake said.

"Yesterday, Kevin and I were so busy preparing for today's meeting, he was only able to give me an overview of the updated plan. I understand he is staying on at the university as Nathan Stevenson and I am going on to FERN to resume my work. This presents a few problems for my personal life, but he assured me I did not need to worry, everything is under control. He told me you would fill me in on the next steps. So where is FERN and how do we get there?" Nathan asked.

Jake looked over at Alo. They had decided on the way over it would be best if Alo did most of the talking. Alo began. "We understand your concerns. We had the same ones, but everything is going to be okay. We are going with you to FERN today, so we will know where it is and what the conditions are like. We have been assured you will love it at FERN."

"That's what Kevin said. This must be one hell of a place for all of them to be so confident I will love it," Nathan added.

"Exactly. That's what we—"

Jake interrupted, "Alo hasn't mastered the art of blurting, so I am going to help him out. As soon as we get home, we are going on a spaceship to FERN. There, Alo, wasn't that helpful?"

"Yes, very. Thank you, Jake."

"Is FERN on Mars or something?" Nathan asked, feeling a little panicky.

"No. It's in rural North Florida somewhere between Tallahassee and Pensacola. FERN is a secure facility, and it has a landing area for spacecraft that is so secret we can land there in broad daylight," Alo explained.

"That sounds cool," Nathan said, relaxing.

"Yes, it does. Your office and lab are already set up. And you will have an apartment right on site. We weren't told much else. Apparently, you have to see it to believe it. The only difficulty, well… Jake do you want to help me out here?"

"No, blurting doesn't really seem appropriate here."

"What are you two talking about?" Nathan asked.

"Well, you've heard of a witness protection program, right? Where a person has to get a new identity to protect him from some bad guys?" Alo asked.

"Yes, of course…oh, shit! I have to get a new identity. Nathan Stevenson is still working at the university. How is that going to work?" Nathan asked as the reality of his situation dawned on him.

"FERN has this covered. They have a whole new identity ready for you, complete with passport, social security card, driver's license, and back story. Apparently, this is not the first time they have done this," Alo explained.

"How does the name David Bridges sound to you?" Jake asked.

Nathan was still stunned and wasn't saying anything. Alo offered, "David is a good name for a warrior. Against all odds, using his slingshot and a rock, he hit an evil giant right between the eyes and killed him."

"I like it, I think I can get used to it," Nathan said.

"Think about the big picture, your invention is all yours now. The university can never sue for the rights to it because Nathan Stevenson did not invent it, David Bridges did," Jake said.

"Oh, that is good. Everything is making a lot more sense now. No wonder I can only call you from this super cool 'bat' phone on my wrist. There would be no reason for David Bridges to be calling Nathan's family," Nathan said as if explaining everything to himself.

"Right, and since Kevin gave me one too, we can call you and the Vermosans will never know that you are Nathan," Jake added. "And another thing, all you have to do when you want to come home is coordinate a vacation with Nathan Stevenson's vacation. You secretly fly home on a spaceship, Nate drives home, and ta da, you're home on vacation."

"Nice, I feel good about this. I'm really tired. I think I'm going to take a nap until we get home."

Jake and Alo looked at each other completely relieved that Nathan was calm and peaceful enough to sleep. They drove the rest of the way home in silence, thinking about the adventure that today was going to bring.

As the tires hit the gravel driveway that led to Alo's house, Nathan woke up. "We're home already? That was fast."

Jake parked the truck and Naomi and Kaia came out to greet them.

"We're so glad to be home. Jake and I have been drinking coffee all night. So please excuse me," Alo said as he hurried into the house.

After everyone had hugged each other, they followed Alo into the house. "The sun will be up in about thirty minutes, so do whatever you need to do and let's get out back as soon as possible. I have snacks in the kitchen if anyone wants anything to eat," Kaia offered.

Once everyone was ready, Alo picked up the bags Naomi and Kaia had packed for the four of them, while Jake and Nathan gathered up Nathan's bags. The five of them headed for the circle behind the house. As they approached, they could see Oscillada standing outside waiting for them. "Good morning, everyone, welcome back. Please come in."

They went inside and found Selena and Anna waiting by an open storage compartment just to the left of the door. "Good morning, it is very nice to see you again. We must quickly get these bags stowed and take our seats," Selena said as she helped them put their bags away.

"Good morning, Nathan, I am Anna, the Commissioner of Plants, Medicine and Health for the Earth Commission. It's an honor to meet you." Anna reached out to take Nathan's hand.

"Good morning, ma'am, I am pleased to meet you," Nathan responded. He was a little embarrassed that she thought it was an honor to meet him.

"You are a brave man of faith and I appreciate your willingness to make the personal sacrifices that are required in order to allow Nathan Stevenson to stay and work with Dr. Peck. I am the one who has asked that you make these sacrifices, and with very little information and understanding, you have agreed. I appreciate your selfless service," Anna said with a warm smile and gentle squeeze of his hand.

"Everyone, please take a seat. Jay, please activate the view screen for our guests," Oscillada said. After they sat down, their chairs adjusted to fit the contours of their bodies, and a safety apparatus wrapped gently over their shoulders and legs. Once the view screen came on, they could see the sun was coming up fast. "Captain Elle, you are cleared for takeoff."

The lights dimmed and they could feel the craft lifting. It did not feel like they were moving quickly, but within a few seconds, they could no longer make out the circle on the ground below.

Oscillada explained, "If you were to drive to FERN from your home, it would be about seventeen hundred miles and it would take you a few days to get there. We could fly at sixty thousand feet above Earth, but that would require us to keep our speed below the speed of sound and it would take us over two hours to get there. If we flew faster than that, we would break the sound barrier, and call unwanted attention to ourselves. So instead, we ascend to above eighty percent of Earth's atmosphere or approximately two hundred and forty miles. Once we are that distance from Earth, we can travel closer to ten thousand miles per hour and then descend into Lake Fern, arriving in less than fifteen minutes."

The beauty of seeing the planet from above was awe inspiring. After a few minutes, Oscillada's words sank in and Jake said, "Into the lake? What?"

"On the grounds of FERN, there is a one-hundred-acre lake. In the lake there are three huge fountains used to aerate the water and to provide cover for us. We will descend into the lake behind the fountains and the water spray will help to camouflage our cloaked ship. That way even if someone sees something, they will discount it as their eyes playing tricks on them," Oscillada explained.

"I think what my Dad is asking is, about the landing in the lake part, then what? I don't see any of those orange life preservers," Nathan clarified.

"Oh, I see," Oscillada said, teasing them. "About fifty feet below the surface of the water, in the center of the lake, we will enter the parking portal for our ship and we will be able to step out of the ship unseen and completely dry."

"But then where will we be?" Kaia asked.

"We are almost there, Oscillada. Stop messing with them," Selena insisted.

"Okay. Hundreds of years ago, the Earth Commission directed the construction of an underground base in North Florida. We used this base for generations, coming and going through the lake, and the humans never had any idea. In 1999, Great Spirit guided the current owner, Mackenzie Martin, to buy the property. She is an engineering prodigy, who was a partner in an international engineering firm by the time she was twenty-eight years old. She was extremely financially successful, and in 1999, at the age of thirty-eight, she died of an accidental morphine overdose following major surgery. It was during this moment of death that Great Spirit gave her a choice. She could go on to the heavenly realms, since she had accomplished all she had come to Earth to accomplish. Or she could choose to live and work for Great Spirit. She chose to live, and since that time, she has co-created FERN and everything that you will see above ground," Oscillada explained as everyone listened intently.

"Of course, she could not do this on her own. Along the way, Great Spirit has inspired her and provided an enormous amount of support in the form of like-minded humans and Star People. Today FERN is a joint venture between humans and the Earth Commission, working together to save the planet," Selena added.

"We are beginning our descent into Lake Fern now. Sit back and enjoy the view," Jay announced.

As Lake Fern came into focus, they could see the grounds around the lake. To the south and west, there was nothing but woods for miles. To the north and the east, it looked like a park with gardens, buildings, and beautifully manicured lawns. Suddenly, they quietly entered the water. The ship stopped descending and they could see a huge opening. It looked like the glass wall of an aquarium, but they were inside the aquarium. As they slowly approached, Nathan braced himself for impact with what he believed was a glass wall. Without any hesitation, they passed right through it and they were out of the water. They were suspended three feet above the ground in a room as big as a giant airplane hangar.

"How did we do that?" Nathan exclaimed. "Go right through the glass that is holding back the water, I mean?"

"An energy force field is holding back the water, not glass. It's very effective and this is the perfect application for this technology," Oscillada said with a smile.

"Nathan, have Jake and Alo help you get your luggage. One of the first stops you will be making on your tour of FERN will be at your new apartment," Anna said. "Selena will be going with you. Oscillada and I will catch up with you later."

"All clear to disembark," Jay said as the door opened and the stairs descended.

Jake, Alo, and Nathan gathered up Nathan's belongings and followed Naomi, Kaia, and Selena down the stairs. Once they were off the stairs, they took a moment to look around and see where they were. That wall of water was amazing to look at, but after looking around, they noticed the white marble on the floor, walls, and ceiling. The entire space glowed with a soft white light.

Naomi said, "It looks like an expensive hotel lobby, paintings on the walls, plants everywhere...beautiful and unusual plants."

"I have never seen these plants before," Kaia said.

"This isn't marble, is it? It looks like polished limestone, but I have never seen anything like it before," Alo said.

"You're right, Alo, this underground facility was carved into the natural limestone that was here, holes were filled with a special polymer and the surface was heat-treated to create the smooth solid surface. These natural limestone caverns are the reason this location was chosen by the Earth Commission for this facility," Selena explained.

As Selena finished talking, a tall, slender woman with short, curly red hair approached them. She was wearing black jeans, KEEN sandals, and a light-green polo shirt with the FERN logo on the left side. "Hi, I'm Mackenzie Martin. Welcome to FERN."

CHAPTER SIXTEEN

WORDS, IN THE English language at least, could not express Nate's joyful anticipation of this Wednesday morning's scheduled events. He was grinning from ear to ear, as he checked in the mirror to make certain his tie was straight and his "dress for success" suit looked good. He was an exact replica of Nathan. At least a Nathan with short hair. Nate wondered how people would react to his haircut since Nathan's hair was always long enough to touch his shoulders. Having a new look was probably a good thing. If anybody was aware enough to think something looked different, they would think it was the haircut. The polished black shoes and business suit, instead of his brown boots, jeans, and casual shirt, probably didn't hurt either.

"I'm ready, time to go to the faculty lounge," Nate said to himself.

As he started down the hall of his apartment building, Tom yelled at him, "Nathan, what happened to you? Job interview? What the hell happened to your hair? It's all gone."

Nate smiled at him and said, "What do you think of my new look? Peck told me I needed to look like a businessman instead of a 'wild Indian.' This is the first time I ever tried it. It's not very comfortable, especially the tie."

"If you ask me, I'd say you look like a million bucks."

"Thanks, Tom. I'm on my way to the faculty lounge to meet some corporate dudes who are interested in my research. The President and Provost of the university will be there along with Peck. I'm a little nervous. I hope I don't embarrass myself."

Tom laughed and said, "Well, if you do, you'll look good doing it."

Nate smiled and waved as he started walking to the parking lot.

Dr. Peck was in the foyer by the window waiting for Nathan. He was the first to arrive and was very anxious about this important occasion. Peck was looking forward to his nice "bonus" from the private military contractor, Global General Aeronautics, for the rights to this new technology. He knew that Nathan would not want his process to be used by the military, but he had already figured out how he could handle Nathan. Peck believed Nathan was naïve and gullible and that is the one thing he liked about him. He would be easy to influence and control.

"Where is Nathan? It's almost 8:45! I told him to be here early!" Peck said to himself.

He was about to call Nathan and tell him to get his ass over here, when the man standing next to him said, "Dr. Peck."

It took a moment for him to recognize Nathan. This was not the soft-spoken Indian cowboy he was expecting. Nathan looked like an intelligent, worldly, successful businessman. *Shit!* Peck thought, *I didn't want him to look this good. He looks better than me.*

At that moment, the representatives from Global General Aeronautics and President Aldon walked through the door which was being held open by the Provost. Introductions were made, and Dr. Peck led them to the side room where a continental breakfast was laid out for them. Peck noticed that the three men from Global General Aeronautics had surrounded Nathan and led him to a chair. One was asking him what he wanted and was going to get it for him, while the other two claimed each side of him. President Aldon and Provost Jones went to the buffet first and were getting their food and drinks. Peck decided to go ahead and get a plate before he sat down. When he got to the table, he took the seat across from Nathan. As he sat down, he heard Nathan asking, "What is the primary business of Global General Aeronautics and what about my research are you most interested in?"

Peck wanted to shut him up and control the conversation, but there wasn't much he could do. The cat was being let out of the bag.

The vice president of the company, Joe Thomas, spoke up, "We are a military contractor of vehicles and weapon systems. Our primary purpose is to make weapons with an increased kill ratio for soft targets and better, safer, faster transportation in the field of battle. Dr. Peck contacted us and explained that your process can change various properties of metal on the molecular level. He said that you have found a way to make some metals flexible and impenetrable by projectiles. Dr. Peck also told us that some metals can be made self-lubricating, thereby reducing the need for oil and grease maintenance. Overheating of automatic weapons can cause significant problems. We are hopeful that, with additional funding, you may be able to help us solve that problem as well. In addition, we are intrigued by your ability to magnetize aluminum, even though we have not yet determined a profitable application for that."

"I see. You are here today to determine how my process can be used for military purposes."

"Yes. The highest levels of the military are waiting for us to report back whether or not this technology works. If it works, your process will immediately receive top secret security clearance. This is essential to prevent our enemies from using it against us," Mr. Thomas explained.

"I understand what you are saying, but I never intended this to be for the exclusive use of the military. My intent was to save lives in auto accidents and save people money on oil and grease. I pictured a very lightweight electric car that would be safe because the metal is flexible enough to absorb impact and return to its original shape. What would a top secret security clearance mean for these things?" Nate asked.

"Well, Nathan, it means that if your process works, it will be so important and valuable that Uncle Sam will immediately want it for Homeland Security operations. We will be the first contractor to use it. After we have used it in several products and it has been successful in real world military applications, it will be made available to other military contractors with top secret security clearance," Mr. Thomas clarified.

"Mr. Thomas, I invented the process and that is not how I want it to be used," Nate insisted.

"Well, Nathan, that is not up to you. As I have said, Dr. Peck contacted us because he has the experience to recognize the significance of your invention for the military. We are very grateful to him for contacting us first." Mr. Thomas continued in his arrogant, self-absorbed fashion. "Remember, Nathan, the university owns the rights to all intellectual property. We will be making a contribution to the university and compensating you and Dr. Peck of course. Also we would like for you to consider working for our company."

Nate managed to maintain the calm look on his face, as he thought about how Nathan would probably be unable to resist the urge to vomit on this pig's shoes.

Dr. Peck spoke up. "So let's go to the lab. Nathan already has the demonstration set up for us."

On the way to the lab, Nate was thankful that he was doing this for Nathan. He knew how hard it would be for Nathan to go through this farce. More than ever, he was looking forward to the fun he was about to have.

Dr. Peck opened the door of the lab and said, "This way, gentlemen. Please put on these safety goggles and step behind the safety partition, while Nathan demonstrates his technology."

"Thank you, Dr. Peck. Gentlemen, first I am going to magnetize this aluminum bar. As you can see, this magnet easily picks up these nails, but the aluminum bar cannot pick them up. After the bar goes through the process in this machine, the bar will be magnetized and it will be able to pick up the nails." Nate placed the aluminum bar into the machine. He typed the program command and said, "The process to magnetize the aluminum will start within one minute. You will hear a humming noise and some sounds that may remind you of the popping of static electricity. The process will take only a few minutes, and the machine will buzz when it is complete."

After the machine buzzed, Nate took the bar out and placed it over the nails. Nothing happened. The aluminum bar was not magnetized. Peck's face turned as red as a beet. One of the representatives, who was a physicist, turned to the other and whispered, "I hope something works or this is a big waste of time."

Nate, looking perplexed and embarrassed, stuttered, "I, I don't know what's wrong. Give me a minute to check the program."

Peck barked, "Nathan, since they are more interested in other processes and checking the program would take a lot of time, please do another process."

"Oh, okay, Dr. Peck. I'm very sorry. I don't know what happened. I'll go ahead and do the process to make steel flexible."

Nate picked up a four inch by eight inch steel plate one quarter inch thick and placed it in the machine. Nate tried to look nervous as he was choosing the flex program on the computer, but inside he was having a blast. The machine made some peculiar noises and then buzzed, signaling the process was complete. Nate took the steel plate out and tried to bend it. He couldn't bend it at all.

Everyone looked at each other. Dr. Peck was beside himself. "Nathan! Something is wrong! You were supposed to have everything ready and working!"

"But, Dr. Peck, it was working! Maybe it's the power supply module. Let me check that." Nate knelt down behind the counter to look at the power supply module that was plugged into the back wall. After a minute, he stood up and said, "The power control knob was down to three and it was supposed to be set on eight. I don't know how it could have been changed. I'll do it again. I am so sorry."

Nate put the steel plate back into the machine and started the program again. Suddenly, the machine started vibrating and making loud crackling noises. The men instinctively made sure that they were completely behind the safety glass panels. The machine exploded and sparks flew in all directions. The computer control module started smoking. Nate grabbed the fire extinguisher as flames erupted. "I'll put the fire out!" Nate yelled, as he enthusiastically swung the fire extinguisher all over the room, sending the foam everywhere. The fire was out, but it was smoky. The smell of wires and plastic melting was disgusting. The building smoke alarms began blaring and suddenly the ceiling sprinklers starting spraying water everywhere.

The men were covered in foam and drenched from the sprinklers. Joe Thomas yelled, "Let's get the hell out of here!"

Peck yelled at Nathan as he was running after the company representatives. "You are fully responsible for this fiasco! Get it cleaned up now! I'll deal with you later."

Nate was laughing so hard, it sounded like he was crying. When the firefighters came in, Nate was sitting on the floor with his head buried in his arms. That worked out well as everyone concluded that he was overcome with smoke. When a paramedic asked him if he was all right, he looked up with tears in his eyes and said, "All my work is ruined. I've lost everything."

The paramedic said, "We need to get you out of here. The fumes are noxious. Come on, it will be all right. There were no injuries and no structural damage to the building. That's the good thing."

CHAPTER SEVENTEEN

"**M**AC, LET ME introduce Nathan Stevenson, Nathan's parents, Jake and Naomi Stevenson, and his grandparents, Alo and Kaia Rivers," Selena said.

"Hi, everyone, I am pleased to meet you. Selena, it's good to see you. It has been too long," Mac said as she hugged Selena. "I understand Oscillada and Anna are here as well."

"Yes, they will catch up with us later. They have some business to take care of," Selena responded.

"Okay then, everyone, please follow me. This parking portal is what we refer to as the sub-basement level of FERN. We will go to the basement level to begin our tour."

"These are very unusual plants you have in here. I've never seen them before," Kaia commented.

"Stand by, Kaia, you are going to see a lot of things you haven't seen before," Mac said with a wink and a warm smile.

They followed Mac into a large elevator and the door closed behind them. Within seconds of the door closing, it opened again and they walked into the security office. It was similar to the parking portal in décor, but the ceiling was only nine feet high. The room was twenty feet long by twenty-five feet wide, and the wall on the far side was covered with an array of thirty security monitors. Before they could grasp what they were seeing, a man who was standing looking at the monitors pushed a button on the desk and all the screens went blank. He turned and walked toward them.

"Greetings, my name is Skyler Browning. I am the head of security here at FERN." Skyler Browning did not look like someone you would want to mess with. He wasn't very tall, only about five foot seven, but he was extremely muscular. His biceps were so big, it looked like the sleeves of his tan polo shirt were going to cut off his circulation. He had on navy blue cargo pants and black boots. He wore a belt with handcuffs and a knife on the left and a unique hand gun on his right. "Welcome back, ma'am. It is very nice to see you again," he said, shaking Selena's hand.

Mac said, "We have a couple of things we need to do here before we proceed with the tour. First, Nathan, I am happy to see that you and Jake are already wearing the FERN watch. In addition to the preprogrammed numbers you have for personal use, Skyler is programmed as number nine and I am number eight. Due to the highly secure nature of our work here at FERN, it is important that everyone here limit their outside communication to these phones. The Vermosan threat is real and we don't take it lightly. If there is anything you need at all, please don't hesitate to call me on number eight. If you feel threatened in any way while you are here, call Skyler immediately on nine. Never hesitate to call either of us. Understand?"

Jake and Nathan nodded in agreement. Jake said, "Nathan told me this watch does some cool things, but he has not had a chance to show me how to operate it."

"Okay, let's take care of that right now. First, the watch automatically sets the time based on where you are. The alarm functions are explained in the manual, and they work like any other watch. In other words, use your cell phone for your alarm. It's not good for anything else while you are here anyway," Mac joked. "I'm kidding. The alarm function works fine and it is simple. For safety purposes, we are jamming all cell phone signals, so your cell phone won't work while you are here."

Skyler continued with the instructions. "There is a dial on the bottom left side of the watch face. As you turn that dial, numbers one through nine will come up on the face of your watch. When you reach the number you wish to call, push the button in. Once the call is connected, look into the watch face because it becomes a video phone. In an emergency, hold your thumb on the watch face for three seconds, and assistance will arrive within moments. Go ahead, Nathan, call Mac."

Nathan dialed his watch to number eight and pushed the button. They could hear her watch ring. Mac pushed the same button to answer it. "Hi, Mac, this is too cool," Nathan said as he looked at her on his watch.

"I agree. Hang up by pushing the same button again," Mac answered. "Go ahead, Jake, call Nathan."

Jake dialed number one and Nathan answered, "Hi, Dad, are we having fun yet?"

"Yes, we are," Jake answered, and then they both hung up.

Mac continued. "Now the next order of business. From this moment forward, Nathan needs to become David Bridges."

"In this folio, I have everything you will need, David Bridges," Skyler said as pulled out a leather notebook, unzipped it, and showed him each item as he pulled it out. "A new wallet, your Florida driver's license with your FERN address, Social Security card, passport, birth certificate, MasterCard, Visa card, Sam's Club membership, Costco membership, and last but not least, your voter's registration card."

"It looks real. Is this stuff real? Nathan asked.

"Yes, they are all legal documents. Your date of birth and physical description are the same, but that is where the similarity ends. Familiarize yourself with these documents. Please believe me, we know how hard this is, but for your safety, you have to get used to the idea that from this moment forward, you are no longer Nathan Stevenson. You are now David Bridges," Skyler explained, while looking intently into Nathan's eyes. "One more thing, please give your Nathan Stevenson wallet to Naomi so she can take it home for you to have when you visit."

Nathan pulled his wallet out of his left back pocket and took the cash out. He handed his wallet to Naomi and said, "Hi, my name is David Bridges and it is very nice to meet you."

Naomi's eyes suddenly filled with tears. She had not expected it to be this hard. She was proud of him, but at the same time, she was sad to think he would never again be known to the world as her son, Nathan Stevenson. Jake put his arm around Naomi's shoulders and pulled her close. He felt the same powerful emotions. They were both at a loss for words as they looked through tear-filled eyes at the son they loved so much.

Nathan hugged them and said, "I love you. I want you to know that I am okay and I am ready to do this."

Nathan hugged Kaia and then Alo and said, "Thank you, Grandfather, for teaching me to have courage."

Alo, taking Kaia's hand, nodded and smiled at his grandson.

Nathan stood up, pulled his shoulders back, took the leather folio with his documents from Skyler, and said, "Hi, I am David Bridges and I'm very pleased to meet you, Mr. Browning."

Skyler shook his hand and said, "The pleasure is mine, Dr. Bridges. Please call me Skyler." Skyler was impressed with this young man's courage and the love and support he received from his family. He already had a really good feeling about them.

Mac spoke up. "Whew, now that the hard part is over, there is one more thing we need to do. Skyler, go ahead with the security protocols."

Skyler nodded. "This machine, while it may look like a typical full body airport security scanner, has been retrofitted to serve as our biometrics scanner. This facility is protected by a combination of artificial intelligence and advanced biometrics. We do not carry security badges or have secret passwords because neither of these techniques is actually secure in a world threatened by Vermosans. Instead, we will use this machine to take a biometrics scan of each of you. Once the scan is complete, the system will be told the areas of FERN for which you have security clearance. If you have the proper security clearance to enter a particular door, it will automatically open for you as soon as you touch the doorknob. If you do not have the clearance to enter that location, the door will not open," Skyler explained. "In addition, the computer screens you saw me watching when you arrived show where everyone is at FERN. If someone who is not in the system happens to get onto the property, I will be alerted immediately. As you can probably imagine, this provides an extensive amount of protection for all of us."

Mac, wanting to be sure they understood this was for everyone's health, safety, and well-being, clarified, "The system monitors your physical location and your energy. For example, as long as you are peaceful, happy, and content, you will show up as a green light on the monitor. If you are in distress from fear or danger or even physical pain, you will show up as orange. An intruder would show up as a red star and alarms will blare. Skyler is aware of who, where, and how you are, but not specifically what you are doing, so your privacy is not being invaded in any way. Does anyone have any questions?"

Skyler asked, "Is everyone comfortable submitting to the biometrics scan?"

"I am, start with me," David volunteered.

"Excellent, David," Skyler said as he walked over to the machine and stood in front of the keyboard attached to the side of it. "I am entering his name, David Bridges. Okay, David, go ahead and walk slowly through the machine, stepping on each of the footsteps you see painted on the floor."

David walked through, being careful to step on all six of the footsteps that were painted on the floor approaching and exiting the machine.

"The scan is complete, give me a minute to enter your security clearance," Skyler said as he typed away on the keyboard.

"Did it hurt?" Jake asked, trying to lighten the mood in the room.

"No, Dad, of course not."

"Okay, I'll go next then," Jake said as he approached the front of the machine.

"Stand by, Jake Stevenson. Okay, I am ready for you to go," Skyler said. Jake began his methodical walk through the machine. Alo lined up to go next as Skyler typed on the keyboard.

"Alo Rivers, I am ready for you to proceed." Alo walked slowly through the machine while Naomi lined up. Skyler continued typing. He really liked this family, and they were making his job very easy.

"Go ahead, Naomi Stevenson." Naomi walked through the machine and as soon as Skyler finished typing, Kaia was in position.

"Proceed, Kaia Rivers." Kaia walked through and Skyler finished typing.

"Excellent, you all have full security clearance for all the above ground facilities and David's lab, which is lab D. The only above ground facilities that are off limits are labs A, B, and C, which belong to three other scientists. In addition, you have clearance for some of the basement tunnels. I would like to thank you for your cooperation and welcome you to FERN," Skyler said with a warm smile.

"Okay, let's get this show on the road. Follow me," Mac said, leading them toward a door at the back of the room.

Once they were outside, they saw two electric vehicles parked there. Each of them had the FERN logo, a wheel with the colors of the rainbow, and a fern in the center, painted on their hoods. One was a four passenger off-road emergency vehicle with lights, sirens, and no doors.

"Is this an electric police car?" Jake asked.

"Yes, all our vehicles are electric. This security vehicle came from the factory with a maximum speed of thirty-five miles per hour, but our mechanical wizard, Robert Mays, made a few adjustments and now it has a top speed of fifty miles per hour. That is even after Skyler decked it out with all the gadgets he needs," Mac explained.

"That is the coolest golf cart I've ever seen," Jake said to Alo, who was nodding his head in agreement.

"You can put David's bags in the rack on the back of this bus. We call it the people mover. No seat belts necessary on the people mover, its maximum speed is only twenty-five miles an hour. Everyone take a seat," Mac said, as she climbed aboard. Selena took the front seat next to Mac; Alo and Kaia took the second seat; and Jake, David, and Naomi took the back seat.

While backing out, Mac explained, "FERN consists of eight hundred acres of property that includes the one hundred acre Lake Fern. The entire perimeter is fenced and monitored by our security forces. When I bought the property in 1999, all the underground facilities were already here, unbeknownst to me. Every building at FERN has direct access elevators to this underground network that we refer to as the basement. The basement is huge. That is why we built all the access elevators large enough to accommodate the electric vehicles. The basement is the ultimate safe place. Our first stop is the basement elevator that will take us up to ground level in my garage."

"Does everyone who works at FERN know about the underground facilities?" Alo asked.

"Everyone who lives at FERN does, but not everyone who works for us. We have forty acres on the northeast corner of the property that is outside of the main security fence. This area houses our office building for legal and accounting functions, a diner that is open to all employees and guests for breakfast and lunch weekdays, and our laundry facilities. These positions are staffed by people from the surrounding counties. These employees know they work for a top secret research facility, but they do not know anything about our otherworldly associates," Mac answered.

"How is the basement, well, um, how is it powered, I mean, climate control, lights, automatic doors, stuff like that?" David asked.

"As far as climate control is concerned, that is courtesy of Mother Earth, she maintains the year-round temperature at sixty-five degrees Fahrenheit. Everything else is alien technology. I am sure Oscillada or your lab assistant, Thax, would be happy to explain anything you want to know in immense detail. When Selena explained earlier that the limestone was coated with a 'special' polymer, she conveniently left out that this 'special' polymer includes a bioluminescence material from some far-away galaxy that is basically fish poop. After I found that out, I stopped asking for specifics," Mac said.

Everyone erupted in laughter including Selena, who said, "There is no way I am adding that detail to my story."

"We are about to enter the elevator to my garage, please hold on to the railing in front of your seats until we are safely parked," Mac advised.

They approached a wall of four garage doors. Three of the four doors had a red light above them. Mac lined up the people mover with the fourth door, which had a green light above it. As soon as they stopped, the door opened and Mac drove into the elevator.

She turned off the key and set the parking brake as the door closed behind them. The elevator lifted them into the garage and they could see three vehicles parked in the other spaces. When the floor of the elevator clicked into place, Mac said, "All clear. We have arrived."

CHAPTER EIGHTEEN

MAC OPENED THE backdoor to her house and said, "Come on in, you can put your luggage right here by the door. I would like to introduce you to Joan."

As they walked into the living room, Joan came from the kitchen to greet them. Joan was a little shorter than Mac, about five and a half feet tall, with mocha skin, brown hair, and beautiful aqua blue eyes. She was wearing loose-fitting black slacks and a white chef's jacket. "Everybody, this is my best friend and business partner, Joan Clark. Joan, this is Dr. David Bridges."

"Hi, David, we are happy to have you here," Joan said, shaking David's hand.

Mac continued, "This is Jake and Naomi Stevenson, David's parents."

"Hi Jake, Naomi, nice to meet you," Joan said as she shook their hands.

"And Alo and Kaia Rivers, Naomi's parents."

"Welcome," Joan said as she greeted them.

Selena was the last to come in the door and as she reached Joan, they gave each other a warm hug. "It's so good to see you. We have a lot of catching up to do."

Selena nodded, "Yes, we do."

Selena turned to the guests and said, "Joan has been on my team for, well, let's say a long time. She volunteered to move to Earth for this assignment, and she is perfect for the job."

At that point Jake thought to himself, *Oh boy. Joan is another alien. She's probably three hundred years old. I've got to start getting used to this.*

"I imagine by now you are thirsty, hungry, and possibly a little tired, so we are making breakfast for you. Please make yourselves comfortable. It will be ready shortly," Joan said as she turned to head back to the kitchen.

Mac spoke up, "There are two restrooms right here for your convenience. The dining room is right around the corner to the left, past the stairs. Just follow the smell of the coffee."

Jake said, "Coffee? I need coffee."

Selena followed Joan to the kitchen. Mac led Alo and Jake into the dining area, while Naomi and Kaia took advantage of the opportunity to freshen up. David walked to the fireplace to look at the pictures on the mantle. When Naomi came out of the restroom, she walked up to David and put her arms around him. "How are you doing, Nathan?" she whispered softly.

"Mom, this seems so weird. Being myself, with Kevin, at home was fun and easy. Being here as David Bridges may not be that easy."

"David Bridges! You are going to be fine. I know this may not be easy, but we raised you to do the right thing, even when it's the hard thing. I've always been extremely proud of you, but never more than now. Remember dial two and we can talk. If you want to come home, you can be there in less than an hour by flying at supersonic speed."

"Thanks, Mom," David said as he kissed her on the cheek. "You always know when I need a pep talk."

Walking into the dining area David and Naomi found Mac, Jake, Alo, and Kaia sitting at a large, rustic, cedar plank table with a plate of pastries in the center. Selena came out of the kitchen, smiled at them and said, "Coffee, herbal tea, juice, and ice water are here on the serving counter, help yourself. How do you like your eggs, Naomi, David?"

"We both like them scrambled," David replied.

"That makes it unanimous. They will be ready soon."

Mac got up to get a glass of water. "Would anybody else like a glass of water?"

David said, "I would. I've been thirsty since the flying saucer ride."

Mac nodded and said, "Supersonic travel has a tendency to dry me out too. If anybody knows the scientific reason for it let me know."

David spoke up, "I believe it is because the supersonic speed squeezes the juice right out of your body." After a pause, everyone laughed. Mac handed David a glass of water and sat down at the table.

"How's the coffee, Jake?" Mac asked.

"I think I need another cup to adequately evaluate its deliciousness," Jake said, as he got up to refill his mug.

Mac was debating with herself about whether she should ask them if they had any questions now or wait until after breakfast. She decided it would be best to wait and see where the conversation led. Nobody seemed shy in this group. She knew the background and personality profiles of each of them, but nothing prepared her for how genuine they were. She found herself wanting to get to know them more. She was enjoying their company, and human friends were hard to find these days.

Selena came to the table with elderberry jelly and strawberry preserves and asked, "Is anyone ready for breakfast?"

"I am. Now that I'm not so nervous, I'm hungry," Jake announced.

"Hungry is Jake's middle name, but this time I think we are all in agreement," Kaia said, as she looked around the table to find Naomi, David, and Alo nodding their heads enthusiastically.

"Good, Joan has cooked a feast, just stay seated and we'll bring it out to you," Selena said heading back to the kitchen.

Shortly, platters and serving bowls filled with scrambled eggs, ham, bacon, hash browns, grits, biscuits, and fruit were on the table. After pouring themselves some juice, Selena and Joan sat down to join them.

Mac said, "Please, let's hold hands and thank Great Spirit. Alo, would you like to say the blessing?"

Alo nodded and took Kaia and David's hands and said, "Great Spirit, we thank you for this new day and this new beginning. We thank you for the gift of this food and for our new relationships. Aho."

Everyone said, "Aho," and started passing the serving platters and bowls around the table and filling their plates.

"This is a wonderful breakfast, but you shouldn't have gone to so much trouble," Naomi said to Joan.

"It was no trouble at all. I enjoy cooking for a lot of people and it's my way of saying welcome to FERN," Joan responded with a smile.

"Well, thank you very much. We definitely feel welcome," Naomi said, as she finished filling her plate.

"Yes, thank you, Joan, this is delicious," Jake added.

David spoke up, "Mac, would you mind telling us the rest of the story about how FERN got started? How did you meet Joan?"

"I'd be happy too," Mac said. "The first morning I woke up in this house was January 1, 2000. It was a very cold day. I was sitting in front of the fireplace with a cup of hot chocolate wondering what was going to happen next. I knew that I was supposed to buy this property, but that is really all I knew. As I sat there, I said out loud, 'Okay, Spirit, now what?' and suddenly the front door bell rang."

"That was a little weird," Jake commented.

"You're right. Joan was at the door with a pecan pie. She said she came to welcome me to the neighborhood. We talked for hours. It was late afternoon before she told me she had arrived that day on a spaceship that had landed in my lake."

Jake laughed. "Believe me, I can imagine how you felt."

"I was pretty sure she was pulling my leg, so I told her to show me the spaceship. When she said it had already left, I was sure she was full of it, so I told her to have it come back. I was shocked when she said, 'Okay, let's go out back.'"

Joan interrupted, "You should have seen the look on her face when that spaceship landed. It was priceless."

Mac and Joan were both laughing. Mac continued, "That was the last time I ever doubted her, and we have been best friends ever since."

"What does your family think about all this, Mac?" Kaia asked.

"My family, well, long story short, when they found out I had cancer, they got pretty excited imagining how wealthy they would be when they inherited all my assets. They were furious when I sold my business and house in Tallahassee and moved out here. I guess they thought I was squandering their inheritance. Well, let's just say, when they couldn't get me to go back to the way I used to be, they got pretty nasty and disowned me."

"Oh my, that's awful!" Kaia exclaimed.

"They were awful. It was very painful for me, but Spirit held onto me and healed my broken heart. The only good part was it completely freed me of all entanglements and obligations. Everyone at FERN is my family now and I couldn't be happier." Mac said.

"Was this house already here when you bought the place?" Alo asked.

"Not all of it. Once I knew what we needed, I designed the complete renovation of the house. We added the upstairs and the four-car garage with elevators to the basement and the two-car garage for our 'going out into the world' vehicles. The original house was gutted and turned into this open concept living room, dining room, and kitchen. Once the house was finished, Spirit started sending people to help us. Lolly Berry, our herbalist, moved in first, followed soon after by PJ Maxwell, our resident massage therapist. I worked with Lolly and PJ to design our medical facilities."

"I can't wait to see that!" Naomi and Kaia exclaimed in unison.

Mac smiled and continued, "Next, our first scientist moved in. She helped me design the ultimate, versatile science lab, and we built four of those. She was an electronics engineer, who went on to become our first success story. After helping invent the FERN watch, she invented the technology that allowed cell phones to be smaller. Once we started receiving royalties from her company, we were able to build the residence hall."

"Speaking of the residence hall, David are you ready to see your new apartment?" Mac asked.

"You bet I am. Thank you for breakfast, Joan, it was delicious," David said, as he excused himself from the table. "Can I take the plates to the kitchen for you?"

Selena responded, "No, dear, I'll help Joan clear the table and clean up. The rest of you go ahead and enjoy the tour. I'll catch up with you in a little while."

Mac cleared some of the plates from the table on her way upstairs. In a short while she joined them in the living room and said, "The residence hall is right next door. We can walk over. The sidewalk is covered, so there is no risk of a Vermosan spy satellite noticing you are here."

Picking up David's suitcase and duffel bag, Jake asked, "Is that really a threat?"

David picked up his briefcase and messenger bag as they followed Mac out the side door. On the way to the residence hall, Mac explained, "Not a direct or immediate threat, but this is the way we look at it. If the Vermosans are watching and they see two people enter the house and suddenly six people walk out of my house they could realize that we have underground facilities here. We try to obfuscate our activities every chance we get. Between the covered walkways and parking facilities and the roofs on the electric vehicles, we make it pretty difficult for anyone watching from above to figure out who is here or what we are up to."

CHAPTER NINETEEN

THE COVERED WALKWAY led them through a beautifully land-scaped garden to the main entrance of the six-story residence hall. The porte-cochere that covered the double driveway in front of the building had double columns at each corner and reached up to the second story. Once they entered the lobby, Mac said, "First, let's go to David's apartment on the sixth floor."

The elevator doors opened and they went in. "I don't think my first apartment was as big as this elevator," Jake joked, as the door closed behind them.

When they reached the sixth floor and the other elevator door opened, they walked out and stopped at the railing. The entire center of the building was an atrium; the sun was streaming in from the roof above, and they could see all the way to the ground floor. There were fruit trees in giant pots reaching up to the second floor, a koi pond with a bridge over it, sofas and soft, comfortable chairs, and game tables in a magnificent indoor park. They could see a balcony walk-way all the way around the building on each of the five upper floors. There were five apartment doors on each side.

"This is incredible." David was not expecting anything like this.

"Beautiful, absolutely beautiful" was all Naomi could say.

At the far end of the building on the right side of the ground level was a dining hall. Looking to the left Jake asked, "Is that a game room down there?"

"Yes, we have it all, billiards, ping-pong, foosball, game tables, you name it. Sunday night is our weekly foosball tournament," Mac answered. After giving them a few minutes to look around, she said, "Let's go down the right side. David's apartment is at the end."

When they reached the door, Mac said, "Go ahead, David, you go in first."

David tried to keep his expectations in check as he opened the door. "What? A full size kitchen, are you kidding me? I was expecting an efficiency…sixty-inch flat screen TV in the living room, nice. This is a comfortable sofa," David said, as he sat down on the living room sofa and looked back to his left. "An eat-in bar and a dining table. Unbelievable!"

David continued looking around the kitchen, dining, and living space. Jake went past him to the screened-in porch and said, "Alo, come here, you've got to see this."

Alo joined him on the porch, "This porch is huge. He is going to go nuts when he sees the hammock and the clear roof on this thing."

Just then they heard, "Mom, get in here, you've got to see this," David yelled from the bedroom. "I'm not talking about the king-size bed, yeah, that's the bomb, but look at this bathroom."

Naomi and Kaia went into the bathroom, "This is the lap of luxury, a spa tub, and a separate shower with wall jets. This bathroom is huge," Naomi said, in amazement.

They were astonished as they walked around, taking it all in.

"Awesome!" David yelled from the screened porch, when he discovered the hammock.

Kaia and Naomi went out to the screened porch through the French doors in the bedroom.

Mac stood inside the living room by the French doors that opened onto the porch. "Watch this." She flipped a switch by the door and the screen retracted into the knee wall. Then the roof retracted into the exterior wall of the apartment building, and the porch was completely open.

"I can sleep outside under the stars," David realized. "I'm going to be fine. Now I have everything I need."

"That's not all," Mac said, as she reversed the process. "There are three settings for the roof; open, clear vinyl glass, and tinted vinyl glass. And three settings for the sides; open, screened, and clear vinyl glass. Even on a hot summer day, this porch will be cool under the tinted roof, especially if you have the clear vinyl glass on the sides and you open both sets of French doors. The air conditioner in your apartment will cool this porch nicely. You can enjoy being out here in any weather."

"This is a fantastic apartment," Naomi said, as she opened other doors looking at the amount of storage he had. "What is this, a coat closet?" she asked, opening the door to the half bath that was to the left of the front door. "Unbelievable."

"What is unbelievable?" David asked as he walked back toward Naomi and looked into the door she had opened. "A half bath too."

"The sofa pulls out into a queen-sized bed, the refrigerator is already stocked and housekeeping cleans on this floor every Friday. Can you think of anything we forgot?" Mac asked David.

"No way," David said as he leaned in to give her a hug. "This is perfect."

Jake opened the refrigerator. "Guinness? David, she wasn't kidding when she said the fridge is stocked."

"Kevin called ahead to let us know what he likes," Mac said with a smile. She beamed as she realized everyone was ecstatic with David's new home. "We try to make sure you have everything you need on the personal front, so you can focus your energy on your work."

"It looks like you have thought of everything, but I do have one question. What about laundry?" Kaia asked.

"David will have to drop his laundry off at the Laundromat next to our diner on Thursday mornings. Housekeeping will return his clean clothes to his apartment on Friday," Mac answered.

Alo spoke up, "This apartment couldn't be more perfect. I can't wait to see his lab."

"Let's head that way now. We can take the elevator at this end of the building. That way we can see the common areas while we are here," Mac said as they left the apartment. Once they reached the ground floor, the elevator opened out onto the atrium. "The dining hall and kitchen are here on the left and over there on the right is the game room that Jake already spotted. Just go ahead and look around, I will meet you at the other end," Mac said.

Mac had barely finished talking when Alo, Jake, and David took off for the game room.

Naomi and Kaia took a quick peek at the dining room and kitchen and then walked through the indoor park. "This is beautiful," Kaia said as they crossed the bridge over the koi pond.

"I love the sound of the water and the smell of the key lime trees," Naomi commented as she stood and looked all around her. "What's that over there?" she wondered out loud.

"Over where?" Kaia asked.

"Past the game room, is that a store? It is. Let's go shopping," Naomi said to Kaia. When they reached the store, they found Mac was already in there.

"Welcome to the FERN store," Mac said. "We have all the basics and then some for our residents. It's a long way to the nearest grocery store, so we try to stock the things they would want in their kitchens. We have three meals a day available in the dining room, plus breakfast and lunch weekdays in the diner, but there are always things you need in your apartment."

Naomi and Kaia looked around at everything and they were amazed at the variety. "I've run through a checklist in my head of the groceries David would want and I have been able to check off everything. They even have his favorite peanut butter," Naomi said in amazement.

"Did you see they have clothes, hats, and coffee mugs with the FERN logo over here?" Kaia said, guiding Naomi to the clothes racks.

"There aren't any prices on any of these things, only a bar code," Naomi noticed, as she came across a shirt she knew Jake would look fantastic in.

"The bar code is for inventory control. Each resident is free to take whatever they need from the store. All we ask is that they run the bar codes by the scanner over there so we know when to reorder," Mac explained.

"Don't you worry about people stealing?" Kaia asked.

"No, the people here have been thoroughly vetted. Besides, there are only two kinds of people in the world, takers and givers. The people here are givers, or they never would have made it through our vetting process. If you weren't a family of givers, you would have balked at the suggestions Oscillada made about giving up on Nathan's university career and coming here. Please take whatever you like."

"Well, thank you. I do love this sage green coffee mug with the FERN logo, can I have one for Alo too?" Kaia asked.

"Of course."

"Don't you worry about givers becoming takers when everything is free?" Naomi asked.

"That's impossible. True givers never become takers and takers never become givers. Takers may pretend to be givers, but eventually, they will be unmasked. If you were pretending to be givers, we would have realized it, most likely by the time Anna showed up with the change of plans that forced Nathan to give up his identity and become David Bridges," Mac explained.

"I never really thought about it like that before, but I think you're right. If I think about it, the people I know that are takers act like givers most of the time, but the givers I know never act like takers." This became a big aha moment for Naomi as she realized the full extent of this truth.

Suddenly Jake, Alo, and David came into the store. "You should see that game room. We could have stayed in there for hours. David and I played a little foosball. He can still beat me and I can assure you he is ready for the tournament," Jake said, shaking his head.

"Jake, do you like this tan, long sleeve Henley with the FERN logo?" Naomi asked.

"I would definitely wear that," Jake responded.

"If you are buying, I would wear one of those too, but I like the hunter green one," Alo volunteered.

Naomi picked out an extra-large tan one for Jake and a large hunter green for Alo, then she picked up two of the coffee mugs like Kaia had. "Mac, may we have these?"

"Yes, you may. Come over to the counter with me so I can scan them," Mac said, walking Naomi and Kaia to the computer. "Here is a canvas FERN bag for each of you to carry your things in."

"Thank you, Mac," Kaia said, as Naomi handed her Alo's shirt.

"Yes, thank you so much," Naomi said, putting Jake's shirt and her two mugs in her bag.

The men were checking out what was available in the grocery store, when Naomi, Kaia, and Mac came in. "Next stop, David's lab. Is everyone ready to go?" Mac asked as she led them past the elevators and out the front door.

CHAPTER TWENTY

A S THEY WALKED out of the residence hall, Joan and Selena pulled up in the people mover. Joan got out of the driver's seat and walked toward them. "How do you like your apartment, David?" Joan asked.

"I absolutely love it. We're going to see my lab now," David said, beaming.

"That's wonderful. Enjoy the rest of the tour. I'll see you later," Joan said as she turned to head back to the house.

Selena joined them and said, "David, why don't you sit up front with Mac? I'll sit in the back with Naomi and Kaia."

David nodded and climbed into the passenger seat next to Mac. Jake and Alo sat in the second seat, while Selena, Naomi, and Kaia slid into the back seat. Mac put the vehicle in gear and drove them around the circular driveway, which took them past the front of her house. She turned left and drove past a two-car garage; then turned left again and passed the four-car garage for the electric vehicles.

"What is this road paved with? I've never seen anything like it," David asked as they drove past the back of the house.

"Solar road tiles. We have covered all our driveways, walkways, parking lots, and recreation surfaces with these tiles, and with the help of the solar panels on our roofs, we have virtually eliminated our electric bill," Mac explained.

"Wait a minute. Are you saying these are solar freakin' road-ways? I read an article about them last year. Were they invented here?" Jake asked.

"Unfortunately, they were not invented here, but yes, they are the solar road tiles you read about. They are amazing. Our electric vehicles are perpetually recharged as we drive on them. They have LED lights that can be programmed different ways. We program the tiles on the roads and paths to light up at night, thereby eliminating the need for overhead lights. In the recreation area, we can easily change the pattern of the lines on the ground from a basketball court, to a volleyball court, to a tennis court. I love these things," Mac explained.

"Why did you say, 'unfortunately they were not invented here'?" Alo asked.

"Was it because they were so expensive?" Jake wondered as they drove past enormous vegetable gardens on their right.

"Well, they were expensive, but being a brand-new technology that is to be expected. The price will drop as they become more prevalent. Besides, we recouped our investment within twenty-four months," Mac paused to point out the maintenance facilities and security building on the left. "This is a technology that if fully implemented in the United States, could dramatically decrease the use of fossil fuels and at the same time make electric vehicles much more viable. This would allow Earth to begin to recover from global warming and heal herself. As it is, the Vermosan propaganda machine is relentlessly trying to discredit the technology. It's a no-brainer. It saves money and the planet, so of course, Vermosans are out to destroy it."

"What would be different if it had been invented at FERN?" Alo inquired.

"First, we would have been able to fully develop the product before the Vermosans even got wind of it. Second, our team of lawyers would have figured out the best strategy for unveiling the product in the market. It would have been changing the world before the Vermosans could even start their propaganda campaign. By the time the Vermosans released their lies on YouTube, it would have been too late, and the technology would have already spread like wildfire," Mac explained.

They turned right and approached three huge greenhouses on their left. "The first two greenhouses are for food plants, the last greenhouse is for landscaping plants. Across the street coming up on the right is our octagon shaped herb conservatory, affectionately known as the Herb House."

"That's huge. I can't wait to get in there," Kaia said.

"Me neither. How big is that thing? Are those roads going through the middle in both directions?" Naomi asked.

Mac was busy pointing out the labs, which were coming up, to the guys. Selena answered, "It is almost two acres, and yes, those are roads. The Herb House was a collaborative effort between Anna and Mac. They hit it out of the park."

They turned right past the Herb House and after they had passed three huge lab buildings on the left, they stopped in front of the fourth one. "This is David's lab," Mac announced.

Grabbing his briefcase and messenger bag, David rushed to the front door of the lab. Jake and Alo were right behind him. Mac looked back at Naomi and Kaia with a smile as they walked to the door. This time David knew he did not need to set his expectations so low. His heart was racing as he opened the door and walked in. The lab consisted of an eleven-hundred-square-foot office space and a nine-thousand-square-foot warehouse production area.

"Amazing. This is the biggest desk I've ever seen," David said as he put his bags down and sat in the desk chair. "Dual fifty-five inch computer monitors, a blueprint plotter, color laser printer. Dad, can you believe this power desk?"

"The whole office is fantastic. I'm impressed," Jake answered.

Naomi and Kaia noticed the kitchen right away. They were both relieved to see it was complete with refrigerator, microwave oven, and coffee maker. David, like his Dad and Grandfather, tended to be very focused when he worked; often forgetting to stop to eat.

Kaia looked at Naomi and said, "I don't think we need to worry anymore, it looks to me like Mac has thought of everything."

"Honestly, Mom, I couldn't have done a better job myself. Let's relax and enjoy the adventure."

Alo opened the door to the attached garage and peeked in. "Mac, whose golf cart is that in the garage?"

"That's for David and his assistant. Thax must be out in the warehouse."

"David, there's a black golf cart out there in the garage for you," Alo told David, as he closed the door behind him.

"Is there an elevator to the basement in the garage?" David asked Mac.

"You bet there is. You would be surprised how often that comes in handy."

The door to the warehouse opened and Thax walked in. Thax was an intimidating figure, six feet nine inches tall with light brown skin, black cargo pants, black t-shirt with the FERN logo. His black Oakley sunglasses were striking against his white crew cut.

"Hi, Mac. Hi, Commissioner, ma'am, it is very nice to see you again," he said as he bowed slightly.

"Thax, I would like to introduce you to Dr. David Bridges," Mac said. "David, this is Thax Clinton."

Thax reached out to shake David's hand. "It's very nice to meet you, Dr. Bridges. I hope I have everything set up the way you like it. Please call me Thax."

"You've done a fantastic job setting everything up, Thax. Please call me David." David turned to introduce the others. "Thax, these are my parents, Jake and Naomi Stevenson, and my grandparents, Alo and Kaia Rivers."

He greeted each of them and shook their hands. "Come on out to the warehouse, let me show you all the great equipment we have at our disposal," Thax said, as he led David, Jake, and Alo into the production facility.

Naomi and Kaia stepped into the warehouse and glanced around. Naomi saw that Alo and Jake were listening intently to Thax and David. She quickly walked across the warehouse, touched Jake on the shoulder and said, "Honey, we will be at the Herb House. Pick us up if you get done in here before we get back."

Jake nodded and managed to say, "Okay."

"I saw welding equipment, hoists, and a bunch of other boy toys out there. Jake is not going to want to leave anytime soon," Naomi said to Kaia as she got back to the office. "I'd rather go see some herbs. What about you?"

"Oh yeah." Kaia immediately started walking toward the door and yelled over her shoulder, "Let's go."

"Mac, would it be okay for us to go check out the herbs while they do whatever they're doing?" Naomi asked.

Mac smiled, "I thought you might say that."

Mac rushed to catch up with Kaia who was already halfway to the Herb House. Selena and Naomi walked together.

When they approached the west side entrance, the two panel doors slid open and Mac led Kaia in. Kaia said, "This is enormous!" They were walking on a ten-foot wide driveway with three feet tall by three feet wide planters on each side, when Selena and Naomi caught up with them.

Mac said, "The Herb House is actually four different green-houses. These planters act as knee walls. The interior vinyl glass panels come down from the ceiling and slide into the back of the planters. This allows us to have different configurations for grow-ing. There are five rows of plant benches in each quadrant that can hold anything from seed starter trays to five gallon pots." Mac and Kaia kept walking. Kaia was interested in all the technical greenhouse specifications, and Mac enjoyed explaining everything to her.

Naomi was interested in being with the plants and smelling the herbs, so when they came across a set of cushioned club rocking chairs, she asked Selena to sit with her so they could talk.

As Kaia and Mac walked away, Mac was explaining, "In the cen-ter hub, we have the control panels for each of the four sections. Each section is programmed to maintain a different climate. The roof and side panels automatically adjust between screens and clear or tinted vinyl glass, as needed, to regulate the temperature. The growing lights suspended above each bench are automatically raised or lowered to adjust the lighting for the different types of plants. The southwest quadrant has cactus and succulents that require hot, dry conditions. The climate in the southeast quadrant is like a tropical rainforest, for plants that require hot, wet conditions. The northwest quadrant has plants that prefer cooler, wetter conditions. The northeast quadrant is for the plants that require cooler temperatures."

After they had disappeared in the maze of the greenhouse plants, Naomi said, "Selena, I've been wondering about something that, well, it seems like you would know, being Commissioner of Politics and Religion for the Earth Commission and all."

"What is it?"

"Well, I used to feel secure, calm, and peaceful most of the time. Now the negative energy is getting to me like it never has before. It makes me angry. It makes me want to cry. I don't know what to do about it. I'm so frustrated, I worry that I'm off track. I don't know if I am doing what Spirit wants me to do anymore," Naomi said as tears started streaming down her face.

"I know what you are going through, dear. Let me assure you, you are doing exactly what Spirit wants you to do. You are being faithful and loving in all that you do. Spirit gave each human being free will, and Spirit never takes that away from anyone, even if their choices are leading to their demise," Selena explained.

"Or the demise of the planet! I don't understand how anyone who says they love God, the Creator, could ever cheer for the pending doom of the planet. They think the destruction of the planet means God is going to return. Maybe so, but do they really think God is going to be happy with them when he gets here? Like God is going to say, good job, my loyal and obedient children, in a few hundred years, you have managed to destroy this beautiful and special planet, which I created for you. See what I mean? Now I'm resorting to sarcasm!" Naomi exclaimed.

"Remember, Naomi, it's all about the energy. Your sarcasm is the result of frustration based on love, not contempt or hatred. You are frustrated because more and more people are making choices based on fear instead of love. This fear shows up as anger, bitterness, resentment, hatred, and greed. It is causing enormous suffering. In your heart there is an overwhelming desire for people to love one another and stop the proliferation of this fear-based negative energy, which is choking the life force out of the atoms of human existence. We are all spiritual beings living a physical life, the purpose of which is to experience in physical terms the consequences of the choices we have made. The plan was for people to learn from their mistakes and make more loving choices the next time, thereby, to evolve and to grow toward Spirit. The problem is these selfish, fear-based choices have reached epidemic proportions on this planet. This negative energy is causing suffering for all humans, not just the individuals making the selfish choices. You cannot change this, and it's really getting to you. The net negative energy is overwhelming the net positive energy. And the planet is on the brink of reaching the point of no return," Selena explained.

"So it's not just me? It is really bad, isn't it?" Naomi asked, feeling on one level relieved, but on another level horrified.

"No, it's not you. And yes, it is really bad. We are all working very hard to reverse this. The core teaching at the heart of all the world's religions is that humans should love one another, forgive one another, and not judge each other. Unfortunately, the actual practice is the opposite. Instead of loving the diversity that is one of the biggest blessings of this planet, extreme religionists judge everyone that is different. It is indeed, very sad and frustrating. All anyone can do is hold onto love in our hearts and continue to choose to be selfless in dealings with others, and have faith that love will prevail in the end. Love is the energy that created all of this, and it is the strongest force of all, never doubt that. It has been a refreshing change for us to get to know a family as loving as yours. Thank you for being faithful and loving," Selena said, as she stood up to give Naomi a hug.

"Thank you, Selena, I feel better now," Naomi said.

At that moment, Anna walked up to them and said with a smile. "Are you interested in seeing our medical facilities? Where's Kaia? I can't wait to show you."

CHAPTER TWENTY-ONE

DAVID AND THAX were deeply engrossed in a conversation about equipment specifications and what needed to be done first. It was a very technical conversation, but it sounded like two buddies talking enthusiastically about a sporting event. Jake was beginning to wonder if he and Alo should find their way to Naomi and Kaia, when he looked up and saw Oscillada walking toward them. Oscillada greeted Alo first with the alien handshake. Jake was still a little intimidated by alien contact, but he held out his arms and was soon relaxed by Oscillada's friendly greeting. Thax wrapped his arms around Oscillada in a big hug and picked him up. Oscillada yelled, "Thax! Put me down!"

Everyone was laughing as Thax put him down. "Oscillada is like a father to me. He's helped me many times and taught me many things. Besides that, I have him to thank for the opportunity to work here at FERN."

Oscillada greeted David and asked, "What do you think of the job Thax did setting up your lab? Does it work for you?"

"You bet it does. I couldn't have set it up better myself. We plan to get started immediately."

Suddenly David was startled by his watch ringing. Looking at it, he said, "It's Nate! Please excuse me, I have to take this."

Walking into his office, David pushed the button to answer his phone. "How did it go, Nate?"

"Ah, David, it was a thing of beauty," Nate said in a thick Irish accent. "Do you want me to tell you about it or would you like to see a video clip on your watch?"

"Tell me."

"Okay, my lad."

"Nate, knock off the Irish accent!"

"Sorry, I thought the accent made for a better story."

"Nate! Just tell me. You're killing me here."

"Okay, I'm sorry. First, I looked so good that 'Pecker' didn't even recognize me when I was standing right beside him. Second, the guys from Global General Aeronautics were arrogant, obnoxious pricks. It was quite apparent that Peck had a financial arrangement with them. And they let me know in no uncertain terms that I had absolutely no control over how the technology would be used. GGA had already contacted the military and if the technology worked, it was to be confiscated, made top secret, and used exclusively for military purposes. They were practically drooling when they talked about using it to kill people more effectively."

"Assholes," David interrupted.

"But, wait I'm just getting to the good part. After they made it clear they would be taking the technology, if it worked, they invited me to consider working for them. I kept calm, but you would have thrown up."

"You're not kidding. I feel like I am going to throw up right now. Too bad the technology was an abysmal failure," David said sarcastically. "How did that part go?"

"It was a beautiful thing, not to mention, the most fun I've had since we went fishing. On the third try, I had the machine making all kinds of loud crackling noises while it was shaking the table and sparks were flying. When the machine exploded, I leapt into action, yelling, 'I'll put the fire out!' I grabbed the fire extinguisher and proceeded to put foam everywhere, especially behind the safety glass where those jerks were cowering. Suddenly the fire alarm went off and the sprinklers joined me in joyfully drenching the lab and all the lovely human beings in attendance. Peck and the GGA guys looked like drowned rats. It was fantastic!"

"Yay! Way to go, my brother," David cheered.

"I was laughing so hard, I had tears in my eyes. The paramedic thought I was overcome with smoke and grief. He helped me out of the building while I was saying, 'All my work is ruined! I've lost everything!'"

David was doubled over with laughter as he pictured the scene. Once he could speak again, he asked, "What did Peck do?"

"Peck looked like he was going to pop his cork. He pushed past me saying, 'I'll deal with you later!' He was mortified as the GGA guys stormed out and left."

"Nate, thank you so much, you did a fantastic job!"

"It was my pleasure, David. Have you met Thax yet?"

"Yes, Thax and I are really hitting it off. We can't wait to get to work. You weren't kidding about FERN, this place is incredible. The university already seems like a distant memory. I'm having no trouble at all letting go of my past. Obviously, you drew the short straw in this arrangement."

"Just remember, David, I'm having a blast. The fun is in knowing Peck can't do anything to hurt me or you. I'm happy, if you're happy. Tell everyone I said hi."

"I will, Nate. Thank you for everything." David pushed the button on his watch to hang up. Walking back to the group, he realized how blessed he was to have such a good friend and the opportunity to continue his research at FERN. He silently vowed that he would do everything in his power to make the technology work for the greatest good for all.

"Well, how did everything go for Nate?" Jake asked.

"Perfect, everything went just as we planned and Nate had a blast. He sent me a video of the whole thing, do you want to watch it?"

"Yes, of course," Jake and Alo answered in unison.

"Here, let me show you how to transfer the video to your monitor," Thax volunteered.

While they gathered around the computer in David's office, Oscillada and Thax excused themselves and returned to the warehouse to talk shop.

When the video was over Jake, Alo, and David were all laughing hysterically. "Boy, I'm glad that wasn't me," David said. "That Nate was something else."

"I'm glad it wasn't you, plus I'm really glad you are continuing your work here," Jake said. "It looks like you, Oscillada, and Thax have important things to discuss. I think Alo and I will go catch up with the ladies."

"We'll see you again before we take off," Alo said as he and Jake headed for the door. Once outside, they saw the people mover was still parked in front of the office. They looked at each other and smiled. Without saying a word, Alo went to the passenger side while Jake climbed into the driver's seat.

"You can drive this thing, right, Jake?"

"Of course, it's just a giant golf cart. I used to drive my Dad all over the golf course when I was young. I say we should drive right down there to the west door of the Herb House, what do you think?"

"I can guarantee Kaia made a bee line for that door as soon as she left the office," Alo confirmed with a big smile.

Jake put the people mover into gear and took the first right toward the Herb House. "This is a fine ride; it has a lot more power than any other golf cart I've ever driven. Do we need one of these? If I could think of a reason we need one, I would get one," Jake said, as they approached the west door.

"I can't really think of why we need one this big, but maybe one of those police cars that goes fifty miles an hour would be good," Alo suggested, as the doors of the Herb House opened for them.

Jake and Alo looked at each other and nodded in agreement as they just kept driving straight through the open doors. "Look, there they are," Alo said.

"What do you want to show us, Anna?" Kaia asked, as she and Mac joined the group. "This Herb House is out of this world, fantastic, so I am really interested in whatever else you have to show us."

"Thank you, Kaia. I want to take you to our medical facilities. Look, here is our ride," Anna said.

"All aboard," Jake bellowed as he put the vehicle in park and started to get out.

"You two stay right where you are, I'll navigate from the second seat," Mac said as she slid in behind Jake. Kaia joined Mac while Naomi, Selena, and Anna got in the back seat.

Kaia turned, looked over her shoulder, and smiled at Naomi. "Those are our boys."

Mac navigated, "The shortest way to get there will be to turn right here, we'll exit through the south door. Next, take a right and we'll go past David's lab again. Stay on this road and in about a half a mile, the road will turn right to take us past the front of the Medical Center."

"What is beyond the fence over there on the left?" Jake asked Mac as they drove past rows and rows of peas, beans, squash, cucumbers, and other vegetables growing on the right.

"Past the fence is a National Forest. It's very swampy back there, so we don't have to worry about neighbors. We built a levee all along the south edge of the property to prevent flooding. On top of the levee, we built a concrete knee wall to put the security fence on. This is very effective at keeping out all kinds of unwanted visitors. That's the Medical Center coming up. Just turn right and go past the front of it, then turn back to the left to enter the covered parking area."

Jake smoothly maneuvered the people mover past the building and around to a slanted parking space next to the front door. "An electric ambulance? I think I've seen everything now," Jake said, as he parked and set the emergency brake.

"No, Jake, I don't think you have seen everything. Look at that parking space that is one of those elevators, I bet," Alo said, walking across the covered driveway to examine the ambulance in the emergency parking lane.

"You're right, Alo, sometimes we have emergencies in the basement too," Mac said, waiting for Alo and Jake to finish their examination of the ambulance.

Anna led Naomi, Kaia, and Selena into the Medical Center, stopping in front of the self-diagnostic kiosk. When Jake and Alo joined them, she began the tour.

"There are three medical practitioners here at FERN. Lolly Berry is the medical director. She is a naturopathic physician, an herbalist, and an acupuncturist. Grace Noble is the intuitive counselor. In addition to mental health counseling, she is a member of the security team. PJ Maxwell is our licensed massage therapist, cranio-sacral therapist, and energy worker.

"Visitors use this self-diagnostic kiosk to notify the staff of their arrival and level of need. When one of these four buttons is pushed, the three of them are notified on their FERN watches. We will push the green button to let them know we are here, but there is no medical emergency. The next three buttons allow you to communicate your level of need. If you need assistance, but it is not an emergency, you push the yellow button. If your need is urgent, but not life threatening, you would push the orange button. In the event of an emergency or extreme need, you push the red button, and they will immediately come to assist you. We can make ourselves comfortable in the waiting room to our left," Anna explained, pushing the green button.

"Look, Alo, these are massage chairs," Jake announced, as he turned on the heat and reclined the chair.

Looking around the waiting room, Naomi and Kaia saw sofas, comfortable chairs, and even a day bed you could lie down on if you weren't feeling well. "Amazing, this is so nice. They have thought of everything. Look, Mom, they even have a refrigerator full of bottled water."

"I could really use one of those. Would anyone else like a bottle of water?" Kaia asked, as she helped herself.

As Naomi drained the last drop of water from her bottle, she noticed a woman wearing a white lab coat over khaki jeans and a purple polo shirt approaching. Anna said, "I would like to introduce all of you to Lolly Berry. Lolly, this is the family I told you about, Jake, Naomi, Alo, and Kaia."

"I am very happy to meet you. Hi, Selena, it's so good to see you again," Lolly said, as she hugged Selena.

Lolly turned to Naomi and Kaia and said, "I am always happy to meet other herbalists. Let's go to the lounge first."

They walked past the self-diagnostic kiosk toward the back of the building. After they passed a couple of office doors on the right, the hallway opened up into a big room with two overstuffed sofas facing each other and eight swivel recliners in front of a wall of windows that looked out over the lake. On the far right end of the room was a small library with floor to ceiling bookcases and two library tables with lamps and four chairs each. Straight ahead they could see floor to ceiling shelves that lined the forty foot wide wall. The rolling library ladder provided access to the bottles on the upper shelves. "Wow, look at all of those bottles of tinctures. How many bottles of tinctures can you hold there?" Naomi asked in amazement.

"That is only one of the four cases we have to store our tinctures. We designed them to maximize the number of sixteen ounce bottles we can store. Between all four cases we can store over four thousand bottles. We use this one and the one behind you to the left to hold the single extracts," Lolly explained.

Naomi and Kaia turned to the left, taking in the sight of the herbalist's dream kitchen, with space for cleaning and chopping herbs, making salves, and bottling tinctures. The amount of work surface and cabinets was mind boggling. "This is beyond my wildest dreams. If I had this setup, I don't think I would ever want to leave," Kaia said, as she took in every inch.

"Jake, can you add a rolling library ladder like that to the shelves you are building for me?" Naomi asked.

"Well, yes. This is a great design. Do you mind if I borrow your design?" Jake asked Mac.

"Not at all, I will get you a copy of the measured drawing before you leave," Mac answered.

"Thanks, Mac, I would love—"

Before Jake could finish his sentence, alarms started going off all around him. Mac, Selena, Anna, and Lolly simultaneously looked at their FERN watches. They looked up at each other, and Mac said, "I will go to my office and call the Ambassador to get more details. Fill them in. I'll be back as soon as possible."

CHAPTER TWENTY-TWO

THAX LOOKED DOWN at his FERN watch and turned off the blaring alarm. "This isn't good," he said, looking up at Oscillada, who was shaking his head as he turned off his alarm.

Thax dialed eight on his watch.

"Hi, Thax. I am going to my office right now to call the Ambassador for more information. Take Commissioner Oscillada and David to the Medical Center. Everyone is in the lounge. I will meet you there with more information as soon as I can," Mac said as she climbed into the people mover and backed out of the parking space.

"Will do, Mac." Thax hung up, looked at Oscillada and David and said, "Come on, let's go."

"What is it?" David asked.

"An Orange Alert from the Earth Commission with the message: EMERGENCY MEETING, TRITON IN TWELVE HOURS. We must hurry," Thax explained, as they rushed to the garage. Thax slid into the driver's seat of the black golf cart, while Oscillada took the passenger seat and David jumped into the back. Thax put the cart into gear as the garage door opened.

"It feels like something really bad has happened. What does this mean?" David asked, feeling a little panicky about the intensity of the situation.

"You're right, something really bad has happened or is about to happen," Thax said. "We will know more when Mac briefs us in a few minutes."

"Do you get Orange Alerts often?" David asked.

"No. They are very infrequent for the Earth Commission," Oscillada replied.

"The last one I experienced was on Vermadon, shortly before it fell under the control of the Vermosans," Thax said as they pulled into the covered parking facility at the Medical Center. "Give me just a minute, I'm going to move this ambulance off of the elevator for Mac."

As the doors to the Medical Center opened and David saw the self-diagnostic kiosk for the first time he said, "What's this? It says we have to push one of these buttons."

"If they didn't know we were coming, we would push the green button to let them know we are here, but since they are expecting us, we can go straight to the lounge," Thax explained as they passed the kiosk and hurried down the hall.

David could see his parents and grandparents sitting on the sofas. Naomi waved him over to come sit with them. Oscillada and Thax joined the other commissioners and Lolly who were talking by the windows that looked out over the lake.

Mac pulled up and saw that the ambulance had been moved to allow her to park on the elevator. She said to herself, "That Thax, he never misses anything." She parked the people mover and rushed to the lounge.

Everyone turned their attention to Mac as she took a deep breath and began, "In the wake of the recent terror attacks, an epidemic of fear has been unleashed on the planet. While the attacks were perpetrated by radical, extremist Muslims who are agents of the Vermosans, people all over the world are responding with hatred, judgment, and blame toward all Muslims. Worse yet, this overt hatred is spreading like wildfire. It is rapidly becoming socially acceptable to hate. Fearful societies are dividing themselves into groups and choosing to hate and judge one another. This spike in negative energy is unprecedented. The spread of negative energy must be curtailed or the time horizon for the survival of the planet will be cut in half. For this reason, an emergency meeting of the Earth Commission has been called to determine what can be done to reverse this trend, before it's too late," Mac paused to wipe a tear from her eye. "Alo, Commissioner

Crying Hawk has received permission from the Ambassador to extend a formal invitation for you, Kaia, Jake, and Naomi to attend."

"Kaia and I have discussed this possibility. We would be honored to attend and feel it is our destiny," Alo answered.

Jake was suddenly very pale and turned to Naomi.

Lolly quickly went to the kitchen and returned with some medicine. "Jake, you look a little pale. Will you please drink this for me?" Lolly said, handing him a glass.

"What is it?" Jake asked, taking the glass from her and smelling its contents.

"Water with a little lemon balm, skullcap, and St. John's wort tinctures," Lolly said as she sat down beside him and took hold of his wrist to check his pulse.

"It's Peaceful Warrior, Jake, go ahead and drink it," Naomi said with a reassuring smile.

"That's the perfect name for this mixture. Sometimes I call it, You Can't Possibly Be in a Bad Mood Medicine, but that name doesn't always fit. I would like to call it Peaceful Warrior from now on, if you don't mind."

"Of course, you can call it Peaceful Warrior. I was just wishing I had my medicine bag when you walked up. Jake, you are pale and you look completely stressed out, how are you feeling?" Naomi asked, as he finished drinking the medicine.

"Well, I'm starting to relax a little now, but honestly, the prospect of taking a spaceship ride to Triton to meet maybe countless aliens, well—"

"That's a bit much, isn't it? I have a better idea. Why don't the two of you stay here at FERN, until Alo, Kaia, and the commissioners get back from Triton?" Lolly suggested, as she took the empty glass from Jake.

David spoke up, "Yeah, Dad, I'd like it if you and Mom stayed here with me. I could use your help in more ways than one."

Naomi looked at Jake with compassion and said, "I think that sounds like a really good idea, don't you, Jake?"

Jake took hold of Naomi's hand and a little bit of color started to return to his face. "That sounds good to me. Do you think it will be okay for us to stay here?" Jake asked.

"It's more than okay, it is the doctor's orders," Lolly said, as she switched into her more direct doctor mode. "Jake, please stick out your tongue for me. Good. Let me assure you, you are not having a heart attack. The chest pain you are feeling is stress-related. After the commissioners are on their way, I want PJ to give you a massage and some craniosacral therapy. Are you okay with that?"

"A massage sounds great, I don't know what that other thing is, but if you say I need it, well, okay."

"Basically it is a gentle manipulation of the bones and energy of the skull, it is deeply relaxing," Lolly explained.

"Naomi, is all of this okay with you?" Jake asked.

"Of course, honey. I'm relieved; you look better already. Besides, while you're getting a massage, I'll be having a wonderful time talking herbs with Lolly." Naomi squeezed his hand. "Just relax, we are not going anywhere."

Jake took a deep breath and relaxed. The experiences of the last ten days had turned his life upside down and completely changed his view of the world. He needed time to process. Being here, working with David sounded normal and he could really use some normal right now.

"Jake and I would prefer to stay here, if it's okay with you," Naomi said to Mac.

"Yes, of course, that's fine. Alo, I brought you a FERN watch so you can keep in touch with us at all times. I've had your watch programmed; one is for David, two is for Nate, three is for Jake, eight is for me and nine is for Skyler. The numbers are written on the back of the instruction manual," Mac said, as she handed the watch to Alo and the manual to Kaia. "Jake and David, Skyler has remotely reprogrammed your watches so that six is for Alo on his FERN watch."

"We can reach Alo, even when he's billions of miles away?" Jake asked.

"Yes, it's amazing, but true. Now we need to get going. For those of you who are going, Elle and Jay have lunch ready for you on the ship. For the rest of us Joan has lunch ready at the house. I'll be back shortly with your luggage and we can go to the house together," Mac explained.

Alo went over to say good-bye to everyone. After he hugged David and Naomi, he pulled Jake to the side. "Jake, I have been friends with Commissioner Crying Hawk my whole life, so it is easy for me to imagine traveling to Triton. You have been exposed to an awful lot of new and mind expanding experiences in the last ten days. I am proud of you for all the courage you have shown and the way you have kept your heart open. I am honored to call you my friend. Rest up, because in a few days, I will return and have many stories to tell you."

Alo pulled Jake into a man hug as he shook his hand.

"Thanks, Alo, have a great trip. I am looking forward to hearing all about it."

Kaia hugged David and Jake and then went over to hug Naomi. "Take good care of Jake. He just needs to process. Alo and I could not be any happier if we had won the lottery. Don't worry about us. Learn all you can from Lolly, I expect a full report with notes and everything." With that Kaia kissed Naomi good-bye and joined Alo.

Jake, Naomi, David, Thax, and Lolly said good-bye to each of the Commissioners, then watched as the people mover filled with Mac, Alo, Kaia, Selena, Anna, and Oscillada disappeared into the basement.

CHAPTER TWENTY-THREE

M AC MANEUVERED THE people mover into the parking space next to the basement security office. She opened the door and led them through the office onto the elevator that took them to the sub-basement parking portal. The stairs to the ship were down, so Anna, Selena, and Oscillada led the way into the ship. Anna went directly to the luggage storage and asked for Kaia's help picking out Jake and Naomi's luggage. Mac hugged each of the commissioners, Alo, and Kaia goodbye, grabbed Jake and Naomi's luggage, and said, "I'm sorry I've had to rush so much, but you have got to get going. Have a safe trip."

As soon as she was off, the stairs retracted and the door closed behind her. "Please take your seats, we are ready to take off," Jay announced over the loudspeaker.

The five of them sat down and the chairs conformed to their bodies. Then the safety apparatuses enveloped their shoulders and legs. Just as they could feel the ship start to move, the view screen came on. Suddenly they were out of the water and they watched FERN shrinking below them. "This never gets old if you ask me," Oscillada said. "We must remain seated until we get outside of the atmosphere, then we will be able to move around freely."

Alo and Kaia watched in joyful amazement as the beauty and splendor of Earth came into focus beneath them. "From this perspective, I can see why it's called the blue planet. This is incredible," Alo said.

"In a few more minutes, Earth will look like a star in the sky and then we will be able to move around. Is anyone else getting hungry?" Oscillada asked.

Alo and Kaia looked at each other, a little nervous about what lunch might be like. Anna noticed their nervousness and said, "Don't worry, we have spent enough time around humans to know what you like to eat and how to make it. We gave up on bugs and worms a long time ago."

Oscillada and Selena burst into laughter, and Alo and Kaia joined in. Anna said, "Good, I'm glad you're both starting to relax. There is no reason to be nervous; we'll take good care of you. After lunch you will have about eight hours to rest. We will wake you up in time for you to shower and eat before we go to the meeting. We'll even have coffee ready for you."

Selena spoke up, "Do either of you have any questions at this time?"

"Well, about Triton. What is it? Even more importantly I guess, where is it?" Alo asked.

Oscillada explained, "Earth's astronomers would tell you Triton is Neptune's largest moon. Our space station is actually inside this huge sphere. Its massive size provides us with environmental protection and an excellent disguise. Its retrograde orbit around Neptune provides perpetual energy to meet all of our needs."

"Neptune? That is an awfully long way from here!" Kaia exclaimed.

"Yes, it is. Triton is nearly three billion miles from here. If we could travel at the speed of light it would take us over four hours to get there; unfortunately, it is impossible for a physical object to travel at the speed of light."

"But you can travel almost half as fast?" Alo asked.

"No, that is also impossible. Even if we could travel at one million miles per hour it would still take us over one hundred and seventeen days to get there. Therefore, it is not practical to travel within the confines of linear time. Interdimensional travel is the only way we can get there in less than ten hours. Using magneto aerodynamic propulsion, we are able to shift into the eighth dimension and then it is a smooth sail on the ion wind into Triton."

"Okay, I'm going to have to trust you on that one," Alo said.

"Interdimensional travel! That would have pushed Jake right over the edge," Kaia added. "We're just going to relax and enjoy the ride. Right Alo?"

Alo nodded as the safety apparatuses on the chairs retracted.

Oscillada stood up and said, "Let's go eat. Right this way."

***

Meanwhile, back at FERN, Mac walked through the front door of the Medical Center and straight back to the lounge. Lolly, Jake, and Naomi were sitting on the sofas talking. "Where are Thax and David?" Mac asked.

"They wanted to get back to work, so they ordered take out from the diner," Lolly said. "The rest of us are ready to go eat lunch now. Jake has an appointment with PJ in a little over an hour."

"Then let's go eat, Joan is waiting," Mac said, as she turned to head back outside.

They drove past the pool and recreation area on their way to Mac's house. As Mac pulled up, the door on the far right side of the garage opened, and she pulled the people mover in and parked. The garage door closed behind them, "Lolly, if you don't mind, I would appreciate it if you would show them to their room. They will be in the suite next to mine. I want to see if Joan needs any help."

"I would be happy to," Lolly answered.

Jake picked up their luggage and followed Lolly and Naomi up the stairs. "Your room is here on the right."

Naomi and Jake followed her into their room. It was an enormous suite with a king size bed, French doors onto a screened porch, a sitting area, and a large bathroom with a whirlpool tub. "I think this will do. Don't you, honey?" Jake asked, with a smile.

"Oh, it will more than do. Mac doesn't cut corners, does she?"

"No, she does not. The way she sees it, you should do your very best or you shouldn't do it at all. That's the way she lives her life. She inspires all of us here. Go ahead and get ready for lunch, then come on down to the dining room," Lolly said as she closed the door.

Once the door was closed, Naomi turned to Jake, put her arms around him and said, "Jake, are you really okay?"

"Yes, I'm fine now. I don't know how she knew my chest was hurting. But after I drank the Peaceful Warrior and realized I wasn't going to Triton, it stopped hurting. I think one day I might be able to go there, but it was all happening so fast and—"

"It's okay, Jake, I understand, I'm glad you're feeling better. I can't think of a better place to be right now."

"Yeah, I know. Everyone is so kind and loving. I feel very safe here. Did you see the guns on that, Skyler? Man! That guy could probably crush a Vermosan with his bare hands. I want whatever he's having for lunch," Jake said, as they finished washing their hands and headed down the stairs for lunch.

"It sure smells good in here!" Jake exclaimed as they reached the bottom of the stairs and turned left toward the kitchen.

"We have salad from the garden and fresh homemade bread on the table; grab a plate and help yourself to the lasagna," Joan directed.

Jake, Naomi, and Lolly fixed their plates and took a seat at the table. Mac and Joan joined them as they passed around the salad bowl and the bread. Once everyone had what they wanted, they held hands and Mac said the blessing. "Great Spirit, thank you for this food and all of our blessings, please be with our friends as they travel to Triton and keep them safe. We love you, Aho."

Everyone said, "Aho," and they started eating.

"I was wondering," Jake asked, "are Orange Alerts very common?"

"No, they are actually quite rare. The last one I remember was in March 2011 when the 9.0 Earthquake caused the tsunami that destroyed the Fukushima Daiichi Nuclear Power Plant in Japan," Mac said.

Joan added, "That's right. The Earth Commission made the decision to secretly intervene and by doing so the damage at Fukushima was limited to a level seven meltdown. It would have been much, much worse. Why humans have moved forward with the use of nuclear technology without bothering to figure out how to neutralize the toxic waste is beyond our comprehension. And frankly, beyond the understanding of all the other species in the galaxy, except Vermosans of course."

"The nuclear waste products can be neutralized?" Jake asked.

"Remember, Jake? Selena told us that she tried to convince President Eisenhower that nuclear waste could and must be neutralized," Naomi reminded him.

"That's right, it can be, and on most planets in the known universe it is neutralized. It doesn't take long for a species developing nuclear technology to realize the extreme danger posed by nuclear radiation. Usually this danger motivates the search for the antidote before the widespread deployment of the technology. There really is no other way to explain why humans didn't develop the antidote other than to chalk it up to some combination of laziness and greed," Joan explained.

"Yeah, that explains it. It would take too much time and money. When compared to the health and welfare of all humans, there is no such thing as too much time and money. Oh, unless you are being influenced by Vermosans, of course. What a sickening thought," Jake added, shaking his head. "I really don't like Vermosans."

"We don't like them either, Jake. Unfortunately, a whole lot of humans do like Vermosans," Mac said. "It's hard to fathom."

"That is one thing you can be sure you have in common with everyone you meet at FERN. None of us like Vermosans," Lolly added.

"Are there planets besides Earth, where the nuclear waste products were not neutralized?" Naomi asked.

"Only the five planets which are under the direct control of The Vermosans. They are all in the Hyades Star Cluster, which is in the Taurus Constellation. That is the most horrible section of the known universe. That is one place you do not want to go," Joan explained.

"Have any of you ever been to Triton?" Jake asked.

"Joan worked there for years before she took the assignment to come to Earth to help me. Joan and I went there for two weeks during the house renovation, when all the finish work was being completed. It is absolutely incredible. That is when I met all the commissioners and the Ambassador to the Council of Intergalactic Enlightenment," Mac answered.

Jake kept eating while he was thinking to himself, *Joan is an alien, so what? She is a really good cook. She is very nice and intelligent. The only thing that is noticeably different about her is her aqua blue eyes that are beautiful in contrast to her warm brown skin and hair. Nothing scary about that. What's not to like? Nothing. I like her.*

"Joan, everything is delicious. You are a very good cook," Jake said with a warm smile.

"Well, thank you, Jake, I'm glad you like it. The fresh vegetables from our gardens are the secret."

"He's right, Joan. Everything is wonderful, thank you. I would like to hear more about Triton if you don't mind," Naomi added.

"Certainly. Triton, disguised as a moon, is a giant sphere that the Earth Commission put into orbit around Neptune, hundreds of years ago. Let me just say the place is huge. Like seventeen hundred miles in diameter, huge. The outside ring of the sphere is basically a two hundred mile thick layer of insulation. There are two hundred and sixty different doors for the ships to enter through. Most doors lead to one particular docking point inside the base. After a ship enters an exterior door, it must travel through a series of air locks until it clears the insulation layer. This process is necessary because the interior space station itself is climate controlled," Joan paused to take a drink of water. "At the center of this hollow sphere is the actual space station. There are a total of eight hexagonal ten-story buildings that are all connected via sky bridges at levels one and ten to a center circular hub. Can you picture this?"

Jake nodded, "Yes, I think I can. What is going on at the center?"

"On level one, the center is the receiving and storage area for the entire facility. At this level the sky bridges lead to a balcony roadway that goes all the way around connecting the buildings to each other."

"So at level one, the balcony roadway is like the wheel and the sky bridges are like the spokes that connect it to the center hub, is that what you mean?" Jake asked.

"Exactly. Okay, at level ten the center hub is the common community area with places to eat, relax, and visit with each other. The sky bridges connect each of the eight buildings to the center, in the same way as on level one," Joan explained, pausing to eat more of her lunch.

Mac jumped in, "There are docks on each of the three outward facing sides of the hexagons on all ten levels of every building. One building is for the Ambassador, one is for the Watchers, and the other buildings are assigned to the staff and crew of each of the six commissioners. The commissioners actually live and work in the Ambassador's building, but they are responsible for supervising everyone in their building and the thirty-one ships under their command. It is really something amazing to see, an engineering marvel."

Naomi responded, "That sounds fantastic. I cannot imagine humans working cooperatively with other cultures to create something so elaborate and expensive to help a foreign race of beings, billions of miles away. Talk about the ultimate in selfless service. People here have trouble sharing with their neighbors, much less helping seemingly ungrateful strangers. That's what really amazes me. If they could make enough money, Disney might build it, otherwise it would never happen on Earth."

"Yes, the contrast is very stark," Jake added.

Naomi, regretting she had used her out-loud voice to reveal her inner most thoughts, said, "I'm sorry. I don't want to digress into thinking about the sad state of affairs on Earth. I don't want to be a Debby Downer, I am very blessed to be here and to meet all of you who are working so hard to make a difference."

"We understand, Naomi, it can be really disappointing to think about how many humans have unwittingly become megaphones for the voice of the Vermosans. It's a tragic epidemic. I sometimes think people become infected with it, just like they might catch a virus. Too often, I am shocked by the selfish words that come out of the mouths of some people, when I know they have more love in their hearts than they show. Once they catch this infection, their hearts no longer seem to get a vote. I wish we could come up with an herbal remedy for this, but then we would probably have to tie them down to get them to take it," Lolly suggested.

"There's that free will thing again. I think force feeding an antidote for selfishness would be against the rules," Mac said. Everyone at the table burst into laughter.

Lolly couldn't let it go, "What if we could put it in a mister and go into crowds spraying a little on everyone?"

"Well, there's an idea. You and Naomi come up with the formula and I will run it by the Ambassador," Mac promised.

"Now you're talking," Lolly said, as she stood up from the table and gave Joan a hug. Joan, lunch was outstanding as always, thank you. It's about time for Jake's massage, so we had better be heading back to the Medical Center."

Jake and Naomi took their plates to the kitchen, then thanked Joan and gave her a hug. Lolly led them out the side door for the short walk to the Medical Center.

CHAPTER TWENTY-FOUR

WHILE PJ WAITED in the lounge for Jake to arrive for his appointment, she watched a family of wood ducks swimming along the edge of the lake. "Oh good, PJ is ready for you." Lolly said, as she, Jake, and Naomi entered the room.

Hearing Lolly's voice, PJ walked over to greet them. She had short, salt-and-pepper curly hair and bright blue eyes that matched the color of her scrubs. "PJ, this is your two o'clock, Jake Stevenson and his wife Naomi. Jake and Naomi, this is PJ Maxwell."

PJ shook Naomi's hand and said, "It's nice to meet you, Naomi. Please have Lolly put you on my schedule. A little extra relaxation never hurt anyone."

"Thank you, that sounds wonderful."

"Hi, PJ, I'm happy to meet you. I could really use a massage," Jake said, shaking her hand. When he felt the firm grip of her handshake, he realized she reminded him of Skyler. She was about the same height and seriously strong. He figured she must do a lot of massages.

"I'm pleased to meet you, Jake. I'm ready, if you are. Right this way," PJ said as she led Jake back toward the front door, then through the waiting room on the right.

Jake followed her into the therapy room. She had the top sheet on the massage table pulled back and soft, relaxing music playing in the background. "I'll step into the hall while you take off as much of your clothes as you are comfortable with, then get under the top sheet, face up. Just let me know when you're ready."

When she heard Jake's okay, she entered the room and closed the door.

PJ sat down on the stool and placed her hands on Jake's head. Jake closed his eyes and began to relax. After about ten minutes, he was putty in her hands and she began working on the muscles of his neck and upper back. "I can't believe how relaxed I feel already. What did you do to my head?" Jake asked.

"I was using craniosacral therapy to manipulate the bones and energy of your skull."

"That was like magic. Where did you learn that?"

"At the Atlantis University of Body and Energy Therapies."

"I didn't know there was an Atlanta University."

"Not Atlanta, Atlantis University."

"Oh, where is that?"

"On the planet, Atlantis, where I am from," PJ clarified.

Jake thought to himself, *Oh boy, she just told me she's an alien. I'm so relaxed from that cranium thing she was doing that it's not bothering me. Why should it bother me anyway? What difference does it make where she comes from? Being weirded out about it, is just as silly as being racist. It makes no difference what color your skin is, no more difference than what color your hair is or what color your eyes are for that matter. Then what difference does it make if you were born in Florida or Paris or Atlantis? I'm not a racist and I'm not a "planetist" either.*

"Well, you must have been practicing for a long time because you're really good at it," Jake said.

"Thank you. To become a licensed practitioner of body and energy work on Atlantis requires the completion of an eight-year course of study. We study anatomy and physiology of multiple species; as well as, a wide array of therapies including massage, chiropractic, craniosacral, and other energy therapies. When I came to Earth I took the licensed massage therapy exam and I scored one hundred percent. Frankly, it was pretty basic."

"How did you find your way to FERN?"

"After school I went to work at Triton. That's where I met Joan. I worked on her for years before she took the assignment to move here. Joan was in desperate need of a massage and it wasn't long before she managed to talk Mac into going with her to Triton. I worked on Mac daily while she was there and fixed the chronic hip pain she had suffered with since childhood. Before she left, Mac promised to figure out a way to get me transferred to FERN. So here I am."

"Do you like being here, on Earth I mean?"

"Oh, yes, Earth is beautiful. The colors, the variety of wildlife, well, the variety period. The diversity on Earth is unparalleled. I love being here at FERN."

"This is a special place. Frankly, I'm glad you're here; I feel so much better than I did this morning."

"That's good, I'm glad, but now I want you to totally relax. Let go of all of your cares and concerns. Drink deeply of the positive energy and be at peace."

Jake took a deep breath and let go. He let go of his fear, he let go of his tension, he let go of all of his anxiety, and he felt like he was floating on a cloud.

***

While Jake was enjoying his massage, Lolly and Naomi were sharing herbal remedy formulas. Naomi was impressed by Lolly's vast assortment of extracts; as well as, her extensive knowledge of herbs and health. Lolly loved the creative names Naomi had made up for her compound tinctures.

"We grow our own medicinal herbs, so I had to modify some of my formulas, since not everything in my original formulas grows here," Lolly explained.

"I love that about herbal medicine. Great Spirit created different herbs that grow all over the world, so herbal medicine is available for everyone," Naomi added.

"The scientist side of me came up with most of my medicine names, so they don't really sound as creative as your name, 'Peaceful Warrior.' Do you have any other favorite names?" Lolly asked.

"Well to be fair, Mom and I collaborate on our names; some I thought up, some are hers, but once we agree on a name, we both use it. One of my favorite names is 'Fire Breathing Dragon Slayer'—"

"Oh, don't tell me, let me guess, it's for heartburn, indigestion, and flatulence."

"Bingo."

"I love that, what else?"

"Sciatica Quiatica."

"Low back and nerve pain?"

"You got it. We have some obvious names too like Bronchitis Eliminitis, Asthma Blaster, Flu Fighter, things like that. I guess both of us had a cold when we invented the medicine for that because the name is Cold Medicine."

They both laughed. "It's hard to be in a playful mood when you have a cold," Lolly agreed. "I'm getting low on my parsley tincture, and we have lots of parsley growing in the Herb House. Do you want to help me collect it and get the tinctures started?"

"Sure, I'd love to. Will we be back before Jake gets out?"

"Yes, this will only take us about fifteen minutes." Lolly grabbed four gathering baskets and two pairs of scissors from the cabinet and said, "Since I have help, we might as well stock up."

Lolly put the baskets and scissors in the metal cargo box on the back of the red two-seater golf cart that was parked in front of the Medical Center. Naomi climbed into the passenger seat. "This is a mighty sporty golf cart with the front brush guard and off-road tires. I guess you have to be prepared for when Mother Nature plants some medicine out in the fields or at the edge of the lake."

"Exactly. Last summer, I found a huge crop of wild lettuce growing on the other side of the lake, and the pecan grove in front of Mac's house has an endless supply of our favorite antibiotic, Grey Beard. PJ and I have been on some pretty wild gathering adventures in this baby. I've been known to use the brush guard to climb up into the basket on the front, to harvest the herbs we couldn't reach from the ground. But only when PJ is there to spot me, of course," Lolly said, with a wink.

"A girl has got to do, what a girl has got to do," Naomi added, grinning.

They arrived at the west door of the Herb House. As they approached, the door opened and they pulled in. They parked on the left; Lolly jumped out, handed two baskets to Naomi, and took two for herself. "The parsley is right back here."

"You weren't kidding, this parsley is thriving. It smells so good."

"Snip away, the more we trim it, the happier it is and the more it grows." Lolly began cutting the tops off the parsley. As she trimmed, she thanked each plant and told it how beautiful and strong it was.

Naomi joined in the fun, and within a few minutes their baskets were full. On the way back to the red cart Naomi said, "I noticed your self-heal is thriving too. We could easily fill four baskets with self-heal."

"I'll have to check to see how much I need, but that sounds like fun for tomorrow. I like driving over here, so I usually get one herb at a time," Lolly said, as they pulled out of the Herb House. "I've been busy lately writing my book, so I am a little behind on my medicine making. Would you like to help me tomorrow?"

"I would love to. Tell me about your book."

"It's about how being healthy and happy requires a holistic mind, body, and spirit approach. There is no such thing as a pill that will fix everything. Each person has to listen to our own body to know what we need and should avoid, not the mass media. I explain how easy it is to make herbal medicine, and I am including my favorite recipes for the most common ailments. The title is *Lolly Berry's Guide to Health and Happiness.*"

"Oh, I like that. I imagine you are very busy with your responsibilities here at FERN, so what inspired you to write a book?"

"You aren't kidding about being busy. Still, I felt it was important for me to write it. I'm trying to explain that the key to health and happiness is having self-awareness. Once a friend suddenly developed an allergy that made her sneeze. The first time she asked me for my allergy medicine, I gave it to her without thinking much about it, because seasonal allergies are so common here in North Florida. About a week later, she came back for more. That time I asked her what was new in her life. After she thought about it for a minute, she said, 'Nothing, but I did find a lactose free cheese I've been eating. I love cheese and it doesn't make my stomach hurt, so I've been eating it every day.' I told her the lactose intolerance was her body telling her that she should avoid dairy products. Since she had found a work around, her body had to find another way to give her the same message. She immediately stopped eating the lactose free cheese every day and never asked me for allergy medicine again. Now she can occasionally enjoy a small amount of the lactose free cheese without any problems."

"Wonderful, I can't wait to read your book, I'll probably buy it by the case and give a copy to every client." Naomi smiled, as they pulled up to the Medical Center; she felt that she had met a new best friend.

Lolly parked and the two of them gathered up their harvest and entered the Medical Center. As they walked in, a very tall woman in black jeans and a sage green polo with the FERN logo emerged from her office. "Hi, Grace, I'm glad you're free. I would like to introduce you to my new friend, Naomi Stevenson. Naomi, this is Grace Noble, our Intuitive Counselor."

"Hi, Naomi, it's nice to meet you. Can I carry one of those for you?"

"Sure. It's nice to meet you too, Grace."

The three of them walked together into the kitchen and put the baskets down on the counter. "Naomi and I are having a grand time, while her husband, Jake, is in with PJ getting a massage," Lolly said, as she walked across the room to get a couple of gallon jars for the parsley tincture.

"I'm glad you're both having fun," Grace said.

After Lolly returned with the jars, she pulled out two chopping boards and knives. They began chopping the parsley into small pieces and stuffing the jars. "Grace, I have a feeling you have something important to tell us," Lolly said.

"You're right. Mac got a call from the Ambassador. The Commission meeting will be tonight at eleven via video conference. Mac has everything set up in the library at her house. The Ambassador feels it is important that Jake and Naomi join us. This is a very serious situation, and I want to make sure Jake is ready to participate," Grace explained.

"Naomi is on PJ's schedule after Jake. Why don't you hang out here and visit with him while Naomi is getting her massage? After that the two of them would probably be more than ready for a long nap before the meeting," Lolly suggested.

"He was already much better after lunch. I'm sure he will be fine after PJ is finished. It has been a really long day for us, so a nap sounds perfect. He will want to attend the meeting," Naomi assured them.

"Good. He should be out in just a little while. I'll stay here visiting with the two of you until then."

Lolly and Naomi finished chopping and had to get a third gallon jar to hold all the chopped herb. They covered the parsley with one-hundred-proof vodka and screwed the lids down. After putting a label on each lid with the date and type of herb, Lolly updated her computer records and put the gallon jars in the cabinet to "cook." She studied her wall of single extracts and confirmed, "Yes, tomorrow we need to gather the self-heal; three gallons would be nice."

PJ stopped at the sink behind the emergency treatment area to wash her hands, then joined them in the kitchen. "Jake is no longer stressed out. We had a very enlightening conversation, and I think he has processed everything now." PJ opened the cabinet and got out a glass, filled it with ice water and said, "This is for Jake. Please make sure he drinks all of it when he comes out. I need to check my appointment book."

"I can save you the effort. Your next appointment is with Naomi; after that you're free until seven o'clock," Lolly told her.

"Thanks, Lolly. As soon as Jake gets out, I'm ready when you are, Naomi."

"Wonderful. Here he comes now. Hi, Jake, how do you feel?" Naomi said, as she went over to give him a kiss.

"I feel fantastic. That PJ knows her stuff, you should have her give you a massage."

"I am, right now. Are you okay hanging out here?"

"Yes, of course."

"Let me introduce you to Grace Noble," Naomi said, as she and Jake walked to the kitchen. "Grace, this is my husband, Jake Stevenson."

"It's nice to meet you, Grace," Jake said, reaching out to shake her hand.

"Hi, Jake, I'm pleased to meet you, too. We can sit over there on the recliners and visit while Naomi has her massage."

"That sounds wonderful. I will be there in a minute." Jake went over to PJ, gave her a big hug, and said, "Thank you so much. You truly have a gift."

"You're welcome, Jake." PJ turned to Naomi and said, "Naomi, if you're ready, please come with me."

Lolly handed Jake the glass of water that PJ had fixed for him and said, "I'm pleased to see you look much better, Jake. It's important that you drink all of this. I have some work I need to do, so relax and enjoy your visit with Grace."

Jake thanked her for the water and went to sit in a recliner across from Grace. "So Grace, what do you do here at FERN?"

"Well, I am part of the security team and part of the medical team. I do energy work and craniosacral therapy and I am the Intuitive Counselor."

"That's an interesting combination of skills. Don't tell me, let me guess, you're part of the security team, because you are telepathic; you can read minds, right?" Jake said.

As he realized he had just used his out-loud voice, Grace answered, "Well, yes, as a matter of fact that is correct. Did PJ tell you?"

"Oh boy. No. Well . . . frankly, I am so relaxed right now my lips were moving before my brain was in gear. I hope I didn't offend you."

"No, you have not offended me at all."

"PJ did tell me she is from Atlantis. So I started thinking about the people I have met here, and I just thought with such a unique combination of skills you might be from Atlantis, too."

"I am not from Atlantis, but you are right, I am not from Earth either. I am from Lemuria, which is not far from Atlantis."

"Where are they?"

"They are both in the Constellation of Orion. Atlantis orbits Rigel which is the bottom right star in the constellation, or the hunter's left foot, and Lemuria orbits Alnitak which is the left star in Orion's belt when you look at Orion from Earth."

"That is interesting and weird at the same time."

"How do you mean?"

"Well, both Atlantis and Lemuria are supposed to be lost civilizations on Earth."

"They were never lost. This misconception is simply the mistranslation of historical documents. Both Atlantis and Lemuria had mother ships that stayed on Earth for a very long time. Eventually they had to leave to go home."

"That makes sense. I imagine most of what we consider to be human history is wrong. Either it has been intentionally or unintentionally distorted. With all the new information I have been given in the last ten days, I'm pretty sure most of the time it has been intentionally distorted. When I was very young, I was taught that lying was wrong, even the little 'white' lies. So I've just never done it. For the longest time, I thought most people always told the truth too. I thought lying was the exception. Recently I started realizing, I have that backwards."

"I know it's sad, but true. The Vermosans have had a big hand in corrupting humans for a very long time. I've been working for the Earth Commission for the last twenty years and I still struggle to understand why humans so easily join with the Vermosans. I think the reason is they lack faith in the Creator. On all the planets I've been to, it is well understood that we were all created by the love of Great Spirit and as long as we strive to be loving and selfless we will have everything we need. The opposite of the Creator's love is the fear that the Vermosans encourage. The more a person has fear, the more they become selfish and greedy. This causes them to turn their back on love and create misery for themselves and everyone around them. It's a shame."

"Tell me about some of the other planets in the Federation."

"Well, let's see, Thax and I are both from Lemuria. Lemuria is smaller than Earth, and the gravity is not as strong, so the average height is taller than on Earth. Atlantis, on the other hand, is bigger than Earth, so the gravity is stronger and people are not quite as tall. PJ and Skyler are both from Atlantis. You may have noticed that people from Atlantis are muscular and physically very strong. There are many other planets where the intelligent beings are humanoid, but height varies from two feet to ten feet, depending on the amount of gravity. Intelligent life takes all kinds of different shapes and exists in all types of environments. There are as many unique species of intelligent beings as there are different types of creatures in your oceans. The differences may be vast, but most are kind, loving, and selfless beings. The notable exception is the race of narcissistic sociopaths, known as the Vermosans."

"So, not all the beings who work for the Earth Commission are humanoid?"

"No, but we understand that suddenly meeting non-humanoids would be shocking for humans, who have been led to believe that they are on the only planet with intelligent life. So the non-humanoids work mostly behind the scenes. You do not need to be afraid, even if you were to stumble upon one."

"Like in the tunnels under FERN?"

"Yes, or at a meeting of the Earth Commission."

"Well, I am not on my way to Triton, so I don't have to worry about that."

"Would you be opposed to attending an Earth Commission meeting via video conference from the comfort of Mac's library?"

"No, not at all. Actually, I would like to attend. I do want to help."

"Good, the meeting will be at eleven o'clock tonight. As soon as Naomi finishes her massage, it would be advisable for the two of you to take a long nap so you will have the energy to attend."

"Really? That sounds great."

CHAPTER TWENTY-FIVE

ALO, KAIA, AND the commissioners returned to their seats on the main deck of the ship, for the approach and entry into Triton. As the safety apparatuses locked into place, Jay turned on the view screen and announced, "We have been cleared to enter Triton through Indigo gate LV, and we are beginning our final approach."

Alo and Kaia watched in anticipation as the ship closed in on the moon's surface. They were beginning to think they were going to crash into the surface of Triton, when the massive doors of Indigo gate LV began to slide apart.

"The surface is divided into eight quadrants; each quadrant has thirty-one gates that allow the Earth Commission ships to dock directly to the buildings. This is the fifth of the ten gates in this quadrant that are large enough for this craft. We are entering the Indigo Sector, which will allow us to dock on level five of the Ambassador's building. After we dock, we will take the elevator to level ten," Oscillada explained.

Once the doors were fully open, the ship began moving forward and passed through them. As soon as the doors were cleared, they began closing again. The forward movement of the ship steadily continued, and as the door behind them closed completely, a door in front of them began opening. Without any change in speed the ship passed through the second door.

"These doors function to keep the bad air out and the good air in. We must travel through three more doors and then we will be in the climate controlled atmosphere of Triton. The temperature is maintained at a comfortable seventy-two degrees and the oxygen level is twenty-two percent. You will have no trouble breathing," Anna said.

The ship passed through the last door and entered the vast open space of the Triton atmosphere. The view screen revealed another ship just above and slightly ahead of them heading toward the same building.

Jay said over the loud speaker, "That is Commissioner Crying Hawk's ship arriving just above us. We are the final group to arrive, so the Ambassador has asked that you proceed directly to the meeting room. The video conference is set up at FERN and everyone who has been invited to attend is present."

Alo and Kaia looked at each other wondering what to expect. "Jake, Naomi, Mac, Joan, Lolly, and Grace are in attendance via video conference," Selena told them.

The mood was very serious. Somehow it made Alo and Kaia feel more peaceful to know Naomi and Jake would be watching with them. The ship flew up to the docking port on the balcony of the building, and locked into place. As the safety harnesses retracted, Elle announced over the loudspeaker, "Welcome to Triton."

The doors opened, and the commissioners led Alo and Kaia off of the ship and onto the elevator. They ascended one floor; when the door opened again, Commissioner Crying Hawk joined them. "Alo, Kaia it is wonderful to see you again, my friends," he said, as he greeted each of them. The elevator resumed its ascent to level ten while Crying Hawk greeted Oscillada, Anna, and Selena. "It has been awhile since we have seen each other. I am happy to see all of you again, but the purpose of our sudden reunion is most unfortunate."

The three of them nodded in agreement. The elevator door opened, and the four commissioners led Alo and Kaia down the long hallway and into the Commission Meeting Room. As the door opened onto the upper level of a huge octagonal amphitheater, Alo and Kaia paused to look around the room. Each section of the octagon was a different color, red, orange, yellow, green, blue, indigo, violet, and pink. Six rows of seats led down to the octagonal conference table at the center of the room.

Crying Hawk said to them, "You are both my honored guests, so please come and sit behind me." They followed him to the red quadrant. The symbol of a red hand was imprinted on the backs of the seats in the red section. Kaia noticed the hand symbol was etched into the fabric of Crying Hawk's uniform.

Crying Hawk took his seat at the table; Alo and Kaia sat in the two seats directly behind him. On the wall across the room was a huge monitor with the Earth Commission logo on the screen. This logo had the same wheel of eight colors as the FERN logo, but it had a picture of Earth from space in the center, instead of a fern. There was a similar view screen for each of the eight quadrants. They watched as Oscillada took his seat in the orange section, Selena took the violet and Anna took her seat in the green section. Kaia noticed the wave pattern she had seen in Oscillada's uniform on the conference table in front of him. After looking around the room, she noticed the circle symbol in Selena's violet section. And in Anna's green section the triangle symbol was prevalent.

Then a beautiful voluptuous woman with long brown hair took the commissioner's seat in the pink section. The symbol all over the pink quadrant was the triple spiral. Crying Hawk looked over his shoulder and said, "That is Leilani, the Commissioner of the Divine Feminine, taking her seat in the pink quadrant. Sitting in the yellow section is Binh, the Commissioner of Peace and Diplomacy." Binh wore a yellow robe with three concentric circles in the fabric. He was thin, bald, and had a calm, peaceful demeanor. "That is Crunch, captain of the Elite Corp of Watchers taking his seat in the blue section." The all-knowing-eye was the symbol for the Watchers.

"Crunch? Really?" Alo asked, knowing Crying Hawk was famous for his sense of humor.

"No, I'm joking. It makes him laugh every time I call him Captain Crunch, so I can't help myself. His real name is Guardian. The Watchers come from the planet Enyan in the Pleiades Star Cluster. The white hair that covers their bodies and catlike heads comes with the gifts that make them unsurpassed as Watchers. Anytime you see that unusual physique you can be assured they are members of the Elite Corp of Watchers, a very prestigious group."

They watched as all the seats in the room filled up, "The seat in the indigo section is for John, the Ambassador to the Council of Intergalactic Enlightenment. He will be the last to arrive."

After all the seats were filled, a burly man with olive skin, dark brown hair, a full beard and moustache arrived at the table in the indigo section. The symbol of his section was the wheel of eight colors. The room was filled to capacity with all three hundred and forty-four seats filled.

All eight of the view screens lit up with John's face as he began to speak. "Before I get started, I would like to confirm that our six friends at FERN are present via video conference and our communication link is established."

His assistant, sitting at the console behind him, pushed some buttons and Mac, Joan, Lolly, Grace, Jake, and Naomi appeared on the view screens. "We can see you and hear you loud and clear, Ambassador," Mac said.

It was an exceptionally clear picture and sound. The screens appeared to anticipate who was going to speak next, because they instantaneously displayed whoever was speaking.

"Thank you, Mac. First, I would like to say, I am sorry for the short notice about the meeting. I did not have any control over the notice because I did not call the meeting; the FATES did."

The room suddenly filled with a collective gasp. John continued, "Hundreds of years ago the Watchers deployed the First Alert Terrestrial Energy Sensors or FATES on Earth. These sensors are constantly monitoring the negative energy levels on Earth. They were programmed to automatically issue an Orange Alert whenever the negative energy reached seventy-five terajoules. The negative energy on Earth has been steadily increasing for the last one hundred years at a relatively predictable pace. Based on this rate, we were projecting that approximately twenty-five years remained until the level would reach one petajoule and Earth would have reached the point of no return on its march toward destruction. In the forty-eight hours leading up to the Orange Alert, the negative energy level suddenly and unexpectedly jumped five terajoules. During the last twelve hours, it has steadied itself at the seventy-six terajoules level."

A low hum filled the room. The concern and anxiety were palpable. Kaia put her hand on Alo's knee and squeezed. They looked at each other as tears welled up in Kaia's eyes and a lump developed in Alo's throat. Alo put his arm around Kaia and pulled her close to him.

The Ambassador took a drink of water and continued, "We have a lot of projects in the works on Earth that have a six to ten year time horizon, before they could lead to any significant decrease in the negative energy on the planet. Taking this new data into consideration, the FATES are currently projecting the evacuation warning at ninety terajoules to sound within two years. Six months after that we expect to reach ninety-five terajoules at which time all Earth Commission projects must be abandoned and all non-essential commission staff will be evacuated. Then within six more months we expect to have reached the one petajoule level and the complete evacuation of all commission members and human friends will need to be completed within two months."

Kaia felt nauseous, as she buried her face in Alo's chest.

"I feel like I've just had the wind knocked out of me," Jake said softly to Naomi, not knowing how sensitive the view screens were. Kaia heard his voice and looked up to the view screen to see Naomi, Mac, Joan, Lolly, Grace, and Jake with tears streaming down their faces.

The Ambassador continued, "We feel the same way you do, Jake. When the Orange Alert sounded, the Council was also notified. What this means is that in approximately seventy-two hours, the commissioners and I must be on the Indigo Mother Ship departing Triton for our eighty-four hour trip to Orion, for the meeting with the Council of Intergalactic Enlightenment. We need to brainstorm to come up with any and all ideas we can recommend to the Council, so I won't be forced to deliver the following speech."

Earth Commission Ambassador's Speech to the Council

Seven hundred Earth years ago, we were
charged by this Council with the Earth Mandate.

Our mission was to assist in the evolution of the Human Species. We were charged with educating, inspiring, and guiding earthlings in an effort to enlighten and help them to raise their vibration and consciousness. Within the boundaries of our mandate, we have inspired their scientists, monitored their progress, and attempted to guide their religious and political leaders. We have been met with countless obstacles that have sabotaged our ability to make comprehensive progress. While science has made some dramatic advancements and changed daily life, selfishness and greed have made overall enlightenment impossible. The arrogant belief that they are the only advanced species in the universe of universes has closed the majority of the people to the possibility of our existence, and to our messages and teachings as well.

The indigenous peoples all over the planet have remained open to us, and we have been able to communicate with them on a regular basis. They understand that the planet is on the brink of destruction due to the fact that negative energy is expanding at an alarming rate on Earth. The problem is, they are the least respected people on the entire planet and no one listens to them.

The arrogance of the "civilized" people, who have the power on Earth, has kept them blind, deaf, and dumb. Their goal, above all else, is monetary gain. They willingly sacrifice everyone and everything in their pursuit of physical riches. They have no comprehension that the negative energies of arrogance, greed, hatred, prejudice, resentment, lust, and laziness are choking the life force out of the atoms of material existence. They do not acknowledge that these negative energies are the cause of the heating up of their atmosphere, which is leading to the pending doom of the entire planet. While they have some understanding of the forces of electromagnetism, they have not figured out that negative thoughts equal negative energy. When the negative energies overwhelm the positive energies, the poles of the planet will shift. Their scientists acknowledge that the geographic poles are out of phase with the magnetic poles and that the rate of this shift has been increasing in recent years. However, they have not realized that this is due to the vast increase in the negative attitudes and energies of the planet's inhabitants. They even take their understanding that the Earth sometimes flips on its axis in stride, as if the weakening of the magnetic field that is protecting the planet from solar radiation will not result in their certain demise. The inhabitants of Earth are masters of one thing above all else, self-deception. So it is with a heavy heart, I must report to you today, our mission has failed.

CHAPTER TWENTY-SIX

"**I** DO NOT WANT to give that speech to the Council. It would constitute a failure of unparalleled and epic proportions. The grief would haunt all the citizens of the civilized universe for eternity. We have to work tirelessly to develop a plan that will immediately spur the increase in love on the planet, to turn back the ravages of fear and hate. We are open to all ideas that you may have. I am speaking to everyone in the audience. If you have an idea, a thought, do not hold back, please share it with the group. There is no way to predict who will be the source of the divine inspiration which we will need in order to save Earth and its misguided inhabitants. We will take intermittent breaks for refreshments, but we will not stop until we have at least a glimmer of hope. Is everyone in agreement?" John asked, as he surveyed the room.

The roar of the voices in the room grew louder and louder as the participants nodded their agreement and began wiping the tears from their eyes. At first they started sitting up straight in their seats, then suddenly everyone in the room was on their feet, clapping their hands, and chanting "We will!" The chanting died down as the magnificent sound of one voice filled the room. "Amazing Grace, how sweet the sound, that saved a wretch like me. I once was lost, but now am found, was blind, but now, I see." When Leilani and the chorus of beautiful voices throughout the room that had joined her finished singing, she said, "Great Spirit, God, Goddess, Creator of all, we pray for your Divine guidance and inspiration so that we might help our brothers and sisters of Earth find their way out of the darkness. Amen."

Everyone took their seats and John announced, "Binh, the Commissioner of Peace and Diplomacy, would like to begin."

Binh appeared on the view screens as he began talking, "Forgiveness. Humans do not understand the true significance of forgiveness. Vermosans have led them to believe that forgiveness means to condone and accept the wrong that has been done. As if to forgive and turn the other cheek means accepting what has been done and granting permission for it to be done again. This is not forgiveness; this is foolishness! Forgiveness is a two-way street that provides spiritual growth for both parties. The victim must release resentment, blame, hatred, and fear and by so doing, be healed and evolve. Forgiveness requires an apology. Being sorry you got caught does not constitute an apology. Apology requires true regret, the process of acknowledging your mistake, as well as your sincere intention to avoid repeating it. Apology heals the perpetrator; forgiveness heals the victim, and these two actions working in concert can heal a planet." Binh paused to survey the room.

"The victim negates the negative energy perpetrated against them by forgiving, whether an apology is forthcoming or not. The perpetrator negates the negative energy they have created by apologizing for it. Apology and forgiveness in combination results in the creation of a net positive outcome from what began as a negative. We must get humans to understand this. People will always make mistakes. A mistake can be a very potent teaching tool. Currently, even small mistakes are generating large amounts of negative energy. For example, mistake minus apology minus forgiveness equals three net negative units of energy; whereas, mistake plus apology plus forgiveness equals one net positive unit of energy. How can we create an epidemic of forgiveness?"

The mathematical equation explaining the positive benefits of forgiveness made so much sense to Mac, she exclaimed, "He is right! That explains the recent five terajoules jump in negative energy that came on the heels of the worldwide reaction to the terrorist attacks. These attacks were extremely bad, and nearly the entire world erupted in resentment, fear, and hatred!"

Crying Hawk, the Commissioner for the Preservation of the Truth, spoke up, "You are right. We must encourage victims to forgive. At the same time, we must encourage the perpetrators to apologize. Vermosans have deceived humans into believing that as long as they do not get caught, they have not done anything wrong. This has led to an unmitigated epidemic of lying, which is destroying the fabric of society. Lying and healthy loving relationships are mutually exclusive. Loving relationships are required in order for people to have the opportunity to make mistakes and be forgiven. Unfortunately, most people will not admit they have done anything wrong, unless and until they get caught. We must teach them to have honor. Only then will they consider the consequences of their choices before they make them. As difficult as it may be to speak the truth, it is much more difficult to surrender the ego and have humility when one has intentionally made a wrong and selfish choice.

"We must teach them to have the courage to be honest and admit when they have made a mistake. First to themselves, then to others as necessary. Humans generally do not take responsibility for their actions. They will lie, blame or deceive rather than have the courage to admit the truth regarding the choices they have made. Only when they learn to be honest about their choices will they have the courage to take responsibility for them. Self-deception thrives in an environment of secrecy and lies. We must expose the lies. And we must get humans to realize their choices define who they are."

Feeling the pressure of the urgency of the current crisis, John said, "Time is of the essence. How can we possibly teach them to have the courage to be loving, honest, and forgiving in the next few weeks? They have had two thousand years to study and reflect on the life of Jesus which was dedicated to teaching these very things and yet, they have not learned. Jesus had the courage to keep his heart open and forgive in the face of the unbearable emotional pain of betrayal and excruciating physical pain. How can we make it clearer than that?"

Binh was expecting this reaction, and he had given it a lot of thought. "We cannot make it any clearer. Martin Luther King, Jr. taught that 'darkness cannot drive out darkness, only light can do that. Hate cannot drive out hate, only love can do that. Love is the only force capable of transforming an enemy into a friend.' His assassination proved that the Vermosans have the upper hand on Earth. The truth has been taught in numerous ways at numerous times by numerous people, but it does not change behavior. Vermosans invariably manage to wrap their nasty lies in and around the truth so well, that it turns people away from the truth. Hate is hate even when it comes out of the mouths of people proclaiming to be religious leaders. A person who is judging and hating another, in the name of Jesus Christ, is nothing short of a Vermosan, because Jesus taught nonjudgment and love, period. To acknowledge that this hate spewing person is a Vermosan is to have discernment, not judgment. Vermosans have managed to confuse humans into believing that discernment is judgment and therefore it is wrong. Yet hating in the name of God is somehow right."

Binh paused to take a drink of water, so Crying Hawk said, "The insidious nature of the Vermosan attack has destroyed discernment worldwide. Humans have one by one given up truth for the right to believe whatever they want to believe. They are so jumbled, confused, and infected by the lies and hate, they don't even believe the truth when they do hear it. For every word of truth that is heard, one hundred lies will be heard discrediting the truth. If there was any discernment left, Vermosans would not be winning."

"That presents a huge problem. If they don't believe the truth, even when they do hear it, how can we possibly get through to them?" came a very discouraged voice from the audience.

Selena, the Commissioner of Politics and Religion, spoke up, "We cannot change the attitudes of group consciousness. We have to change the attitude of one person at a time. It may appear that the loudest voices on the planet represent most people, but it is not true. The group that called themselves the Moral Majority was one of the loudest voices at one time, but they were neither moral nor the majority, and in time they lost power and fell apart. The most destructive tool the Vermosans use is prejudice. They encourage artificial lines separating people into groups with the like-minded. Then each group sits in judgment of the other groups. 'We are better than you because, fill in the blank.' Prejudice is judgment born of arrogance, pride, and ego."

Leilani, the Commissioner of the Divine Feminine, added, "Prejudice, based on stereotypes, is an energy of hatred that spreads into every aspect of a person's psyche. Prejudice drowns out each individual's conscience. A prejudiced person may think he or she is only prejudiced against one group, but that is impossible. The one group may be all they currently focus their attention on, but the group consciousness of prejudice spreads. This is how Adolf Hitler gathered the support to murder millions of Jews, Soviets, and ethnic Poles, as well as hundreds of thousands of disabled people and others that he decided were inferior. Religious prejudice is the root of all religious wars. Joan of Arc was burned at the stake for wearing pants, not for listening to God when she led France into battle. This prejudice against strong, wise, and talented women led to two hundred years of burning women to death. Even today, women are still fighting against this prejudice. The prejudice against women, one half of the species, underscores the absurdity of all prejudice. The antidote to prejudice is respect. Respect for the diversity and the freedom for all people to be who they were created to be."

Leilani looked at Selena, and Selena continued, "Absurd is an excellent word to describe prejudice, but I would like to add illogical, illusional, and perhaps even delusional. We are all in reality spiritual beings living a physical life, the purpose of which is to experience in physical terms the consequences of the choices we make. The differences in our physical appearances, talents, birthplace, etc. all provide for different potential experiences and different potential choices. This diversity is evidence of the magnificence of the grand design of the Creator and should be admired. Prejudice is hatred fueled by anger, blame, and resentment that thrives in fear, which is the opposite of love. If one chooses to be prejudiced, he or she is choosing to be an agent for the Vermosans; therefore, they are on a path of self-destruction. Respect, love, and selfless service are the way to wrestle power from the Vermosans."

Selena paused to collect her thoughts. "The other major problem as I see it is government corruption. Some political leaders are selfish, totally corrupt, and greedy egomaniacs. Other political leaders have altruistic motives and try to do what is best for their country, but they are blocked at every turn by the greedy and corrupt politicians who have control of other branches of government. On more advanced planets, this betrayal of the public trust is considered the most heinous of all crimes. This is a wise approach, since one egomaniac can destroy a civilization. On Earth, the biggest egomaniacs have the loudest voices and the most determination to have financial riches and power over everyone else. They spew hatred for their enemies under the guise of patriotism and they manage to fan the flames of prejudice, thereby garnering undue support. There is no limit to the lies these greedy politicians will tell, and they are such practiced liars it is virtually impossible for the undiscerning masses to know they are lying. Greed is insatiable, so no matter how much money and power these people acquire, they will never be satisfied and they will never stop pillaging."

As soon as she mentioned greed, Oscillada, the Commissioner of Scientific Advancement, was nodding his head. When Selena finished talking, Oscillada began, "Greed and arrogance are without a doubt the primary stumbling blocks to major scientific advancements for the benefit of all. Existing technology is very entrenched. Costs associated with research and development and related changes to infrastructure can be extremely expensive. Companies are in the business to make money for their shareholders, so reinvesting corporate profits in technology that will make their current technology obsolete is unheard of. Venture capitalists will not invest in projects that benefit mankind unless they can make a lot of money doing it. In the early twentieth century, investor JP Morgan refused to continue funding Nikola Tesla's research, when Tesla was on the brink of discovering free energy that could be extracted from the atmosphere and transmitted wirelessly. That single invention would have revolutionized life on Earth, but since it was not profitable, it did not happen.

"Without humility and cooperation, scientific advancement is impossible. Mistakes are a necessary part of evolution. If scientists refuse to consider that a well-established theory may be wrong, no major advancements can be made. In order to revolutionize science on Earth, scientists will have to free their minds. They must suspend their disbelief, in order to be open to be inspired with advanced knowledge. We have tried in vain for years to get their attention by creating elaborate, extremely complex patterns in the crops around the planet. Our drawings have divulged advanced mathematical and scientific equations, yet we cannot get the attention of the scientific community. In the early nineteen nineties, two clowns from the United Kingdom claimed to be responsible for making these circles. To this day, the consensus of the scientific community is that all these crop circles are created by human beings as hoaxes. No scientist dare take it seriously or risk being shamed out of a job. Just to make sure the status quo was maintained, one researcher was paid to say he believed eighty percent were hoaxes and the remaining, less elaborate twenty percent could be explained by a shift in the Earth's magnetic field that causes a current to shock the crops causing them to flatten and form the circle. Can you believe that?"

The entire room erupted in a groan. Oscillada's expression did not change. Anna waited to see the smile emerge on his face. When it did not, Anna, the Commissioner of Plants, Medicine and Health, said, "You are not kidding, are you?"

"No, I am not kidding. People actually believe that cockamamie lie," Oscillada said, as he shook his head.

Anna said, "I should not be surprised. Greed is also the cause of immense suffering when it comes to medicine and health. The Vermosan propaganda machine wants humans to believe that herbal medicine is dangerous. Meanwhile, pharmaceutical companies work to determine the active ingredient in the herbs for the purpose of creating and patenting a chemical version of this ingredient. The side effects of the medicine are often worse than the illness they were designed to cure. All the components of an herb work together synergistically to alleviate suffering and prevent side effects. There are no unnecessary ingredients in an herb.

"Another major barrier to human health is laziness. The average human chooses to take a pill or twenty pills rather than take responsibility for the emotional and physical choices they have made which created dis-ease in their bodies in the first place. We need to get humans to understand that it is always the energy that matters. Chickens raised in healthy, loving environments produce eggs that are healthy and nutritious. Chickens that spend their entire life in unnatural and inhumane environments produce eggs that are detrimental to human health. Lovingly grown and prepared food is always more beneficial than food prepared out of resentful obligation or produced by greed. Humans must take responsibility for what they choose to put into their bodies. Or Vermosans will gladly continue to feed them poison, as food and medicine."

John surveyed the faces at the table with him. When he saw the commissioners had completed their opening statements, he turned to Captain Guardian of the Elite Corps of Watchers, who was seated on his left. "Guardian, do you have an opening statement you would like to make?"

"Yes, Ambassador, I do." Guardian took a deep breath before addressing the group. "My friends, the commissioners have eloquently and accurately described the conditions and attitudes I have witnessed on Earth. I have been observing human behavior for a very long time, and it is my conclusion that the majority of humans are good and loving beings. Given the extremely negative conditions on the planet at this time, it would appear my conclusion is incorrect. This contradiction has caused me to ask myself, how have the Vermosans managed to lead so many of these good and loving beings astray?"

Guardian looked around the room as if to see if anyone could answer this question for him. "Good people expect that everyone is good. These good humans tend to interpret the behavior of others through this filter. This tendency, which is born out of compassion and love, makes a person unwittingly naïve and gullible. Vermosans actively and intentionally exploit this goodness. Over time, the pain and disappointment of this exploitation makes good people cynical and even vengeful. When someone realizes she has been betrayed, she asks herself, 'Why would he do this to me?' When no answer to this question is forthcoming, it cannot be released and cynicism festers. Vermosans do it because it is their nature. That is what a

Vermosan is, a selfish being who is motivated by only his own needs and desires. These evil beings are completely unconcerned about the effects of their behavior on others. Humans have to learn to accept Vermosans as Vermosans and not to expect anything different from them. Vermosans are not nice, even though they may be skilled at acting nice. A Vermosan will do or say anything, if he believes it will get him what he wants. In my opinion the decimation of human discernment can, in large part, be blamed on the human inability to understand Vermosan behavior resulting from the refusal to acknowledge the existence of evil."

Guardian nodded at the Ambassador. "Thank you, Guardian, and thank you, commissioners. This has been very informative, and we have a lot to think about. At this time, I think it would be appropriate for us to take an hour break. Refreshments are available on the promenade deck behind the green and yellow sections of this room. When we return we will open the floor for all thoughts and comments. Thank you."

CHAPTER TWENTY-SEVEN

THE EARTH COMMISSION logo returned to the view screen. "Is that thing off?" Jake asked.

"It is muted, but the connection is not lost," Mac answered.

"Good, then I can say, wow! That was intense! I'm glad it's not up to me to come up with the solution. I don't know what to say. I am hungry and thirsty, though," Jake said, getting up to stretch his legs.

"I imagine everyone is," Joan said. "Grace, would you mind helping me with the refreshments?"

"I don't mind a bit," Grace said, as she got up to follow Joan downstairs.

Jake sat down on the king sized bed in their room and waited for Naomi to finish in the bathroom. After she came out, he took a turn. Naomi stood by the French doors watching the moonlight dance with the spray of the water fountains in the lake. Jake came up behind her and wrapped his arms around her. She turned around, hugged him and said, "I knew the negative energy was really bad, but I never imagined it was this bad."

"I know, honey. Let's not panic, we have a lot of very intelligent and loving beings here to help us. Just stay open, have faith and listen for Spirit to talk to you like always. Great Spirit doesn't want us to destroy ourselves or this magnificent planet, so I know we will be inspired with what to do."

"You're right, let's go brainstorm with our new friends," Naomi said, as she took Jake's hand and they left the room.

Back in the library, Mac and Lolly had just finished filling everyone's glasses with ice water from the library wet bar. Within minutes, Joan and Grace came up the stairs with an assortment of sandwiches, cheese, crackers, vegetables, and dips and put them on the coffee table.

"What a spread. How did you manage to pull this together so fast?" Naomi asked.

"I have some very talented helpers who anticipated our needs," Joan said with a smile.

"I should have known. Please tell them how much we appreciate it."

Back on Triton, Crying Hawk led Alo and Kaia up the stairs to the promenade deck.

"We are going to want to eat here in the yellow section. Trust me, you don't want that food over there in the green section," Crying Hawk said, as he squinted his eyes and made a face. "That's Watcher food over there. We have all the good stuff right here."

Kaia surveyed the tables of food in the yellow section thinking it looked pretty tasty. She was feeling relieved to have Crying Hawk's guidance when she asked, "Oh really, what do the Watchers eat?"

"The same thing we do. I was just teasing you," Crying Hawk said, laughing.

"You have to watch out for that guy, Kaia, he has to entertain himself," Alo said, as he smiled and shook his head.

Crying Hawk admitted, "Seriously, everything is good. We're supposed to eat over here because the yellow section is closest to our red section. That fruit is from Atlantis, it may look a little strange, but it tastes like a banana. I promise, you will like everything, so don't be afraid to try things."

"It's safe to trust him now that his joke is out of the way," Alo assured Kaia with a wink.

"The situation is so serious, I wasn't expecting a joke."

"I know, but being stressed out and worried is not going to help anyone come up with a solution to this problem. We need to be in a free and lighthearted state of mind in order to be open for Spirit's guidance," Crying Hawk explained.

"You're right, and I have to admit I like your silly sense of humor," Kaia said, as she filled her plate.

Once they had finished eating, they returned to their seats in the meeting room. It was still five minutes before the allotted hour was over, and the Ambassador was already back in his seat. He had his head bowed and eyes closed. As the participants realized this, they quietly took their seats. The image of the six in attendance via video conference from FERN reappeared on the view screens. As soon as the last person sat down, John raised his head and opened his eyes. "Welcome back. I trust everyone is rested and full of good ideas. Who would like to begin?"

The view screen stayed focused on John's face as he looked around the room. No one moved. No one made a sound. "Don't be shy. The only bad idea is the idea that would have worked, but you kept it to yourself."

Still the room was silent. John stood up and scanned the faces in the room. He looked closely at the people behind him in the indigo section. Finally his eyes stopped on one of the two sitting directly behind him, "Leo, you are always thinking of new and innovative solutions, don't you have an idea you could suggest?"

Leo sighed and began, "Ambassador, I have come up with no less than fifty different proposals, but the problem is we have already tried them all. Based on the outcomes of our past experiences, I believe them to be ill-advised at this juncture. I am sorry, I have no suggestions."

The Ambassador was surprised by Leo's response. "Does anyone have a suggestion?" Looking up at the view screen he asked, "Do any of you at FERN have any ideas?" The view screens scanned the participants at FERN.

Mac broke the silence. "Well, I'm sorry that I don't have a solution and as much as I hate to add insult to injury, something else is bothering me that I would like to bring up."

"By all means, Mackenzie, please tell us what is on your mind."

"Well, I could be wrong, but it seems to me that ever since the computer revolution, people have become more and more self-absorbed and disconnected from each other. It seems people get so caught up in what they are reading and doing on their phones that they hardly interact with the people they are with. They can have hundreds of 'friends' on social media and yet they are not connected to the humans that are right in front of them. People will post mean and hateful things on social media that may reach thousands of people that they would never dream of saying to someone in person. Without a governor of decency negative energy and negative attitudes are expressed instantaneously, before a person has had a chance to reflect and consider the consequences of what they are about to say. I don't know what can be done about this, but I'm sure it's adding to the negative energy, and it really bothers me."

Guardian responded, "She is exactly right. We have recorded a direct correlation in the spread of negativity with the rise of social media."

Grace sat up on the edge of her seat and added, "This outcome is inevitable due to the mode of communication. Interpersonal communication consists of context, tone of voice, facial expressions, and body language, in addition to the spoken word. At least, telephone conversations include context and tone of voice to enhance communication. A friend might not object to the words you speak, but she can still have a problem with your tone of voice and call you out on it. In texts, email, and social media there are none of these enhancements to communication and the governor of decency is totally absent. There is no mechanism to douse the flames of hate. Even if someone speaks out against the spreading hate speech, it will be ineffectual without the governor of decency. In addition, movies, television shows, and computer games have normalized violence, hatred, and disrespect."

Mac, feeling validated after Grace had clearly stated what had been bothering her, said, "That makes a lot of sense to me. Before the advent of instantaneous communication, when a letter was necessary, due care was taken to insure that the written words clearly communicated what needed to be said in a respectful manner. My Grandmother taught me, 'If you don't have something nice to say, don't say anything at all.' In my experience, this was, for the most part, the way people used to behave. Not anymore."

Jake was squirming in his seat as he listened, but he didn't say anything. He cleared his throat and shifted in his seat again. Suddenly from the red section, Alo called out, "Blurt, Jake, blurt!"

"Well, um, I was thinking, what about using some kind of parental controls?"

When Jake paused, the Ambassador said, "Jake, please go on and tell us what you mean."

"Don't you guys have the technology to block the negative texts and emails? Sometimes, I will try to send a text and for some reason I get a message back 'Not delivered.' Why don't you block negative texts and say 'Not delivered due to your negative energy, clean it up and try again' or something? I'm just saying."

A low hum filled the room as the participants talked amongst themselves. "Jake, I think you might be on to something!" The Ambassador, turning to Guardian, asked, "Can we precisely trace the source of the negative energy in that kind of detail?"

"Yes, sir, we can."

Oscillada, discussing the feasibility with a group of his scientists, looked up, "Yes, sir, technically we can do this, but it could be considered a violation of our primary directive."

"It may be, but that's my problem. When we meet with the Council in a few days, I would rather present a plan and ask for permission, than offer no plan at all. Oscillada, you and Guardian will be in charge of deployment once we have the requisite approval. The rest of us will focus on determining the sources of negative energy to target, the messages to send, and the reactions we might expect. If the recorders are ready, I will open the floor for all ideas."

Once the Ambassador checked with the recorders for each division and received the requisite nods, he gave the go ahead to Binh, who wished to speak.

"We can only hope to change the world one person at a time. We must block the negative energy and teach them about it at the same time. I believe each message we send needs to precisely define the negative content that is being blocked. For example, 'Delivery blocked due to the negative energy of hate, remove the negative energy and try again.' Maybe it could become progressively more instructive when they get it wrong the second time like 'Your religious prejudice is hateful, messages containing negative energy are not permitted, have a nice day.'"

"I agree with Binh, and this will apply to all negative texts, emails, and social media posts." The Ambassador smiled at Binh and looked around for the next hand. "Kaia."

"Sometimes when you place a phone call you get a message 'I'm sorry your call cannot be completed as dialed, please check the number and try again.' Can you disconnect phone calls that are filled with negative energy? You could give a message like 'Your conversation has been blocked due to your negative energy of jealousy, please adjust your attitude and try again.' Then the victim's message could be 'I'm sorry, your call has been disconnected due to the negative energy of jealousy being projected by the other party. If they are able to adjust their energy they may call back, have a nice day.' Can you do that?"

"I like that, Kaia, especially if we can use that same non-threatening voice that humans hear when their call is not completed. That hardly seems like a violation of our primary directive to me. Who wants to go next? Mac, go ahead."

"How about blocking all spam, phishing emails, and any emails with computer viruses attached? Maybe you could return those emails to the sender and have them wreak havoc to the sender's machine, instead of causing damage to the intended recipient. That would eliminate a lot of negative energy of anger and stress from innocent people."

"Clearly these types of emails are full of negative energy by the very nature and purpose of their existence. If we can shut them down, we will. A handful of people cause an enormous amount of suffering this way. It has always bothered me." John looked around to see a lot of people nodding. Then he noticed Naomi had her hand up. "Go ahead, Naomi."

"What about the evil parts of the internet, like the dark web, child porn sites or websites for terrorist and hate groups? Can you take those down or block them somehow?"

"Thank you, Naomi, I think that is something we should do. Jake, do you have another idea?"

"What about the computer games that promote violence; the type of game where you win by robbing, raping, and killing people? I wonder if you could instruct people that the program has to be updated. Then the new update changes the rules so that you get points for helping people and you lose by hurting people."

"I like it. I think we have come up with some really good ideas about how to curb the negative energy being spread by these technologies. Now let's talk about television."

Crying Hawk's hand went up. "Go ahead, Crying Hawk."

"Thank you, sir. First, let me say, there are some good shows on television. But these good shows are sprinkled among an enormous amount of lies. Lies in the commercials, in the news, and in the shows. After we come up with the programming that we think should be removed from television, I would like for us to consider transmitting alternative programming. I would suggest the True History Channel which would chronical ancient history through today as recorded by the Watchers and my Commission for the Preservation of the Truth. Also, I recommend the True Universe Channel which would reveal information about the planets in the civilized universe. It could show details of each planet's people, food, politics, and way of life. I cannot think of a better way to open humans up to the reality of sentient, benevolent beings throughout the universe, than letting them watch it on television. My final suggestion for replacement programming is the twenty-four hour live feed of the FATES monitor, including a ticker running across the bottom of the screen explaining how to interpret the data."

"Excellent, Crying Hawk, I like the way you think." John was thrilled with the progress that was being made when he saw the next hand go up. "Alo, talk to me."

"I would like to suggest the removal of all the pandering for money that is disguised as religious programming and replace it with the truth about how they are spending the money. The so-called religious programs that are preaching hate, judgment, and prejudice should also be removed. I don't know if you have this, but if you do, I would like to see this religious programming replaced with the Life of Jesus Channel, actual recordings of the life and teachings of Jesus as recorded by the Watchers. Thank you."

"Thank you, Alo. As a matter of fact, we do have that available and I think that is an excellent idea for a channel." The Ambassador again surveyed the room. "Go ahead, Anna."

"I would like to recommend the removal of all prescription drug advertisements on television. These commercials are deceptive and completely inappropriate. I also believe the diet food and drink commercials should be removed. In addition to diet foods being unhealthy, the subliminal messages of these commercials that only skinny people are worthy of love are very destructive. Not all human bodies are built to be tiny, and the food that is best suited for one body is not always the best for another body type. I recommend we replace this programming with a live feed of the Atlantis University Health Channel which teaches the truth about food, medicine, healthy eating habits, and cooking techniques."

"Thank you, Anna. That is another excellent recommendation. Selena."

"Deceptive political advertisements and contentious political talk shows serve to enrage audiences for the purpose of generating income, and I think they should be removed. Or better yet, maybe we should continue to run the ads and shows, but interrupt them whenever a lie is told. We could reveal to the audience that the speaker is lying and tell them the truth instead. I would like to offer the Lies Exposed Channel, which would reveal the truth about a wide array of subjects as reported by the Watchers."

"Okay, that sounds good. I would like to thank everyone for the suggestions and ask that you continue to send me any others that you may have.

"At this time, I would like to articulate the goals we hope to achieve through this effort. First, it is our desire to make humans aware of the energy they are generating and that each individual choice to generate negative energy is contributing to the demise of the planet. Second, each human will suffer the consequences of their choices, individually and collectively. Third, the tendency to justify negative choices because 'everyone else is doing it' is misguided and destructive. It is our hope that by shining the light of truth we will be able to teach humans to make each of their choices with a conscious awareness of the consequences.

"While it is my intention to offer this plan to the Council and I am hopeful that we will be granted permission to deploy it, I expect we will be permitted to continue for a limited time. We must remain cognizant of this restraint while we consider the possible positive and negative repercussions of our endeavors. To our friends at FERN, I would appreciate a report from you, as soon as possible, regarding your collective assessment of the human reactions we should expect. I would like to thank each of you for your participation and continued efforts. This meeting is now adjourned."

CHAPTER TWENTY-EIGHT

THE COMMISSIONER OF the Divine Feminine, Leilani, stood up and made her way toward Crying Hawk's guests. "Greetings, Kaia and Alo, I am very pleased that you are here with us on Triton. Kaia, I am working on my proposal for the Ambassador, and I would like to get some input from you before I deliver it to him. I wonder if I might take you away from these two gentlemen for a little while."

"Certainly, that sounds like a wonderful idea," Kaia said. She had been hoping for an opportunity to talk to this wise and strong woman.

Crying Hawk said, "Kaia, my offices are right across the hall from Leilani's. Alo and I will be working there."

Alo took Kaia's hand and gave her a smile as they turned to follow Leilani and Crying Hawk up the stairs that led to the promenade deck. Once outside the meeting room, Kaia noticed the long wide hall. "I didn't even notice this hall before."

"My office and the offices for my executive staff are right down here on the right. At the end of the hall, just past the elevator is the balcony that goes all the way around the building. Our section of the balcony is attached to the sky bridge that connects us to Triton City. If you like, we can take a walk over there later," Leilani suggested.

When they reached the center of the long hallway, they came to two sets of double glass doors. Painted on the doors on the right was "Commission of the Divine Feminine." On the left, the double glass doors said "Commission for the Preservation of the Truth."

"We will be right in here," Crying Hawk said to Kaia, as he opened the door to his office.

Kaia nodded and followed Leilani into the offices for the Commission of the Divine Feminine. The doors opened up into a huge room that was abuzz as the executive staff was hard at work. In addition to Leilani's private office, there were three other private offices and twenty workstations facing the giant view screen on the far left wall of the room.

Kaia followed Leilani into her office on the right. Immediately her attention was drawn to a beautiful glass sculpture on the wall. It was framed with dark walnut wood on the top and bottom and two copper rods on the sides. The three panels of glass were filled with brilliant and vibrant blue, green, pink, yellow, and purple shapes and patterns. "This is an incredibly beautiful glass sculpture. I have never seen anything like it. Is it from Atlantis?"

"No, as a matter of fact, I got that from a very talented woman who lives in Tennessee. She started with three pieces of black glass and then added four separate layers of hand-cut dichroic glass. Since she doesn't use any adhesives, that sculpture had to spend thirty-six hours in the kiln after each layer was added. It is a masterpiece."

"I agree. I love it."

"Thank you, please make yourself comfortable. Can I get you anything?"

"I would like some water."

Leilani got a glass of water for Kaia and sat down across from her. "Kaia, I am having a difficult time understanding human beings and their seemingly insatiable desire to label and categorize each other. The Vermosans have exploited this tendency so effectively that there is an endless number of attributes that humans use to judge each other. This judgment feeds the ego of the judge, and the shame causes immense damage to the psyches of the judged. While racism, classism, nationalism, ageism, sexism, and religious prejudices are ridiculous and damaging, I would like to focus our discussion on genderism. On the civilized and evolving planets in the known universe, people are people, love is love, and each individual is appreciated and respected as a unique being. We have managed to teach most humans that each individual snowflake is unique, yet we cannot get them to acknowledge that each individual human being is also unique. Even so-called identical twins are not actually identical."

Kaia was smiling and nodding her head. "I completely understand what you mean. It really doesn't make sense that humans are so obtuse about this."

"You just said one of the magic words that indicates the Vermosans are at work, obtuse. If a person fails to acknowledge that which is completely obvious, it is for at least one of a number of selfish reasons," Leilani explained.

"That makes sense. By refusing to acknowledge the obvious, a person is able to maintain the status quo. Change is to be avoided because with change always comes the possibility that you could lose your position of superiority," Kaia realized.

"Exactly. On more advanced planets, it is completely understood that we are spiritual beings living a physical life. The purpose of this life is to experience in physical terms the consequences of the choices we make. Individuals must be free to express or create themselves in the way that they choose. The saying goes 'roses are red'; if roses were not free to express themselves, if they felt obliged to be red because that is what is expected of them, then we would never experience a yellow rose. The polarization of the masculine and feminine energies is extremely destructive to civilization. In a polarized society, masculine energy gains control and power because of its physical strength. By its very nature masculine energy is always working toward conformity, which is unnatural and unattainable without severe oppression. The ideal is the balance of masculine and feminine energies within each human being," Leilani explained.

"That's it. That's what is different here on Triton and at FERN. Everyone I have met has their masculine and feminine energy in balance. The atmosphere of love, acceptance, and encouragement is all that I feel here. In the meeting, I leaned over to Alo and said, 'Matt and Luke would love it here.' At the time, I wasn't completely sure why I was saying that, but now I understand."

Leilani nodded and said, "There is no greater blessing than to be appreciated and accepted for who you are, just as you are. This is the only way to truly experience freedom. Most human beings never experience this. On the contrary, the majority of people, whether they are conscious of it or not, feel that they must prove their worthiness every day of their lives. If humans would simply learn to love one another, all prejudice would vanish in an instant and everyone would be free."

"That is so true!" Kaia exclaimed.

"Why did you think of Matt and Luke in particular?" Leilani asked.

"Twenty-six years ago, my daughter, Lisa, had a child that she named Matt. Two days later another member of our tribe, Ruth, had a child that she named Luke. Matt and Luke have loved each other and been virtually inseparable from the first time they met. Both of them were always interested in caring for the animals and helping people and very opposed to violence in any form. When Luke was fifteen, his parents moved off the reservation. Luke's parents understood that taking Luke away from Matt and the tribe would be cruel and unhealthy for him, so they helped Luke move in with Matt and his family. Matt and Luke are perfect examples of two people with their masculine and feminine energies in balance. They are strong, courageous, and determined, and at the same time they are loving, nurturing, and compassionate. They have always been accepted for who they are, and their love for each other is honored because in our tribe we teach that all love is good." Kaia sat back in her seat and smiled as she thought of how dear Matt and Luke were to her.

"That's wonderful. Now, what can we do to get the rest of the planet to think that way?" Leilani asked.

"That is a good question. In our tribe, we have always understood that gender is not binary. While some people may be male and others may be female, there are still other genders in between these two extremes. Like all that has been created by Great Spirit, it's complicated, and it is arrogant and inappropriate to judge one another," Kaia said.

"Hopefully, we can block the bigoted and judgmental texts, emails, and social media posts. In addition, I am thinking about recommending the Real Life Channel to combat all prejudice by illustrating just how ridiculous it is. Each human being is unique, so the archetype of the perfect man and the perfect woman is as much a myth as the story of the Easter Bunny. Gender is a continuum, at the center of which a full one percent of the population cannot clearly be classified as either male or female, based on their physical attributes. It is very damaging for a child to not be accepted for who she is. A little girl who wants to play ball with the boys and isn't interested in dolls, doesn't recognize that anything is wrong with her behavior. The unexpected ridicule she experiences is incomprehensible to her. It causes a deep emotional wound to a developing young psyche that she will likely spend her entire life struggling to understand and over-come. We can explain that loving and accepting people for who they are, and were created to be, leads to a healthy and happy society," Leilani explained.

"I like it, I think it sounds like you're on the right track. I can't understand why a parent would turn on their child in the first place. How is that even possible?" Kaia asked.

"Vermosans. Greed, the desire to keep up a false appearance, self-deception, and prejudice. So much of society is based on a false reality presented in television and movies. Advertisers spin their lies to sell products that they claim will help you attain this perfection. People become deceived into believing this false idea of perfection is reality. It's all lies designed to sell products. The same patterns lead to the destruction of self-esteem for millions of young girls, who feel inferior because they aren't emaciated and underweight. Some people have small frames and will naturally be skinny, and some humans were not made that way," Leilani said.

"Variety is not just the spice of life, diversity is essential to life! If somehow this false perfection was reached by all humans society would fall apart," Kaia realized.

"That is exactly right. That will be the theme of the Real Life Channel. We will work on all the ways to demonstrate and explain this. Thank you so much for your help, Kaia. This conversation has really helped me to focus my thoughts. Now I can finish my recom-mendations for the Ambassador," Leilani said, as she stood up to give Kaia a hug.

Kaia hugged her and said, "I do have one question that has always bugged me."

"What's that?"

"If white skin is the ideal, why would they use tanning booths?" Kaia asked with a grin.

Leilani laughed and shook her head, "Now that is a good question."

CHAPTER TWENTY-NINE

EILANI LED THE way to Commissioner Crying Hawk's private office. As they reached the door, it opened. Crying Hawk said, "Perfect timing. I just sent my proposal to the Ambassador. I'm ready to take Alo and Kaia over to Triton City, can you join us, Leilani?"

"I can't. I still have work to do on my proposal. Thanks for your help, Kaia," Leilani said, as she turned to go back to her office.

"Would you like to take a walk around Triton City and get some lunch?" Crying Hawk asked.

Kaia and Alo nodded at each other and Alo said, "Yes, we would love a tour and lunch. Space travel really makes a person hungry."

"Then let's go." Crying Hawk led them down the long hallway toward the sky bridge to Triton City. The hallway opened up onto the balcony and they turned right. They followed the sidewalk next to the building until they were directly across from the bridge.

"The view from the sky bridge is incredibly expansive. If anyone is afraid of heights, we should probably take the wide road down the middle of the bridge. If you want to see all that you can see, we can take the moving walkway on the right side. For the most part, vehicles park and allow the moving walkways to carry them to their destination. People have the right of way on the roads, so we can meander without having to worry about being run over."

"We have to take the moving walkway at least once, right Alo?" Kaia said, as she led the way across the balcony roadway to the moving walkway on the right side of the sky bridge.

Alo and Crying Hawk caught up with her, and they stepped onto the moving walkway together.

Taking hold of the handrail on the left, Alo exclaimed, "Look down there, Kaia! Do you see that huge ship approaching? That thing is enormous!"

"That's one of the supply ships pulling in. Here on level ten the sky bridges attach each of the eight buildings to Triton City. On level one the sky bridges attach the buildings to the receiving and storage area. The supply ship will be docking there," Crying Hawk explained.

"What an incredible view. What is that I see way down there in the distance?" Kaia asked.

"Those are just a few of the many ships for the non-humanoid beings. They require different environmental conditions than the rest of us, so they live and work on their ships. In a few minutes, we will reach the end of the sky bridge, then we'll need to step off of the moving walkway. If we were to stay on it, we would travel all around the perimeter, but that would take more time and it's not the best way to experience Triton City."

Exiting the sky bridge, they stepped off of the moving walkway and onto the wide road that went between two buildings. After they were past the buildings, they reached an intersection. Crying Hawk stopped to give them an overview. "This road makes a complete circle around Triton City that would bring us right back to this point. I guess you could call this Main Street, because you can find anything you could need or want along this road. We have eight different restaurants to choose from; each one serves the cuisine of a different planet. They are all really good, but I thought you might like to eat lunch at my personal favorite, the Earth Restaurant."

"That sounds perfect," Alo said, feeling relieved, "Which way?"

"The shortest route is to go through the park," Crying Hawk said, as he led them straight ahead. They walked past outdoor restaurant seating on the right that was packed with the lunch crowd, while other people were relaxing playing board games at the tables on the left.

They came to a bridge that crossed a wide river, and Crying Hawk stopped. "This is the first of three circular rivers that flow around the park. The network of waterways here in the park is part of the bio filtration system for our water. The water flows from this outer river through the streams in the hydroponic gardens, like the one here on our right, then into the second circular river we will cross next."

On the right, as far as they could see, was a lush green garden filled with fresh vegetables. On the left people were skating in an elaborate skate park, playing basketball and other sports they did not recognize. "It looks like there is plenty to do here," Kaia said, as they reached the top of the bridge over the second river.

"Indeed there is. Across the path, straight ahead is the third and final circular river. The island at its center is the home of the cultural center and amphitheater. There are performances in the amphitheater every other evening and the cultural center displays are changed out monthly. So there is always something new and interesting to see."

Kaia said, "That reminds me, I have a question that I have been meaning to ask."

"What's that?"

"How do you measure a month on Triton? I mean, I thought Alo's FERN watch was supposed to change to the time wherever we go and it hasn't changed. So—"

"Very observant. Triton is the permanent home base of the Earth Commission. Therefore, we are on Earth time. More specifically, we are on FERN time, since FERN is our primary base of operation on planet," Crying Hawk explained. "We are going to turn right here."

"Oh, that makes sense," Kaia said, as they crossed over the bridge and turned right.

After they passed a hydroponic garden, on their right, there was a large swimming lake with a beach, waterfalls, and huge boulders. They paused for a few minutes to look at the lake. There were people enjoying swimming, boating, and jumping off the boulders into the water. "I am amazed how natural this lake looks. If I worked here, I know where I would be every afternoon," Alo said with a big smile.

Kaia and Alo were actively taking in all the sights as they followed Crying Hawk past another hydroponic garden and over the two bridges that led them out of the expansive park. As they approached restaurant seating on the left, Crying Hawk said, "Here we are."

"That was quite a long walk. It felt really good to get my blood pumping and at least feel like I was outside for a while," Alo commented, as they approached the door to the Earth Restaurant.

The door opened and Crying Hawk led the way in. "Good, my favorite table is available."

Kaia slid into the booth seat and Alo sat down next to her. Sitting down across from them, Crying Hawk said, "We can go to the buffet or order from the menu. This time of day, I recommend the buffet. Is that okay with you?"

"Yes, that sounds fine," Kaia replied.

"Welcome back, Commissioner, it's nice to see you again."

"Hi, Kay, it is good to see you too. I would like to introduce you to my friends, Alo and Kaia Rivers. They just got in from Earth last night."

"Welcome to Triton, I hope you enjoy your time here. Please, help yourselves to the buffet, and I will check back with you later."

Crying Hawk led the way down the cafeteria style buffet line. They each selected a fresh garden salad, a variety of vegetables, and the hand carved roast beef. When they returned to the table, there were tall glasses of ice water waiting for them.

Kaia asked, "I was wondering, are there any humans working on Triton?"

"As a matter of fact there are. Kay is one of the twenty humans that live here."

"I thought she might be human, that's why I asked. How did they come to be here?"

"Now, that is a good story."

Just then Kay walked up with mugs and a pot of fresh coffee. "Does anyone want coffee?"

"Thank you, Kay. Would you have time to sit with us and tell Kaia and Alo the story of how you came to live and work on Triton?" Crying Hawk asked.

Kay filled everyone's coffee cups. "I would love to, and this is a good time for me to take a break."

Kay sat down next to Crying Hawk and began, "Years ago, I'm not really sure how many, I was taking an evening walk along a country road near my home in Montana. Suddenly out of nowhere, a bright light appeared in the sky above me. Before I could react, I was paralyzed and lifted into the air and into a spaceship. There was nothing I could do about it. My memory of this time is very sketchy. I faded in and out of consciousness and was completely unaware of the passage of time. Periodically, I was aware of being in a room with other human beings, but it was obvious they were just as helpless as me. The beings that were holding us were hideous and disgusting creatures. At the time I didn't know, but now I know they were Vermosans. I don't remember everything they did to me and I'm glad, because what I do remember was horrible."

Remembering this period of her life caused tears to well up in her eyes. Kaia reached across the table and squeezed her hand. Kay took a deep breath and accepted the compassion from Kaia, who reminded her of her Grandmother. Kay blinked back the tears and continued, "One day, I woke up as a very tall, muscular man with a white crew cut was carrying me in his arms. When he saw that I was awake, he looked into my eyes and said, 'You're safe now. Don't be afraid. I'm getting you out of this hell hole. Please trust me.' I tightened my grip around his neck as he ran with me down a hall and onto another ship. He put me down on a reclining chair and said, 'Wait here. I have one more soul to save. I'll be right back.' I looked around and there were eighteen others in similar chairs sitting around me. In a few minutes, he came rushing in with another woman and as he cleared the doorway of the ship, he yelled, 'go, go, go, go.' The door closed behind him and the ship took off."

"Wow!" Alo exclaimed, "Sorry to interrupt, please continue."

Kay smiled at Alo and continued, "After he put the last woman on a chair, he checked a few things with some of his associates and then he said to us, 'I am Thax Clinton, Commander of Team Bravo of the Rescue Forces of the Federation of Orion. We have rescued you from the Vermosans, the only evil beings in this sector of the universe. We are taking you to the nearest Federation space station which is known as Triton. You are still under the influence of sedatives, so for now rest assured you are safe and your nightmare is over.' I will never forget those words, even though I promptly fell back to sleep."

"Thax Clinton? Is that the same Thax Clinton we just met at FERN?" Alo asked Crying Hawk.

"One and the same. Kay, if you don't mind, I'll fill them in on the back story and then you can continue with the rest of your story."

"Of course, Commissioner."

"Thax and his team were on an extremely dangerous mission to rescue fifty Greys when they stumbled upon the twenty human captives and managed to rescue them too. The Greys are a race of benevolent, subterranean beings whose planet, Vermadon, was the most recent to fall under the control of the Vermosans. The heroic rescue of these fifty beings prevented the extinction of their species. They are loving and loyal and are completely devoted to Thax. They insisted on helping Thax with his assignment no matter what. Thax took the assignment at FERN for a new challenge for himself and a safe home for the Greys." Crying Hawk sat back in his seat and drained his coffee cup.

"That is amazing," Kaia said. "Kay, please continue."

"Once the sedatives were out of our systems and we had a few days to recuperate, we started group therapy at the health center. We talked about our experiences and our feelings and after a few weeks, our counselors started talking to us about returning to Earth. They gave us the choice from the beginning. There was never any pressure for us to decide to stay or to go. They helped each of us get the information we needed in order to make the best decision for our lives. One by one, we went with our counselors to the Watchers building to watch our families and friends back at home. I realized that the whole experience had changed me dramatically and I knew I couldn't fit into my old life. I think my family and friends would have been glad to see me at first, but they would not have been open to the truth about what had happened to me. All I could imagine if I returned to Earth was isolation. The love and acceptance I have experienced here on Triton is wonderful. I decided to stay. Each of us notified the counselors of our respective decisions. Once everyone had decided, the counselors shared with the group that every single one of us had decided to stay. That was the day our new lives began with our new family here on Triton. As far as I can tell, none of us has ever looked back."

"What an extraordinary story. Thank you so much for telling us," Kaia said.

"Our grandson is now working with Thax back on Earth. Kay, I am really proud of you and the others for having the courage to seek your own destiny. Can I give you a hug?" Alo asked, as he stood up. Kay stood up, hugged Alo and let him hold her. The fatherly affection from another human being healed her deep down inside.

Kaia slid off the seat and hugged Kay and gave her a kiss on the cheek. Kaia said, "Kay, I am so happy we met you."

"Thank you, Kaia. I'm happy I met you too. I hope we can get together again before you leave, but right now, I had better get back to work."

CHAPTER THIRTY

KAIA SAT BACK down and slid over to the far side of the booth. Alo sat down next to her and said, "What an incredible story. It takes a lot of courage to choose to walk your life path into the unknown, rather than return to the comfort of the life you are familiar with."

"Not just Kay and all the other humans, but also Thax. He gave up his position as a heroic leader that traveled the galaxy saving souls and accepted a position on Earth as an assistant to a scientist, so he could keep the Greys safe. Talk about selfless service," Kaia added.

"Before we leave, there is something else we need to discuss," Crying Hawk said as he refilled their coffee cups.

Alo finished the last bite of his lunch, sat back and said, "We're all ears, what's on your mind?"

"While we were in my office, I received a message from the Ambassador that the Commission of Scientific Advancement and the Watchers are reporting that they will be ready to deploy the plan within the next four days. Since it takes three and a half days to get to Orion, the Ambassador would like to leave within the next five hours. The meeting with the Council of Intergalactic Enlightenment has been moved up in hopes of getting the necessary approval for our plan as soon as possible. On behalf of the Earth Commission, I am authorized to extend a formal invitation for the two of you to travel with us to Orion to attend the Council meeting." When Crying Hawk paused, Kaia and Alo looked at each other. "We hope that you will choose to join us, but we understand if you would rather not."

"Are you kidding?" Alo exclaimed. "Of course we want to go to the Council meeting. This is the adventure of a lifetime. Besides what if they won't give you the approval? We'll beg them on behalf of the entire human race, if necessary!"

"Alo is right. We should go with you," Kaia added.

"Excellent. Your presence at the meeting could be a tremendous help. Now, it will be at least a week, maybe closer to ten days, before we will be able to get you back home."

"I need to call Jake on this FERN watch and let him know," Alo said.

Kaia's mind was racing, "I'm sure Matt and Luke will be fine continuing to take care of everything at home. We just need to let them know we'll be gone longer than we expected. It's not like we can call and tell them what we're doing."

"We just need to call Jake and Naomi and work all of that out. Now, let me see, I'm supposed to turn this button until the three appears and then push it, right Kaia?"

"Yes, that's right, go ahead."

Jake's FERN watch began ringing and Jake pushed the button to answer. "Hi, Alo."

"Hi, Jake, is Naomi there with you?"

"Hi, Dad, I'm here." Naomi leaned in close to Jake so Alo and Kaia could see both of them on Alo's watch.

Kaia said, "Hi, it is so good to see both of you."

"We are glad to see you, too," Jake said. "That was one heck of a night last night wasn't it?"

"Yes, it was very intense," Alo answered. "Assuming they can get the Council's approval, the Earth Commission expects to be ready to begin the intervention within four days. They will be leaving soon to go to Orion for the meeting, and have asked us to go with them."

Kaia spoke up, "So you know us, we have graciously accepted their invitation."

"Of course you did. We wouldn't have expected anything else," Naomi said with a smile.

"Alo, don't you dare leave there without getting the Council's permission. I don't care what you have to do, but you have to make sure you get it. Okay?" Jake added.

"That's our plan, Jake. Frankly, I'm pretty sure that's exactly why we have been invited." Alo and Kaia looked at each other and in unison said, "It's a good day to die."

Jake took Naomi's hand as the gravity of the situation overwhelmed him.

Alo explained, "It will probably be close to ten days before we get back home. So we were hoping you would let Matt and Luke know we will be gone longer than we thought."

"Don't worry. We'll take care of everything," Jake assured them.

"Thanks, Jake." Alo looked at Kaia.

Kaia said, "We love you both and we will see you again soon."

"Be safe and enjoy the experience. We love you too," Naomi said as the four of them smiled at each other and waved goodbye.

Jake and Naomi sat back in their chairs and looked up at Mac and Joan who were sitting across from them. They had just finished lunch when Alo called. The four of them sat in silence for a few minutes.

Mac was the first to speak, "Jake, last night you came up with the idea for the plan to save the planet, so the way I see it, it's time for someone else to come up with a plan. Do you want to hear my plan for the next ten days?"

"Right this moment, I am completely out of plans, so I would really appreciate hearing your idea," Jake said, feeling uncharacteristically speechless.

"There is too much going on right now for the two of you to go home and act like everything is fine, while you are waiting to find out what is going to happen. You both need to stay here with us until Alo and Kaia get back. There is plenty for you to do while you are here, and in four days we will attend the Council meeting together. If that works for you, then all you have to do is call Nate on your FERN watch and ask him to call Matt and Luke and tell them you have decided to extend your vacation for a well-deserved two weeks," Mac suggested.

Jake and Naomi looked at each other and thought for a moment. "She's right, Jake. I don't want to go anywhere right now. We would be sick with worry and feel completely isolated, being unable to talk to anyone about the reality of the current situation."

"I don't want to go anywhere either. I'm sure Matt and Luke can take care of everything at home just fine. I'll call Nate in a little while and ask him to call them. Thanks, Mac. That's a great plan," Jake said, feeling relieved.

"Grace and Lolly will be here any minute for our meeting. Why don't the three of you go on upstairs to the library and relax for a few minutes," Joan suggested. "I'll make arrangements to get this kitchen cleaned up and be up shortly."

Jake and Naomi followed Mac upstairs and took a seat on one of the sofas in the library. Mac went to her room and returned with some note pads, pens, and her tablet computer. "I started our memo to the Ambassador, but I didn't get very far. 'Collective Assessment of Anticipated Human Reactions' . . . That's as far as I got. I'm glad we are going to work together on this," Mac said with a grin.

"I know, the whole thing is overwhelming. Let's just stick together and we'll come up with something," Naomi said as Grace, Lolly, and Joan came up the stairs.

Once everyone was settled, Grace began, "I have been giving this a lot of thought, so please bear with me for a moment. The Ambassador is going to ask the Council of Intergalactic Enlightenment for permission to interfere with human lives in an effort to teach humans to stop creating so much negative energy or they will destroy themselves and their planet. Is that correct?"

"Yes, I would say that sums it up," Mac answered.

Grace continued, "When an angry person sends a negative text and it fails to send, how do you think they will react?"

"Oh crap! That won't work. They'll just get angrier," Jake blurted. "Especially if some smart-aleck text tells them it was blocked because of their attitude. If they try to resend it and it's blocked again, they'll blow up."

"Exactly. So my point is, I don't think we can start interfering and expect humans to say something like, oh gee whiz, I've been an asshole, who knew. I am going to be sweet now," Grace said.

"No! You're right. That will never happen. It's against human nature to admit mistakes and repent," Lolly added.

Grace could feel the despair that was rapidly filling the room. "Hold on, everybody, don't panic. My point is we can't start interfering without any explanation or warning."

"That is a really good point," Mac said.

"So I suggest we look at this a little differently. We have to reveal the following: First, humans are not the only intelligent beings in the universe. Second, negative energy is choking the life force out of the atoms of human existence. Third, Vermosans are effectively influencing humans to destroy themselves with negative energy. Fourth, good aliens are trying to help humans and are not impressed with current human behavior. And finally we have to teach them which of their individual choices is creating negative energy. Some people have completely aligned themselves with Vermosans; therefore, nothing that we do or say will change those people. Our target audience consists of the humans who have been so beaten down by the negative energy that they have, perhaps unwittingly, joined in the effort to destroy the planet." Grace sat back and took a deep breath while the others processed her words and Mac typed notes on her tablet.

Mac finished typing and said, "Grace, I think you have nailed it. Correct me if I'm wrong, but the implementation of the plan that is currently being formulated must be the final step. If we deploy the plan without first covering the first four steps you outlined, we believe the plan will be a colossal failure. Is that what we are saying?"

"Yes, that is exactly my assessment," Grace said.

"I agree completely," Naomi added. "If the plan was suddenly deployed without explanation, I believe it would cause a tremendous amount of frustration, fear, and anger which the Vermosans could easily exploit. But when I think about the plan being implemented after an explanation and irrefutable proof that it is being implemented by good aliens, I believe it would be well received, by the good humans anyway."

"So let's figure out step one. How do we provide irrefutable proof that humans are not alone in the universe?" Grace asked.

"That's easy, fill the skies with thousands and thousands of alien spacecraft for all the world to see," Jake suggested.

"Did you see the movie *Independence Day*?" Lolly asked. "In the movie, when the alien spacecraft filled the skies, it caused widespread fear and panic. We have to be very careful here. The Vermosans have convinced most people that all aliens are evil and are out to destroy humans. At the same time they have managed to incite so much fear that a large number of humans believe they must exercise their right to carry guns everywhere they go. If they all start shooting, thousands of innocent people could be killed by stray bullets. Besides, how many spaceships would it take?"

"That's a good point. Clearly, I temporarily lost my mind when I said it would be easy. None of this is easy. Crap! It would take an enormous number of ships. I don't even know how many they have. I guess I was expecting the Earth Commission to have some miracles up their sleeve," Jake confessed.

"We could recommend that the ships appear in the skies one hour after the sun comes up across the world. As the ships appear, we could send texts and blanket the airwaves with a message, something like 'Look up in your eastern sky. Greetings from the Earth Commission. We represent the Federation of Orion and we are here to warn you that your negative energy must be curtailed or you will destroy yourselves and your planet,'" Mac offered.

"I like that idea," Joan spoke up. "I think we have the technology to send holographic images of ships to increase the numbers dramatically. I believe it is even possible for the actual ships to be in orbit above the Earth's atmosphere each projecting hundreds of holographic images just above the surface. Maybe we could prevent most of the shooting if we include a message in the greeting explaining that these ships are holograms and the actual ships are cloaked in orbit above the atmosphere."

Grace added, "I think we would have to immediately follow these initial messages with the widespread deployment of the live feed of the First Alert Terrestrial Energy Sensors monitor on television and the internet. This visual representation, of the level of negative energy on the planet, ought to quickly grab the attention of the viewer. Every human being who has ever driven a vehicle knows that when the temperature gauge is in the red there is a serious problem. The FATES is in the red danger zone and humans should immediately relate to this meaning. We could have a ticker running along the bottom of this live feed explaining what it means, how to read it, who is broadcasting the information, and why. The greeting message could end with instructions to go to www.spreadlove.help for more information."

Naomi had been carefully listening and considering all that was being said. "I think this will work. The information provided on the ticker of the FATES live feed could be continually expanded and become steadily more informative. Beginning with how to read and interpret the FATES monitor. Followed by in-depth information about the Earth Commission and why they are interfering. Next an explanation of the Vermosans would be in order, including who they are and how they are manipulating humans to destroy themselves. After forty-eight hours of this information being disseminated all around the globe, we could reveal that direct intervention to disrupt negative energy will begin at a certain time and continue for the amount of time approved by the Council."

Except for the sound of Mac clicking away on her tablet, the room was silent. Each of them was carefully contemplating what had been said and considering what may have been overlooked. Grace broke the silence, "In my opinion, this approach would alleviate all the problems I have outlined. I would recommend that an intuitive from Lemuria be stationed on each of the spacecraft that are being deployed. If the humans below are on the brink of using weapons and launching an attack against the ships, the intuitive would be able to alert the ship's captain to stop projecting the holograms before anyone starts shooting."

"I guess I hadn't lost my mind after all," Jake said. "This seems to me like it would work."

"I really like the idea that all the ships are holograms and we acknowledge this upfront. That might allow curiosity to outweigh the fear," Lolly added.

Joan spoke up, "I think it will work. If humans become curious, they will be interested in the information that will be available on the new television shows. In my opinion that will give us the best hope that they will actually choose to change."

Naomi nodded her head and said, "I agree."

Mac finished typing. "I love it. I think we have dodged a bullet, no pun intended, with this assessment. I am proud of all of us and if there are no objections, I will forward our report to the Ambassador."

CHAPTER THIRTY-ONE

MAC SETTLED INTO her U-shaped desk and waited for the communication link with the Ambassador to be established. She had received notice that he read the FERN assessment and recommendations and wished to speak with her. Suddenly the Ambassador's kind and loving face appeared on the view screen. "Excellent work, Mackenzie! Once again you and your team have proven to be invaluable members of this Earth Commission. Please extend my highest regards to Joan, Grace, and Lolly for their outstanding service."

"Thank you, sir."

"Based on your report, I understand the tremendous contribution Jake and Naomi have made. Alo and Kaia have proven to be valuable friends of this Commission as well. Currently, Alo, Kaia, and the commissioners are assembled in the Commission Meeting Room for an important meeting before we embark on our journey to Orion. Following the termination of this transmission, please establish your library link for this final Earth Commission meeting before our departure. After the meeting you may proceed with the dissemination of the current status among the executive members of FERN. And Mac, do not worry. I know things have never looked this bad before, but I am encouraged by the formal reports I have received and the progress that is rapidly being made by the Watchers and the Commission of Scientific Advancement. Just hold on to your faith, my friend. Somehow, everything is going to work out for the good. Love will always prevail."

"Thank you, Ambassador. I will see you again in a few moments."

The transmission terminated and Mac took a deep breath. She had been so focused on the task at hand that she had not allowed herself to have an emotional reaction to the current crisis. This unexpected reassurance from the Ambassador caused emotions to wash over her like a tidal wave. She got up, splashed cold water on her face at the bathroom sink, took a deep breath, and returned to the library.

Mac walked to the view screen, initiated the communication link and turned to face Joan, Grace, Lolly, Jake, and Naomi who were waiting with anticipation to hear what she had to say.

"The Ambassador was extremely pleased with our assessment and asked me to convey his appreciation for your excellent work. So on behalf of the Ambassador and the entire Earth Commission, thank you all." Mac smiled at them with warm appreciation. "I have initiated the communication link, because he has asked us to join the final Commission meeting before they depart for Orion."

Mac took her seat on the sofa next to Joan, and they all turned to face the view screen as the Earth Commission logo came into focus.

The Ambassador's face filled the screen. "Greetings. We are in the final stages of our departure procedures for Orion and our meeting with the Council of Intergalactic Enlightenment. I have now received the formal reports and recommendations from all of you, and I am extremely pleased with everyone's work and the progress that is being made. Before we leave, there is one important matter that we must attend to." The Ambassador turned to face Alo and Kaia who were sitting behind Commissioner Crying Hawk. "Alo, Kaia, Jake, and Naomi, I would like to personally thank each of you for your courage and assistance in our endeavors. Even though some of you have known of our existence for a very short time, we have been aware of you and your energy for a very long time. Time and time again, you have proven to this Commission that you are of the highest order of human beings with hearts filled with love and the selfless motivation to help others. At this time, I would like to formally induct each of you into the Earth Commission." The commissioners and FERN's members of the Earth Commission erupted in applause.

Mac quickly went into her office. When she returned, she asked Jake and Naomi to stand in front of her at the view screen. The Ambassador handed something to Commissioner Crying Hawk who stood in front of Alo and Kaia.

The Ambassador continued, "Alo, Kaia, Jake, and Naomi, in appreciation for your love of the Creator, your love of your fellow beings, and your selfless service, it is with great pleasure that I welcome you, on behalf of the Council of Intergalactic Enlightenment as full-fledged members of the Earth Commission with the highest security clearance. At this time, I would like to bestow upon you the silver and gold medallion of the Earth Commission as evidence of your membership."

Mac put a gold chain with the Earth Commission medallion around Jake's neck and one around Naomi's neck. At the same time Crying Hawk was putting the medallions on Alo and Kaia.

"Wear this medallion as a constant reminder that you have nothing to fear. You are a valued member of the Earth Commission and you are loved. Rest assured that you and your loved ones will be evacuated to safety in the event the negative energy on Earth reaches the point of no return."

Jake and Naomi looked at each other. They both had tears in their eyes. They never expected anything like this. The promise to be evacuated to safety with their loved ones caused a flood of emotions to overwhelm them. Jake put his arm around Naomi as tears started pouring down her face. "Thank you, Ambassador, Naomi and I are honored to be counted as members of such a loving and selfless group."

Naomi nodded in agreement as she realized she could not speak.

"Thank you, Ambassador," Kaia said as she took Alo's hand.

"Thank you, Ambassador, we are all honored to join with you and the Earth Commission. We appreciate all that you have done for our planet, and all of us will do everything we can to help you," Alo promised.

The Ambassador continued, "Crying Hawk and Mac, please see to it that both Kaia and Naomi are presented with their own FERN watches as soon as possible. This meeting is now adjourned.

We will all be together again via interstellar communication link when the Council meeting begins. Until then remember, love will always prevail."

With that the Earth Commission symbol returned to the view screen.

Mac hugged Naomi and Jake. "There is just one more thing we have to do before we can take the rest of the day off…does anyone else want a Guinness?"

"I don't think I have ever wanted a Guinness more than I do right this minute," Jake said, plopping down on the sofa.

"I feel the same way," Naomi said as she fell onto the sofa next to him.

Joan opened the small refrigerator at the wet bar and pulled out six bottles of Guinness Extra Stout and began removing the tops, while Mac passed them out to Lolly, Grace, Jake, and Naomi. Then Mac and Joan joined them on the sofa.

Mac raised her bottle and proposed a toast. "Here's to good friends and a job well done."

The six of them clinked their bottles together and took a refreshing drink of the ice cold brew. After a few moments of relaxing silence, Mac spoke up, "The Ambassador asked us to do one more thing, but if the rest of you feel like I do right now, I think we will agree it can wait until tomorrow morning."

Grace spoke up, "Let me assure you, everyone in this room is wiped out. You can tell us what it is, but my vote is we do it tomorrow."

Mac took another sip of her beer and said, "We are supposed to let the executive members of FERN know what is going on. So when you are up to it, Jake and Naomi, will you please update David and Thax?"

"Absolutely, we will be glad to do that," Naomi answered.

"Good. Then, Lolly, please tell PJ. Grace, you can tell Skyler. Then Joan and I will tell the rest of the scientists," Mac said. "Just not right now."

The six of them held their bottles in the air and exclaimed in unison, "Tomorrow!"

CHAPTER THIRTY-TWO

T HE FOLLOWING MORNING, the door to the lab opened, and David looked up to see Jake and Naomi walk in. "Hi, Mom. Hi, Dad, what a pleasant surprise."

"Hi, son, it's good to see you," Naomi said as she walked over to give David a hug.

"It's good to see you too. Mom, are you okay?" David asked, when he noticed his Mom seemed somewhat subdued.

"I'm fine, honey. How is the work going?" Naomi asked.

"Thax and I have been hard at it, and we're making great progress."

"We're really glad to hear that," Jake said as he gave David a hug. "A lot has been happening since the Orange Alert and we came over to update you and Thax. Where is Thax anyway?"

The warehouse door opened, "I am right here, sir," Thax said, walking over to shake Jake's hand. "Morning, ma'am."

"Good morning, Thax. Can we get you guys to take a break from work for a little while so we can talk?" Naomi asked.

"Of course, please have a seat." Thax grabbed four bottles of water from the refrigerator and passed them out. As he handed a bottle to Naomi, he noticed her FERN watch, and then he focused his attention on the medallion hanging from the chain around Jake's neck.

"I see the two of you have been inducted into the Earth Commission. Obviously, a lot has been happening since we last saw you," Thax commented.

"Inducted into the Earth Commission, what are you talking about?" David asked.

"Yes. Alo, Kaia, your Mom, and I have been inducted into the Earth Commission, and indeed a lot has been happening. That is what we want to talk about," Jake explained.

Jake and Naomi looked at each other for a moment, wondering where to begin.

David noticed their hesitation, "Okay, start at the beginning. What was the emergency?"

"Well, there is no way I can explain this as eloquently as the Ambassador did, so let me put it into my own words," Jake offered.

"Sure, go ahead, Dad."

"The negative energy on Earth has been increasing steadily for a long time. We have been aware of this in our personal lives for years now, right Naomi?"

Naomi nodded.

"The Earth Commission has been aware of it too. They were projecting we had about twenty-five more years before the negative energy would reach a level that would destroy the planet. They have all kinds of projects in the works, and they expected to be able to turn things around before we are toast. But suddenly, in the wake of the terrorist attacks, the negative energy rapidly escalated to the seventy-five terajoules level and the FATES issued the Orange Alert," Jake explained.

"FATES? Seventy-five terajoules? What the heck is that?" David exclaimed.

Much to Jake's relief, Thax spoke up, "The First Alert Terrestrial Energy Sensors or FATES is a network of sensors used by the Watchers to monitor the level of negative energy on Earth. When the level of negative energy reaches the one petajoule level, it will be too late to stop it. The magnetic field around Earth will rapidly deteriorate and cause the magnetic poles to flip. During this period, life on Earth will become absolutely unbearable, culminating in the extinction of all life on the planet. The Orange Alert means the negative energy has reached seventy-five percent of this level. This is very bad."

Naomi said, "That's right, and to make matters worse, the FATES are currently projecting the evacuation warning at ninety terajoules will sound within two years. So there is not enough time for the current Earth Commission projects to become fully implemented and help turn this around."

David was shocked, "Holy crap! What the hell do we do now?"

"Exactly, that was the reaction of everyone at the meeting. I felt like I was going to throw up when the Ambassador read the speech he would have to give to the Council of Intergalactic Enlightenment if we didn't come up with a solution," Naomi said.

"It was some kind of intense and stressful when we came back to the meeting after a break and the Ambassador asked for ideas and there was nothing but silence," Jake added.

"Yeah, I can imagine, the suspense is killing me now." David shifted uncomfortably in his seat and let out a deep sigh. "What are they going to do?"

"As we speak, the Earth Commission, along with your grandparents, are on their way to Orion to meet with the Council of Intergalactic Enlightenment to ask for permission to implement a plan of direct intervention in human lives," Naomi explained.

"Wow! That is unprecedented. But then again, how could you not intervene when the crisis is this bad?" Thax added.

"What kind of intervention are we talking about?" David asked.

"We talked about a lot of different things, and some of the ideas we discussed are being further developed by the commissioners and their teams. But long story short, the plan is to reduce negative energy by blocking negative texts, emails, and social media posts, and disconnecting negative phone conversations. Also by taking negative and deceptive television programs and commercials off the air, and shutting down negative internet sites. They are planning to replace these negative energy generating abominations with the truth and messages of love and forgiveness," Naomi said.

Jake jumped in, "They're going to try to teach people about negative energy. What it is, what choices are creating it, and how it is choking the life force out of the atoms of our material existence. They are going to explain that Vermosans are influencing us to destroy ourselves with our own negative energy. For example, if someone tries to log onto a website promoting prejudice and hatred, they will be redirected to a site that teaches diversity is essential to life and prejudice is hateful nonsense."

"The meeting with the Council is scheduled for three days from now. If the plan is approved, the implementation will begin immediately," Naomi said.

"If people really get the messages of love and forgiveness and choose to stop spewing negative energy, life on Earth would change dramatically. I believe it could work, but what if the plan is not approved?" David asked.

"We don't even want to think about that." Jake leaned back and ran his hands through his hair. "Besides, Alo and Kaia are prepared to beg the Council on behalf of the entire human race if they have to."

Thax sat back, slowly shaking his head.

David was in shock. He closed his eyes and took a deep breath, trying to regain his composure. "Well, I, for one, choose to believe the plan will be approved. Love and forgiveness will win out over fear and resentment. So I am going to work harder than ever, and pray for approval and success."

David's positive attitude encouraged Thax, who began to smile. "I'm with you, David."

"That's right. Focus on your work and stay positive. We will be staying here at FERN until Alo and Kaia get back, which will be at least ten days. So if there is anything I can help you with, let me know," Jake offered.

"Thanks, Dad. We can certainly use your help any time. We are here each morning by eight," David said as he and Thax started to get up.

"Before you get back to work, there is something else we would like to discuss," Jake said.

Thax and David sat back down. "Sure, Dad, what is it?"

"This morning, I called Alo to let him know that all the arrangements had been made with Matt and Luke, and everything at home was fine. We had a few minutes to talk, and he told me about meeting a human woman, named Kay, on Triton. He told me that she had been kidnapped by Vermosans and was rescued by Thax Clinton, Commander of Team Bravo of the Rescue Forces of the Federation of Orion." Jake paused, and looked at Thax. "Thax, I was hoping you would tell us more about this."

All eyes were on Thax. Naomi spoke up, "Less than two weeks ago, we had never even heard of Vermosans, the Federation of Orion, the Earth Commission, FERN or Triton. While we have learned a lot, we feel like we missed the beginning of this story. Now that we have time and you seem to know, will you please fill us in?"

"That explains it," Thax said under his breath.

"That explains what?" Jake asked.

"This morning I got a cryptic message from Mac, telling me that the three of you have the security clearance for me to tell you anything I know. I had no idea what she was referring to, but somehow she must have known this was going to come up," Thax explained.

Jake and Naomi looked at each other wondering how Mac always manages to be one step ahead.

"Prior to accepting the assignment here at FERN, I was the Commander of Team Bravo of the Rescue Forces, but that is not the beginning of the story. If I start there, I think it would bring up more questions than it answers. So I am going to fill you in on some ancient history that has long been forgotten on Earth," Thax said.

"That would be great." Naomi said, sitting back in her chair with great anticipation.

Thax took a deep breath and began, "It's complicated, but I will do my best to put it into a story that is easy to understand. First of all, you must realize the universe is huge. There are as many different types of beings in the universe as there are different types of creatures in the sea. We are what is referred to as ascending mortals. We incarnate as physical beings on physical planets with the goal of evolving into more loving and selfless beings by learning lessons. As long as we desire to be like God, who is pure Love, we will have eternal life. God also created spiritual beings, whose purpose is to guide us, teach us, and show us how to evolve into loving and forgiving beings. About two hundred thousand years ago, one of these spiritual beings known as Lucifer proclaimed that he was the Supreme Being and that there was no God greater than himself. He convinced his first lieutenant, Satan, this was true. Satan advocated for Lucifer's cause on Earth.

War broke out between the followers of Lucifer and the followers of God. When that happened, in order to prevent this rebellion from spreading, this entire sector of the universe was put into quarantine."

"Let me get this straight. You are telling us that Lucifer was a real being, who somehow developed such a huge ego that he actually believed he was greater than his Creator?" Jake asked.

"Yes, that's right. Egoism leads to self-deception and stupidity that is beyond comprehension. Allowing yourself to become arrogant and egocentric is worse for your survival than playing Russian roulette," Thax answered.

"I always thought Lucifer, Satan, and the Devil were all names for the same mythical being," David said. "So if Satan was a different jerk who deceived our planet, who the hell was the Devil?"

"The Devil was the nickname given to Caligastia, the Planetary Prince of Earth, a spiritual being who was sent to Earth by God, to teach humans about God. He too, was corrupted by Satan and Lucifer, and that is why Earth got cut off from the heavens in the quarantine," Thax explained.

"So from the earliest days of human existence this battle has been raging. It's no wonder there is so much confusion on Earth," Naomi said. "Please go on with the story."

"Over the last two hundred thousand years of this conflict clear sides have developed. The Federation of Orion represents God, the Creator, who is Love, against the Vermosans, who represent the egocentric teachings of Lucifer. The Vermosans control the five planets in this sector known as Hyades, and the Federation controls everything else. Except for Earth, the separation of these forces was complete after Team Bravo and I rescued the twenty humans and the last of the beings known as the Greys that were being held captive by the Vermosans. Earth is the final frontier of this battle, and it is still up for grabs." Thax paused to take a drink of water.

"If I am hearing you right, you didn't resign your commission as Commander of Team Bravo of the Rescue Forces of the Federation. Your mission was accomplished. There is no one left, who needs to be rescued," Jake realized.

"That's right, Jake. The Rescue Forces were deployed to make sure not one innocent soul was held captive by those horrible Vermosans. We have gone over Hyades with a fine-toothed comb and there is not a single drop of love left. The Council of Intergalactic Enlightenment received word from the Creator that the mission of the Rescue Forces was accomplished. Now it is all about Earth. One of two things has to happen. If the negative energy on Earth reaches the one petajoule level, Earth will become the sixth and final planet under the control of the Vermosans. If this happens, the humans that have remained loving and loyal to the Creator will be evacuated by the Earth Commission to other planets in the Federation. In this scenario, the six Vermosan planets will remain under quarantine from the heavenly circuits for eternity, while the Federation of Orion will be reunited with the energy circuits of the heavens," Thax explained.

"Or to put it another way, the Federation of Orion and all of its citizens will go to heaven and the Vermosans and the planets in Hyades will be in hell!" Jake exclaimed.

"I would say that sums it up," Thax agreed.

"You said, 'one of two things has to happen.' What's the other thing that could happen?" David asked.

"If the plan gets approved and works, and humans learn to accept responsibility for the choices they make, the negative energy on Earth will drop dramatically. If the majority of humans begin behaving like the loving, forgiving, honorable beings they were created to be, then the planet as a whole will become a member of the Federation. Once this happens, the individuals who are aligned with the Vermosans will be evacuated to Hyades. When the Earth is purged of all the selfish, egocentric humans, then and only then will the entire Federation of Orion with all of its planets and inhabitants be reconnected with the energy circuits of the heavenly realms. Ultimately, only Hyades and the Vermosans will remain in quarantine until they are extinguished."

"Holy cow, the stories of heaven and hell are real! I always thought they were made up to manipulate people into behaving themselves. Holy cow! Uh oh, I am repeating myself, I need to shut up and think about this," David said as he leaned back in his chair and put his hands on his head.

"So, no matter which way it goes, some people are going to stay and some people are going to go. The question is, who gets to keep the Planet Earth, the good guys or the bad guys? Isn't that the bottom line?" Naomi asked.

"Yes, that is the bottom line. Of course, all the members of the Federation are doing all that can be done to make sure this beautiful planet is saved with the good guys. That is, by far, the preferred outcome. But in any event, this situation is about to be settled once and for all, and the Federation is on the brink of the much anticipated reconnection with the energy circuits of the heavens."

"Whoa. I get it. You are still a Commander," Jake realized.

"Actually, with the successful completion of our last mission, I was promoted to the rank of Captain. The Rescue Forces have been reassigned to the Security Forces of the Federation of Orion. We have each been assigned to strategic positions on Earth and we are ready, willing, and able to do whatever is necessary. My assignment is to protect and assist Dr. David Bridges and to protect the Greys who are living in the subterranean level of FERN."

"Tell us about the Greys," Naomi asked.

"The Greys are kind, gentle, and loving subterranean beings who lived on the planet, Vermadon, the last planet to fall to the Vermosans. They have tiny little bodies and absolutely no desire to fight. They communicate with telepathy, and their empathy is so sensitive that they can actually die from witnessing someone else's extreme suffering. You would be hard pressed to find a more compassionate species of beings. The Vermosans exploited their kindness and turned them into slaves. Most of them died of broken hearts, but now they are thriving here at FERN. They can't tolerate the bright sun, so they usually stay inside or underground during the day. They are a tremendous help; they cook, clean, and help with the greenhouse plants at night."

"It's the Greys who are helping Joan do miracles in the kitchen," Naomi realized.

"Exactly."

"Well, I would like to meet them sometime, just not suddenly or in the dark," Jake said. Everyone laughed.

"They are unusual looking to say the least, so it could be unsettling to meet one unexpectedly, but don't let their physical appearance dissuade you from pursuing a friendship with any you may meet. Their keen awareness of energy and feelings makes them outstanding friends. Can you imagine a friend who would always be aware of your feelings, who would help you any time, any place, with anything you need, and would never betray you?"

"Well, uh, now that I think about it, I actually can imagine that. You have just described my relationship with Alo. Now, I'm really looking forward to meeting them."

"Thank you for talking to us today and thanks for protecting and helping our son. We will let you get back to work now," Naomi said as she stood up to leave.

"Yes, thank you, Thax," Jake said, standing up and shaking his hand.

"You're welcome. I will see you later." Thax got up and walked back to the warehouse.

David hugged his parents. "I'm glad you're here. My mind is spinning, but strangely, I feel peaceful. Please let me know as soon as anything happens. Do you think Nate works with Thax?"

"That could explain a lot," Jake answered.

"Oh boy, this is amazing stuff. I think I am going to call Nate this evening and try to get more of this story," David said as Jake and Naomi turned to walk out the door.

CHAPTER THIRTY-THREE

JAKE AND NAOMI stepped out of David's lab; their destination was the Medical Center where Jake would have his follow up massage with PJ. It was a beautiful, cool spring morning in North Florida with unusually low humidity, a perfect day for a walk.

"I'm glad we're walking, because I need to talk to you. I need you to help me pull myself together. My mind is blown," Jake said, taking Naomi's hand.

"I know, honey. All that we've seen and heard, it's unbelievable!"

"First of all, let me just clear something up. I know I might have sounded racist because I thought suddenly meeting a Grey alien would be scary, but, I swear honey, I'm not racist! I just think it would be shocking, to suddenly meet an alien who looks so completely unlike anything I have ever seen before. It never crossed my mind, not even once, that there were walking, talking, thinking beings on other planets; much less that I would ever meet one. I'm struggling to get a handle on what it is I'm feeling. But I swear, honey, I am not a racist. Please—"

"Jake, breathe. I know you're not racist. I think your reaction is the result of a natural fear of the unknown. It's not a judgment based on hatred. Aliens are not just outside of your comfort zone, they are completely outside of your understanding of existence. You have to shift your paradigm to even process the fact that they exist. Then to make matters worse, you have to deal with the emotion of fear, which is completely foreign to you. The anxiety worsens because you're having feelings and experiences that you're unfamiliar with, and you don't know how to process them. Usually when people have uncomfortable feelings, they don't want to take the time to process them or work to understand them; they just want to make the feeling go away in the most expeditious way possible. So they attack, condemn, judge or try to destroy the thing they cannot relate to or do not understand."

"You may be on to something. If I went deep sea fishing and caught a strange looking fish that I had never seen before, I would be intrigued. I would probably say, 'Hey, Naomi, look at this weird fish.' But if it started talking to me, I would probably freak out and do something stupid, like shoot it and put a hole in the boat. I'd call that a pretty intense anxiety reaction."

"Exactly. You can't control your emotional reaction or your feelings, but you have a choice about what you do with them. It's this choice that defines who you are, not your initial reaction. If you took the time to listen to what the fish was saying and to process your feelings, then you could choose to not have such a destructive reaction. So now, breathe and open your mind as you allow yourself to process all the new things you've learned."

Jake stopped walking and squeezed Naomi's hand as he took three deep breaths. "It's going to take more than three breaths for me to think about everything that's happened, but I'm starting to feel a little better. You seem to be amazingly calm."

"I'm very calm, and peaceful. Thanks to the history that Thax explained, I finally understand why people choose to believe and continue to spread even the most blatantly obvious lies. I don't have to bother being frustrated anymore."

"What are you talking about? I guess I got hung up learning Lucifer, Satan, and the Devil were real and Thax was still a warrior in a colossal battle. I must have missed something."

"You didn't miss anything. The battle is real, the battle lines are being drawn every day as people make their choices. The ones that lie are either Vermosans or working for Vermosans. It is not about whether they believe or disbelieve the lies they tell; that is irrelevant. Lies are simply a means to an end, the tools they use to connive and manipulate in order to get what they want."

"Now I get it and I understand why you're so calm. No need to try to get a liar to see the truth, they already know the truth, that's why they are lying. The truth does not serve their own personal best interest. That seems so obvious now."

"Exactly. I am not going to waste any more of my energy desperately trying to get a liar to understand the truth."

Jake was smiling and nodding his head, as the full extent of this realization washed over him. "Talk about a paradigm shift. That really does change my perspective, I feel a lot calmer. But there is something more, you are much more . . . peaceful, that's it. What else have you realized?"

"I've realized that our purpose in life is to evolve. To evolve as a species and as a civilization, but first and foremost as individual spiritual beings. As a civilization and as a species we can only evolve as high as the lowest common denominator, the least evolved among us. As individuals we evolve by making decisions that reflect who we are as loving beings striving to become more loving. Loving and selfish are mutually exclusive. It's that simple. We're supposed to make loving and selfless choices to evolve. Great Spirit created spiritual beings to help us in this endeavor. Lucifer rebelled and corrupted the whole process. Now there are spiritual beings and physical beings fighting to make sure we don't evolve. Being evacuated to Hyades to exist with only egocentric Vermosans would be hell, if you ask me. On the other hand, living in a world without selfishness would be heaven."

"I get it. If Thax is right, then we are actually on the verge of living in just such a world. Hopefully it will be on Earth, but if not, we will be on another planet with the rest of the good guys." Jake pulled Naomi close and gave her a big hug. "Thank you so much, honey. I don't feel afraid any more. Now I can just relax and think about everything I have seen and heard. I have to admit this is one amazing adventure."

"Yes, it is." Naomi said as she took Jake's hand and they resumed their walk to the Medical Center.

CHAPTER THIRTY-FOUR

"**H**AVE A GOOD day, Andy," Mac said to scientist, Anderson Montgomery, as she stepped outside and closed the door to his office. He was the last executive member of FERN she and Joan were responsible for updating on the current situation. Mac's FERN watch began ringing as she climbed into the front passenger seat of the people mover.

"Morning, Thax."

"Good morning, Mac. Where are you?"

"Joan and I are parked in front of Andy's greenhouse."

Thax backed the black golf cart out of the garage. "I just got an important security alert from the Ambassador. Please meet me at the security office right away. Do you know where Grace is?"

"She's at the security office, meeting with Skyler."

"Okay. I will be there in a just a minute." Thax hung up and floored it.

Joan put the people mover into gear and drove to the security office. She was just setting the parking brake when she saw Thax barreling down the road toward them. Mac and Joan waited for Thax to join them at the door, and the three of them walked in together.

Skyler and Grace were sitting at the conference table, in the center of the room, facing the door. "What's wrong, Thax?" Skyler asked, as soon as the front door closed.

Mac, Joan, and Thax each took a seat at the table. Thax began, "The Ambassador has issued a Red Alert for the Security Forces of the Federation of Orion on Earth. My mind is racing. There is so much to be done."

"What? What happened to warrant this?" Skyler asked.

"What did the Ambassador say? Start at the beginning," Mac insisted.

"The Council of Intergalactic Enlightenment was very concerned about the rapidly increasing negative energy on Earth. They had already been in session on Orion for a week, discussing what could be done to curb the ever increasing Vermosan influence on Earth, when the FATES issued the Orange Alert. Soon after the Orange Alert, the Council was contacted by Nod, the de facto leader of the Vermosans. Nod proclaimed that the people of Earth had already chosen the Vermosan way and by previous agreement, Earth was now under his control. The Council, representing the Federation of Orion, refused to concede and argued that while the Vermosans did have a lot of support, they did not have the majority of humans on their side. The Council reiterated that the negative energy had only reached seventy-five percent of the level required under the agreement for the Vermosans to be granted control of the planet."

Mac was visibly upset, her face was red, and she had tears in her eyes. "Oh my God! What previous agreement are we talking about?"

"The previous agreement is between the Federation, the Vermosans, and the Creator. But Nod is a liar, Earth is not under his control," Grace explained. "The agreement states that if the negative energy on Earth reaches the one petajoule level, then and only then will the Vermosans have won the battle for the rights to Earth. The one petajoule level is the point of no return and on the sixtieth day following this catastrophic event, anyone who has not been evacuated will be under the control of the Vermosans for eternity. It is not unusual for Vermosans to claim victory just because they are close to winning. Being close to winning is not the same as winning. Don't worry about this part of the story, Mac. So far we haven't heard anything worse than the Orange Alert itself."

"I see what you mean. We are in a bad situation, but Vermosans gloating and claiming a victory they have not yet won, doesn't really make it any worse," Mac responded, as she began breathing normally again.

Joan took hold of Mac's hand and said to her, "Unfortunately, Thax has more to tell us, and I don't think it is going to be good. Are you ready for this?"

Mac nodded. Joan squeezed and released her hand, and they both turned to look at Thax.

Thax continued, "Yes, it gets worse. The Vermosans believe their win is inevitable, and they have threatened to pull out all the stops. They claim to have the right to use whatever physical force is necessary to encourage their followers on Earth to create as much conflict as possible. The Council has received intelligence that the Vermosans believe the remaining Greys are being given sanctuary somewhere on Earth. They do not know where yet, but they are fortifying their efforts to locate and kidnap as many of the Greys as they can find. Using the current climate of fear and hatred toward immigrants and neighboring countries as a starting point, they plan to exploit the physical appearance of the Greys to cause widespread fear, panic, and chaos about aliens arriving to destroy the planet. They want to use the fictional invasion of the Grey aliens as a propaganda tool to create the illusion that the Vermosans and their supporters are the good guys trying to save the planet from the sure destruction the Grey aliens wish to bring. They specifically want to use the Greys for two reasons. One, they are the stereotypical scary-looking aliens, and two, they are not Vermosans, so they are expendable and the perfect diversion."

"What does the Red Alert mean for us and our efforts to protect the Greys?" Mac asked.

"The Red Alert means all the Federation Security Forces have been apprised of the situation, and our security protocol Omega Maximus Gamma has been initiated. Remember, the Earth is the final front in our battle against the Vermosans, and the entire Security Forces of the Federation of Orion are actually assigned to Earth. We have extensive support from our forces stationed on and off planet. For us here at FERN, we need to be extremely careful. The Greys have been instructed to redouble their efforts to remain hidden from view. If they come above ground, it will only be with a security escort and only into rooms protected from view from the outside. Mac, do not worry, Skyler and I have previously drafted the alternate security personnel assignments to accommodate this eventuality. None of the essential services here at FERN will be diminished. On a more personal note, please do not be concerned about your friends. Team Bravo fought hard to save them, and the entire Security Force of the Federation is determined to keep them safe and shielded from the Vermosans' cruelty."

"That is a relief. I trust you and your team have got this. Is there anything else we need to know?" Mac asked.

"Yes, as a matter of fact, there is. Since the entire Council was already on the Orion space station, and the Earth Commission project lies in the balance, the space station has been en route to rendezvous with the Ambassador's ship for days now."

Looking at his watch, Thax said, "Both parties should be reaching the rendezvous point within the hour. The Ambassador asked me to have you assemble the FERN delegation to the Earth Commission meeting with the Council of Intergalactic Enlightenment. He wants you to establish the communication link as soon as everyone is in the library."

"That's an unexpected turn of events. We better get moving. Thank you, Thax. Grace, are you ready to go with us now?" Mac asked.

"Yes. Skyler and I had just finished our meeting when we noticed Thax's energy signature turn orange. We were sitting here waiting to find out what happened when the three of you arrived," Grace said, following Joan to the door.

"Thax and I will take care of everything that needs to be done from the security perspective," Skyler assured Mac.

"Thanks, Skyler, I know you will."

Thax followed Mac to the door. "Mac, if it is okay with you, I would like to enlist David as a member of the security team. He and I have been working very closely together and I could really use his help. Besides—"

"Of course, Thax, you don't have to convince me. Make the arrangements to give him the requisite rank and clearance immediately. Find out if Kevin can be here for David's induction ceremony and security briefing."

"That's a great idea. Thank you, Mac." Thax said, walking to the computer to enter David's credentials.

Mac looked over at Skyler. "Where are Naomi and Jake right now?"

Glancing at his monitors, Skyler answered, "They're at the Medical Center. Naomi is with Lolly."

"Thank you," Mac said over her shoulder as she rushed to the people mover.

Mac slipped into the passenger seat next to Joan and dialed Lolly on her FERN watch.

"Hi, Mac."

"Hi, Lolly. Are Jake and Naomi with you?"

"Yes, Naomi is right here. PJ just finished Jake's massage, so he will be out here any minute. What's up?"

"Stay right there. The Earth Commission meeting with the Council of Intergalactic Enlightenment is set to begin within the hour. We'll be there in a few minutes to pick you up. We'll fill you in on the way to the library," Mac explained.

Joan steered the people mover out of the security office parking lot and headed for the Medical Center.

CHAPTER THIRTY-FIVE

KAIA OPENED HER eyes. She and Alo had retired to their suite for a much needed nap. Alo was sitting in a chair near the bed with his eyes closed; holding his medicine bag in one hand and his Earth Commission medallion in the other. Kaia got out of the bed and sat down in the chair next to him and waited.

Opening his eyes, Alo smiled at her. "Do you feel rested?"

"Yes, I feel much better. Did you sleep?"

"Yes, I've been sitting here for only a little while." Alo held up his hand with the medallion hanging from the chain that was laced through his fingers, "Kaia, does this medallion look familiar to you?"

"Well, now that you mention it, I realize it looks very familiar," Kaia confirmed.

"Do you remember the first time our parents took us to meet the Star People?" Alo asked.

"I will never forget, the celebration, the ceremony, our beloved ancestors had come to visit. That is all I understood at the time. I think I was six," Kaia remembered.

"That's right, we were very young, and we had been looking forward to that day for what seemed like an eternity."

"That is funny to think about. We were way too young for it to have been an eternity of anticipation, but it sure felt like it," Kaia chuckled.

"I just remembered some of those Star People were wearing this medallion."

"Yes! You're right! We met members of the Earth Commission while we were still children," Kaia realized.

"If someone had told us back then that one day we would be on a spaceship heading to Orion with the purpose of convincing Star People to intervene in order to prevent humans from destroying the planet, we would never have believed it," Alo said.

"You're right. I'm still having a little trouble believing it."

"The fact that we are on a spaceship heading to Orion, is no coincidence. This is our destiny, Kaia. We couldn't be in this place, at this time, preparing to convince the Council of Intergalactic Enlightenment to intervene to save Mother Earth, if we had not consistently made right choices in our lives."

"I know that's the truth. Look, I have goose bumps." Kaia held out her arm to show him.

"We have to be ready. We have to get our thoughts together. Jake made me promise we would not leave without getting permission. What do we know, what can we say that the commissioners won't have already said?" Alo asked.

"Alo, we are ready. We've been getting ready for seventy years. All of our life experiences have prepared us. Great Spirit has prepared us and will continue to guide us," Kaia assured him.

Alo took a deep breath and nodded his agreement. "You're right. We are ready. Knowing of the existence of Star People is such a normal and natural part of our lives, it's hard for me to comprehend that people will be shocked to find out we are not alone in the universe." Alo slowly shook his head as he contemplated this. "If you think about it, our view of the world is not like that of most people. We know Great Spirit created us as spiritual beings and accordingly we are connected to all things. Most people don't understand that at all."

"This creates a big problem. People lie, cheat, purposefully deceive, and if you—" Kaia was interrupted by a knock on their door.

Alo opened the door to see Crying Hawk. "The Ambassador has asked me to escort you to the observation deck for an urgent meeting."

"Urgent meeting? What's happened?" Alo asked.

"I don't know. We will find out in a few minutes."

Alo put his medicine bag in his pocket and put the chain holding his Earth Commission medallion over his head. He turned to

Kaia. "Let's go," he said with a smile that conveyed all the love he had for her.

Kaia took his hand, and they followed Commissioner Crying Hawk in silence. As they approached the elevator, the doors opened, and the three of them stepped into the small space. Crying Hawk said, "Deck Five." The doors closed behind them. When they reached the observation deck, the doors opened and they stepped out of the elevator. Without hesitation, Crying Hawk walked toward the left side of the room, but Alo and Kaia stood frozen in front of the elevator.

"This is incredible. It's like being on top of a mesa at new moon. I've never seen so many stars." Alo said as he and Kaia stood, mesmerized by the beauty that was all around them. The room they had entered appeared to be without walls or a ceiling. They were completely immersed in the darkness of space with twinkling bright stars all around them. When Crying Hawk realized he had lost his company, he turned around to go back and get them.

"Beautiful, isn't it?" Crying Hawk said. He had been so preoccupied with the business at hand, he had temporarily forgotten the out of body experience most felt when they walked onto the open observation deck for the first time.

"Stunning," Kaia managed to say.

"The intensity of the view is breathtaking, I know. We can come back here later, but for now we need to take our seats for the meeting." Crying Hawk looked down toward the podium at the front of the room and signaled the Ambassador. The walls of the room became opaque.

Kaia and Alo closed their eyes and shook their heads. "We're sorry, where should we sit?" Alo asked.

"Right this way," Crying Hawk said as he led them down the left side of the room to the second row. Kaia saw Commissioner Leilani seated in the middle of the row, so she went to sit next to her, followed by Alo and Crying Hawk. Kaia and Alo took the opportunity to look around the observation deck. At the back of the room above the elevator door was a six foot high by twelve foot wide view screen with the Earth Commission logo at its center.

The elevator doors closed behind Captain Guardian, who quickly took the ramp on the right side of the room. "That's everyone," Guardian said to the Ambassador as he took his seat near the center of the front row.

The Ambassador touched the control panel on the podium and the starlit sky gave way to a white vaulted ceiling. The Earth Commission logo on the view screen at the back of the room faded, and the FERN delegation came into focus. Standing at the podium, the Ambassador addressed the group. "My friends, let me begin by thanking you for assembling so quickly. Less than twenty-four hours ago, I forwarded our full report to the Council of Intergalactic Enlightenment. Since that time there has been a dramatic turn of events. I was contacted by Emmanuel, the Speaker of the Council. He informed me that the Council members have read our report, discussed it at length, and have adjourned their meeting pending our arrival at the rendezvous point. The Council, while closely monitoring the situation on Earth, realized our mission is in danger of failing. Accordingly, one week ago, the space station, Orion, with the entire Council of Intergalactic Enlightenment on board, began its journey to the edge of Earth's solar system. Their mandate is to stay deployed until the successful completion of our joint mission to save Planet Earth from falling under the control of the Vermosans. I have just been informed that the Orion is currently in position and we will rendezvous with them in fifteen minutes."

Turning to Kaia, Alo blurted, "Our meeting with the Council of Intergalactic Enlightenment will begin in fifteen minutes!" Verbalizing the reaction of many in the audience.

Oscillada spoke up, "Correct me if I am wrong, but it seems to me, the space station has arrived unusually quickly. Traveling at normal speeds, it should take the Orion space station no less than ten days to arrive at the rendezvous point from its home base near Atlantis."

"Very astute observation, Oscillada. The Orion has been traveling at maximum speed for days now, and this is why. Soon after the Orange Alert, Nod, the leader of the Vermosans, contacted Emmanuel, the Speaker of the Council of Intergalactic Enlightenment, to proclaim Vermosan victory in the battle for Earth. Nod became irate when Emmanuel refuted his claim by reminding the Vermosan that the negative energy on Earth had not reached one petajoule."

"Wait a minute, this is the second time I've heard that!" Mac exclaimed. "The Vermosans will win control of Earth when the negative energy reaches one petajoule. What I want to know is how do we win?"

"That is a very important point, Mac. We must focus our energy on winning the battle for Earth, not on the point at which we lose. The Federation wins Earth when the negative energy decreases by twenty-five percent from its highest level. Right now the negative energy is dangerously close to reaching an all-time high of eighty terajoules. Twenty-five percent of that level is twenty terajoules. So if we can lower the negative energy on Earth to sixty terajoules, the Federation will win the battle for Earth. Then all the Vermosans and all their allies on Earth will be evacuated to Hyades within sixty days. After talking to Nod, the Council reevaluated their interpretation of the FATES projections and realized we most likely have less than four months before the evacuation warning at ninety terajoules will sound. From the moment they realized this, they have been traveling at maximum speed to the rendezvous point."

The audience began shifting nervously in their seats. A low hum filled the room.

"I know this is very alarming. The entire Council of Intergalactic Enlightenment is just as upset about this as we are. The Council, aware of the pressure we were under, did not want to distract us from our efforts to come up with a workable plan. That is the reason they did not tell us sooner that they were rushing to meet us.

"In anticipation of our meeting, I would like to convey my gratitude to each of you for your hard work. I am extremely pleased with the final report we have submitted. While we have proposed an unprecedented level of intervention, there has never been a better chance for approval. If anything at all could possibly inspire human beings to abandon their addiction to hatred and fear and embrace love instead, I am convinced, this is it. This will be the final, all-out effort of the Earth Commission, the Council of Intergalactic

Enlightenment, and the Federation of Orion to save Planet Earth from an eternity in the hell of hatred and despair, which is the sure promise of the Vermosans."

CHAPTER THIRTY-SIX

"WE HAVE ARRIVED at the rendezvous point on the outskirts of Earth's solar system and are currently docking our ship to the Orion space station. This observation deck will be attached directly to the emergency meeting chamber of the space station. When the docking procedure is complete and the Council is ready to begin, the wall beyond this stage will become transparent, and they will be able to see and hear all of us, just as we will be able to see and hear them. At this time I will take my seat and we will wait to be addressed by Emmanuel, the Speaker of the Council of Intergalactic Enlightenment." The Ambassador took his seat, next to Captain Guardian, in the center of the front row. The podium disappeared into the floor, and the Earth Commission waited in silence for the meeting to begin.

The wall at the front of the room cleared in an instant. The meeting chamber lights came on to reveal two semicircular rows of seats filled with Councilors in their shimmery silver and gold flowing robes. Emmanuel, sitting at the center of the front row, smiled as he surveyed the attendees. He paused as his eyes met Kaia's and then Alo's. They could feel his warm and compassionate gaze. Suddenly they both realized he was one of the Star People they had met when they were children. Alo squeezed Kaia's hand and knew she understood what he understood. But neither of them looked away from Emmanuel.

Emmanuel began, "Greetings, my dear friends. On behalf of the Council of Intergalactic Enlightenment, I welcome you and would like to thank each and every one of you for your service. We are delighted to see you, and we would thoroughly enjoy the opportunity to spend time with you in a less formal setting. However, as you know, time is of the essence, and it is imperative that we begin this meeting immediately.

"We have received, read, and analyzed your written plan for direct intervention into the lives of human beings in an effort to curb the alarming and astonishing growth of negative energy that has Earth on the brink of destruction. We are aware that the failure to curb this negative energy will result in a disaster of epic proportion. However, we are concerned that your proposal recommends an intervention that is a clear violation of our primary directive against interference in the choices of sentient beings. Due to the dire nature of the current situation on Earth, we have elected to reserve our final judgment and decision, until after we have heard from you. Accordingly, the floor is yours, Ambassador, you have our full attention."

The Ambassador, John, stood up in front of his seat and bowed his head to the Speaker in a show of respect and gratitude. "Thank you. On behalf of the entire Earth Commission and all of mankind, I would like to thank you and the rest of the members of the Council for your prompt response and for your devotion to the survival and advancement of Earth and the human race."

John paused for a moment to collect his thoughts. "Since the time of the default of Lucifer, over two hundred thousand years ago, the Federation has fought against the defectors for the right to be reconnected to the energy circuits of the heavenly realms. One by one, we have fought for the survival of each of the planets that now make up the Federation. In every battle the reward has been worth every bit of the sacrifice and pain that we have collectively endured in the struggle to rid each of our planets of the Vermosans. In every case, the eradication of the Vermosan influence has been the precursor to unbridled emotional growth and spiritual development that has exceeded expectations. On each of our home planets, we live immersed in so much love, kindness, peace, and freedom that the Vermosan influence is a distant memory. But let us not forget the turmoil and confusion that we were forced to endure as a result of the lies and deception they perpetrated. Remember their strategies for manipulation. Repeat a lie three times and people will believe it.

Make false accusations repeatedly, loudly, and incessantly, because this kind of deceptive tactic is impossible for the innocent to defend against. Preach and teach that vengeance and revenge are equivalent to justice and restitution. Those were very dark times on our planets, and this is the darkest hour for the planet, Earth.

"Remember the despair we felt when the loving voice of the Creator was almost impossible to hear amidst the deafening sound of the evil, deceptive, and conniving lies of the Vermosans. Humans have been so completely deceived, it raises the question, are they on the path they would have chosen for themselves, if they truly understood? The Earth Commission and I believe the answer to that question is a resounding no. Furthermore, we suggest that a temporary disruption in the flow of deception is necessary in order to provide humans an opportunity to consciously choose their destiny. While our proposal is extreme and will disrupt their choices, it will not in any way interfere with their free will. It is more, shall we say, a speed bump designed to afford them the opportunity to reconsider the direction they are headed and make different choices. For example, while the negative text an individual tries to send will be blocked and not delivered, we will in no way stop the individual from having the negative attitude or choosing to deliver the same negative message in person.

"We acknowledge there are humans who, with full consciousness, have chosen to align themselves with the self-absorbed, hateful, and oppressive energies of the Vermosans. However, we strongly believe that the majority of Earth's inhabitants are loving beings. Earth and her inhabitants deserve the opportunity to take their place as members of the Federation of Orion. If you will grant us permission to deploy our plan to wake up and educate the deceived and misguided human beings, we are convinced we will win this final battle and Earth will become the tenth Federation Planet. Thank you."

The Ambassador bowed his head and took his seat. His mind was racing as he tried to think of anything else he should have said. He did not expect any of the commissioners to speak, and he did not have a good feeling about the reaction of the Councilors. The gravity of the situation was hitting him hard, when Leilani leaned forward in her seat and placed her hand on his right shoulder. Without words, she was able to reassure and comfort him. John put his hand on her hand to say thank you.

Emmanuel finally spoke, "Thank you, John. You have made a unique yet conceivably valid argument." The Councilors were silent as Emmanuel made eye contact with each of them in turn. Emmanuel turned his gaze to Alo. "Alo, I feel your intensity, and we would like to hear from you at this time."

Alo squeezed Kaia's hand and stood up, reached into his pocket for his medicine bag, and held it in his hand. The Ambassador and Captain Guardian turned in their seats, on the row in front of him, so they could look at him while he spoke.

"Emmanuel, Councilors, Ambassador, Commissioners, and to all my friends gathered here today, please listen to my plea. Mother Earth was a gift to us from Great Spirit. My family and I have always honored Mother Earth. Our people lived in harmony with our four-legged, finned, and feathered friends for thousands of years. We have used all the blessings Mother Earth has given us with thankful and humble hearts. My ancestors died trying to save Mother Earth from those who would dishonor and destroy her. The men who tried to kill us and destroy our way of life were influenced by the Vermosans. They called us heathens and animals to justify destroying us and our way of life. These men were without honor. These men were not human beings at all. Human beings have hearts. Hearts are filled with love, compassion, and forgiveness, not hatred, prejudice, and judgment.

"These people poison everything they touch. The Vermosans rejoice as our entire planet is being poisoned. Young people cannot possibly understand that which they have never experienced. Their hearts and minds are poisoned by lies. Truth is almost impossible to hear over the deafening noise of the lies. If our young people have not chosen to live in truth, it is because they do not know the truth.

"Please step in and stop the noise long enough for the truth to be heard. Give our children a chance. The Creator gave us everything we need to have good lives. The Vermosans try to destroy all that we have been given. I beg you, on behalf of the human race, a race with hearts filled with love and compassion, help us get out of this trap of lies. Help us to see and hear the truth! Now! Before it is too late.

"We have contempt for the selfish deceit of the Vermosans, but we do not have fear. We love our Mother Earth and we will fight until we die to save her from the Vermosans. She does not belong to the Vermosans. She was a gift from Great Spirit to the good people of Earth. We will die fighting even though the odds of winning are stacked against us. We need your help. We pray Great Spirit will inspire you to help us in this final battle to save our beautiful planet and all of our loving relations."

Kaia stood up and took Alo's hand and exclaimed, "Aho!"

Commissioner Crying Hawk stood up and declared, "Aho!"

Commissioner Leilani stood up and exclaimed, "Aho!"

The Ambassador and Captain Guardian stood up, turned to face the Council and together said "Aho!"

Everyone at FERN leapt to their feet and exclaimed in unison, "Aho!"

All the remaining commissioners and guests on the observation deck stood up together and in one thundering voice declared, "Aho!"

Everyone stood waiting with bated breath to see how the Council was going to react. Suddenly without warning the entire Council of Intergalactic Enlightenment stood up. Emmanuel's face broke into a smile and he proclaimed, "Aho!"

The observation deck and the council meeting chamber began to vibrate as everyone present erupted into a thunderous applause.

Alo and Kaia turned to look at the view screen at the back of the room when they heard Jake yelling, "Way to go, Alo, I knew we could count on you, my friend!"

Alo's face relaxed into a warm smile as he watched his best friend, Jake, strut around the library at FERN giving him two thumbs up while Naomi, Mac, Joan, Lolly, and Grace laughed and hugged each other.

The Council stood clapping their hands together and watching with joy as the Earth Commission celebrated the approval of their plan to intervene in hopes human beings would choose to stop hating, stop judging, and finally choose to start loving one another.

Emmanuel spoke up, "My friends."

The cheering and applause died down, and everyone took their seats.

Emmanuel continued, "My friends, just to be clear and for the official record books, let me say, the Council of Intergalactic Enlightenment has read your proposal and we have carefully considered all of your arguments. As a result, we have reached the following unanimous decision. The implementation of your plan of intervention on Earth is in the best interest of Earth and it is for the highest good of all human beings. Therefore, your plan is approved and deployment should begin immediately."

Again the audience erupted in cheering and applause.

"On behalf of the entire Earth Commission, I would like to thank all of you for your time and wise counsel," the Ambassador said.

Emmanuel nodded and said, "Before we adjourn this meeting, let me caution you. We were able to approve your plan in part because we realize it does not interfere with human free will. The success or failure of our mission will be based solely on the choices that human beings make. Their choices will determine their destiny, not anything we have done here today or anything the Earth Commission is about to do. We fully expect the initial reaction to cause the FATES monitor to jump to eighty terajoules, which leaves human beings with a fifty-fifty chance of saving themselves and their planet. In reality everything boils down to a battle for twenty terajoules of energy. If the negative energy increases by twenty terajoules, it will reach the one petajoule level and the Vermosans will have won the rights and control of Earth. If the negative energy decreases by twenty terajoules to sixty terajoules, Earth will become the tenth planet in the Federation of Orion. Please be aware, if the evacuation warning sounds due to negative energy having reached the ninety terajoules level, it is imperative that all evacuation preparation begin as previously ordered. Evacuations of all but Federation Security personnel must begin immediately if the negative energy reaches ninety-five terajoules. This is not negotiable. We must not take any chances with the survival of Federation citizens."

"Yes sir, we understand. All evacuation procedures must be followed without hesitation, regardless of any other activities we may be engaged in. We realize the ninety-five terajoules alarm signals the inevitability of the Vermosan victory and all efforts will be made to secure the safety of all of our friends and associates. All the on planet efforts of the Earth Commission will immediately cease, and we will prepare for the initiation of the sixty-day evacuation protocol, without delay," Ambassador John acknowledged with a solemn vow.

Emmanuel acknowledged John's vow and said, "Now as we adjourn this meeting, let me leave you with some final thoughts. Throughout history, human beings have been presented with numerous opportunities to win this battle over the Vermosans, and they have failed. Finally and most notably the Creator of our universe incarnated on Earth, to live and walk among them, as one of them. His intention was to personally demonstrate in completely physical terms, what was required of them if they were to win this battle for an eternal connection with the heavenly realms. Rather than accept his example, people betrayed him, tortured him, and killed him. Subsequent generations have repeatedly betrayed and tortured him, by permitting Vermosans to turn his teachings of love and forgiveness into dogmas of hatred and judgment. This opportunity is, in reality, their final chance. The Creator's love and devotion to human beings and Earth is apparent in that even now they have even odds of winning. Understand this and let me be clear, whatever the outcome, it will have been their choice."

ABOUT THE AUTHORS

E. Talley Morgan, a certified public accountant in private practice in Tallahassee, Florida, is a professional barnyard carpenter, herbalist, and artist. She survived stage three colon cancer and a near-death experience following an overdose of chemotherapy drugs. After two intensive years attending quarterly weekend workshops to do her emotional work, which she found more terrifying than the cancer experience, she serendipitously met Sheridan A. Morris.

Sheridan, retired from the State of Florida, is an avid reader, master gardener, herbalist, grandmother, and outstanding cook specializing in nutritious comfort food. They live, write, and make herbal medicine together on their private, sixty acre, nature preserve located in north Florida with their chosen family which includes numerous rescued dogs and cats.

CPSIA information can be obtained
at www.ICGtesting.com
Printed in the USA
FFOW03n1341140517
35479FF